MURDER
AMONG
THE
ANGELS

Stefanie Matteson

BERKLEY PRIME CRIME, NEW YORK

MURDER AMONG THE ANGELS

A Berkley Prime Crime Book / published by arrangement with the author

PRINTING HISTORY
Berkley Prime Crime hardcover edition / February 1996
Berkley Prime Crime mass-market edition / November 1996

The Putnam Berkley World Wide Web site address is
http://www.berkley.com

ISBN: 0-425-15548-X

PRINTED IN THE UNITED STATES OF AMERICA

10 9 8 7 6 5 4 3 2 1

Dla Ryszarda,
z miłością

1

As was her daily custom, Doris Snyder saw her husband Paul off on the silver and blue Metro North express to Grand Central at seven-forty, and then, as was also her custom, she took her Border collie, Homer, for a walk along the four rows of railroad track that guided the trains carrying Westchester County's commuters down the Hudson River Valley to their daily labors in the city. Twenty-five miles to the south, the city was readily visible on a clear morning such as this one, when the morning sun glinted off the tips of the distant skyscrapers.

She loved this walk along the railroad, which was one of the few places in the area where one got an unimpeded view of the river. She loved the walk because she loved the river. Living near it was like living next to a majestic cathedral or a great museum: its very presence served to put her own problems into perspective. It was also a comfort, in the way a cathedral could be, the strength of its deep-flowing waters seeming to anchor the soul as well as the landscape. She was especially fond of this stretch of the river's geography, which seemed to her to embody all of its best qualities. At the northern end of the lake-like expanse of the Tappan Zee, it was wide enough at this point to give a sense of peace and repose, but not so wide (the Tappan Zee being three miles across at its widest) that one lost the sense of it being a great river.

After more than thirty years of living on the Hudson, she was intimately familiar with its many moods: the end-of-the-world mood of the dog days of August, the languid mood of Indian summer, the energetic mood of a crisp midwinter day. But the mood of the river on this late April morning was intriguingly out of the ordinary. It had been a hard winter, and spring, which usually arrived at Manhattan about mid-March, and then crept slowly up the Hudson to arrive at the Tappan Zee two weeks later, was taking its time. And so the two seasons of winter and spring, which were usually so distinct in their moods, had blended into an eerie amalgam. The sun shone with the gusto of a fine spring day, but it cast haunting shadows of naked branches on the ground, which swayed as the result of a cold, blustery wind that should have departed several weeks before.

Homer, who tugged lustily at his leash, seemed to share her opinion of the day. After lifting his leg near the old summer house that marked the spot where they usually turned around, he looked up at her imploringly with his velvety brown eyes and uttered a polite entreaty to continue, which took the form of a barely audible whine.

"All right, baby," she said, looking down at the dog, whose black and white face returned her gaze so appealingly. And thus they continued on toward Zion Hill Cemetery, which was their destination when they had the time for a longer walk than usual.

Zion Hill Cemetery was what she called it. She didn't know if it had an official name; she had never heard one. In fact, she had never heard anyone ever mention the cemetery, and she considered it her own private discovery. Although she went there often with Homer, she had never encountered anyone else, though there was occasionally evidence that someone had visited during the night: a cast-off beer can or a soft drink cup. These she picked up and put in a plastic bag that she took along for the purpose. She felt an obligation to keep the cemetery tidy because of her only child, Paula, who had died eight years before at the age of thirty-one. It was in this little cemetery that she felt Paula's presence the most strongly, more strongly than in church, more strongly even than in the cemetery in which Paula was actually buried.

The hamlet of Zion Hill had been founded just after the turn of the century by Edward Archibald, a Scottish immigrant who had worked his way up from ticket taker to railroad tycoon. Archibald was a follower of the eighteenth-century Swedish mystic, Emanuel Swedenborg, to whom the Lord had revealed his teachings in a series of visions. Swedenborg recorded these visions in thirty volumes of theological works that became the foundation of a worldwide church called the Church of the New Jerusalem, or the New Church. Archibald had moved from Manhattan to the shores of the Hudson in 1909 with several hundred Swedenborgians to form a utopian community devoted to the beliefs of the New Church. The community they created was outstanding for its graciousness, which was the product of Archibald's infallible taste and deep pockets. The houses were designed by the finest architects—most notably the firm of McKim, Mead, and White—and the grounds laid out by the prestigious landscape architecture firm of Olmsted Brothers.

But to Mrs. Snyder's mind, the most incredible thing about this utopian religious community was the fact that it still survived, liberally supported by funds from Archibald trusts, and peopled with the descendants of Archibald's offspring, and those of the other original settlers. On the rare occasions when a house did come up for sale, the owner was usually able to sell to another Swedenborgian, there being a waiting list of Swedenborgians from all over the world who wanted to live there. As a result, ninety-five percent of the population of three thousand were still followers of Swedenborg, the exceptions being the inhabitants of the elegant houses on River Road, which was the only stretch of prime residential real estate in Westchester that fronted directly on the river. These properties had been reluctantly ceded by the community to the New York doctors, lawyers, and stockbrokers who could afford them, their price tags being out of the reach of even the richest of the Archibald heirs.

As a lifelong resident of Ossining, the neighboring community to the north, Mrs. Snyder had in the past looked on the residents of Zion Hill with the same benign distrust as the other inhabitants of the area: not exactly as having five fingers and a dead body stowed away in the attic, but not as part of the respectable mainstream either. But her visits to the cemetery had piqued her interest in the church, and she had become quite knowledgeable about its beliefs. She even attended Sunday services occasionally, and had fallen in love with the wonderful neo-Gothic church, with its exquisite design and fine workmanship, which reflected Archibald's opinion that God's dwelling should represent man's highest artistic achievements.

A cardinal belief of the New Church was that of a material heaven: a paradise where one went after death, not to idle one's time away playing the harp in vague adoration of some authoritarian God, but to carry on with the work one had performed on earth. One did this not in the company of strangers who had also managed by virtue of their good works to ascend to the same levels, but in the company of close friends and relatives, and in particular with one's soul mate. It was Swedenborg's belief that everyone had a soul mate, whom they would meet, if not on earth, then in heaven. The two halves of a single soul would merge in heaven into one angel, and live forevermore in eternal bliss. This belief in the afterlife had the effect of producing among its adherents an enviable state of peace of mind. This peace of mind would have been sufficient on its own to attract Mrs. Snyder to the New Church, but the church also offered the comforting prospect that she would not only be reunited with Paul in the next world, but with her beloved daughter as well.

It was with thoughts of being reunited with Paula that, being led by Homer, she headed up the embankment on a narrow path of her own making through the tangled thicket of wild roses, raspberry canes, and bittersweet vines. At this time of year, the path was still muddy from the recently melted snow, though delicate green shoots were beginning to sprout from the excelsior-like mat of dead grass on the ground, and leaf sprouts were pushing their way out of the barren raspberry canes.

The belief of Swedenborg's followers in the afterlife was reflected in the minimal nature of this little graveyard on a wooded hillside overlooking the river. There were no roads to facilitate access to the graves; there weren't even any paths. Nor were there gravestones—not in the usual sense anyway.

There were only markers: some of these took the form of headstones, but they were untended, tilted over in many cases, and usually lacking inscriptions. Others were merely rocks or boulders lying in the grass. Sometimes these had been rudely inscribed with the name of the departed, but more often they, like the headstones, were unmarked. Most basically, the graves were marked only by metal markers of the type used in public gardens to identify plants. In many cases, the names, which had originally been written in black felt tip pen, had been worn off by the weather, if there had been any names on them to begin with. The Swedenborgians clearly saw no point in going to any lengths to mark the spot where the body lay when it was only a material raiment for the spirit.

The most peculiar thing about the Zion Hill cemetery, however, was the arrangement of the graves. These weren't lined up in orderly rows, but were scattered haphazardly around: some off by themselves, others in pairs, still others in a circle, like a family that has carried the porch chairs out to the lawn for a spot of iced tea on a summer afternoon. Actually, it wasn't a lawn so much that the cemetery reminded Mrs. Snyder of as a beach. The arrangement of the graves put her in mind of that of the towels of beach-goers who have left to take a carefree dip, and who will be back momentarily. But instead of their clothes, the dead had shed their bodies. One almost had the feeling that one could wave to them out there on the Hudson, and that they'd shout back: "C'mon in, the water's fine." It was this that gave the cemetery its peculiarly joyful atmosphere, so different from the heavy, somber air of most cemeteries. Usually, in fact, Mrs. Snyder did—wave, that is.

As she gained the summit of the embankment, she sniffed the damp spring air, brimming with the promise of renewal, and turned to wave to Paula. Raising one hand and moving it slowly back and forth, she imagined Paula waving back from the "other side," as Swedenborgians called the afterworld, her dark head bobbing on the sparkling waters, and the silhouette of Hook Mountain, gold-capped in the morning sunshine, looming on the Nyack shore.

Impatient with this familiar ritual, Homer pulled again at

his chain, and Mrs. Snyder leaned over to unleash him. It was their usual procedure: she didn't need to worry about a train coming along up here, and she trusted Homer not to venture from their route. A woman of habit, Mrs. Snyder always took the same loop through the cemetery, and always made the same stops, which included a greeting to one of the family circles of boulders, and a rest on a rock whose distinguishing feature was a surface whose contours fit those of her own amply padded behind. Depending on the time of year, this routine might vary. In recent weeks, she had been watching the progress of the blossoms in a colony of dogtooth violets growing in the leaf mold lining a depression where a body was buried. Though the buds had swollen, there were still no yellow flowers on the stems: only the erect pairs of brown-speckled leaves that guarded the emerging bud like sentries in camouflage garb. They should have been in bloom by now, but the wildflowers were just as dilatory as everything else.

Basically, however, the routine stayed the same. Which was why Mrs. Snyder was surprised when Homer dared to venture from their usual path. But dare to venture, he did. As they were heading back toward the path down the embankment, Homer suddenly bounded off toward the north, ears waving. Vexed at this uncharacteristic breach of decorum, Mrs. Snyder followed him through the woods toward a cluster of three headstones at the northern edge of the cemetery. They stood at the very edge of the embankment, two large ones and a smaller one. Though they were unmarked, Mrs. Snyder had always taken them to be another family group. Reaching the headstones, Homer proceeded to circle them as if he were a working dog of the Scottish lowlands, and they an errant clique of sheep. Then he paused, his forelegs braced against the ground, and started to bark: a sharp, disturbed bark that was distinctly out of character for a dog so mild in manner that he couldn't even bring himself to bark at the neighbor's cat when it deliberately set out to provoke him.

"What is it, baby?" Mrs. Snyder shouted with concern as she hastened her step, knowing that Homer must be very upset indeed to have broken with his own strict code of etiquette.

His response was to run back to her, circle her legs three

times, and then dash back through the woods in the direction of the headstones.

Arriving at the cluster of headstones a few moments later, Mrs. Snyder saw immediately what he had been barking at, though she could hardly believe her eyes. Sitting on top of the most level of the headstones, which was the one in the middle, the patterns created by the sunlight filtering through the leafless branches playing over its gleaming white dome, was a human skull.

It stared out of dark, vacant eye sockets at the choppy surface of the river, as if it too were searching for someone it knew—someone who had decided to take a casual dip, and who was expected back any minute.

2

AS CHARLOTTE GRAHAM drove across town toward the West Side Highway, she found herself pondering one of the weightier questions of her fifty-year career as an actress on the stage and on the screen. It was a question that she'd pondered many times before, both on her own initiative and on that of others. But on the previous occasions, the weight of the argument had always come down squarely on the negative side of the equation, and she'd managed to dispense with the whole issue rather quickly. But with the passage of time, the balance had shifted toward the center, with the result that the question had been dogging her now for several weeks: interfering with her sleep, her daily walks, and even—God forbid—the pleasure she took in a good meal. The question was this: to lift, or not to lift.

The issue had first come to the fore when her career entered the ten-year slump she called her black period: from the ages of roughly forty-five to fifty-five when her work had been limited to cameo television appearances and the occasional Broadway show. "Why don't you get a lift?" her well-meaning friends had advised her, thinking that a younger look might give her career a boost. But Charlotte had resisted, sensing that it wasn't because of her appearance that she wasn't getting work, but because she fell into that awkward category—for female actresses, anyway—in which she was too old to play young parts and too young to play old parts. Which everyone knew wasn't the case for men. Even the most wizened of Hollywood geezers could get away with the romantic leads until he was well into his fifties. Her looks weren't the issue at that point anyway: she had been blessed with good skin, and could easily have played much younger women had Hollywood been willing. The real issue, as she later learned, was politics, but that was another story.

By the time she had aged enough to really warrant a face-lift, her career was back on track. It had taken ten years and a number of false comebacks—a critic had once quipped that her career had been recycled more times than a soda pop bottle—but Hollywood had at last rediscovered her, and she'd spent a busy and productive fifteen years playing women whose ages approximated her own. But she was now seventy-two. She didn't look it. In fact, people said she looked at least fifteen years younger. But she wasn't ready to be put out to pasture yet, and she knew the offers would dwindle if she started looking old. The issue wasn't one of vanity: she didn't really care how she looked. She had inherited a streak of the kind of Yankee righteousness that viewed a face-lift as a frivolity, if not a downright self-indulgence. To such a way of thinking, a face-lift was on par with eating crackers in bed, an act that had always been cited by Charlotte's stern Yankee father as a sign of moral turpitude, and one in which she still indulged with the gleeful perversity of the rebellious child. Apart from that, however, she actually took pride in the contours of her aging face, in the same way that the owner of a fine antique takes pride in its worn patina, as a record of its long and distinguished history. The issue was work. Work was her lifeblood; without it, she would wither and die. Her career was booming now as a result of the publication of her long-awaited autobiography, which had come out five months before to widespread acclaim. But what would happen when the hoopla died down? She remembered well the despair of her black years; it was an experience she didn't care to repeat. Nor did she want to spend the rest of her life being the guest of honor at various awards dinners. If it took a face-lift to prolong her productive years—to function as her ante for a few more years as a player, as her agent would have put it—then so be it (practicality and resourcefulness being two other Yankee characteristics with which she had been amply endowed).

And so, she headed up the west side of the island of Manhattan toward the Henry Hudson Parkway, which would take her to the Saw Mill River Parkway, Westchester County's main north-south artery, and ultimately to the home-cum-office of the renowned cosmetic surgeon, Dr. Victor Louria. Dr. Louria, she had been assured by her personal physician, her Hollywood agent, and a number of friends, was the celebrity's cosmetic surgeon of choice, at least, the East Coast celebrity's cosmetic surgeon of choice. There were a number of celebrity cosmetic surgeons in and around Hollywood, but Hollywood was a place Charlotte preferred to avoid whenever possible. Dr. Louria, she had been assured, had operated with great success on some of the world's most famous faces, to say nothing of the most famous boobs, the most famous tummies, and the most famous posteriors. He could be trusted not to turn her face into a grotesque caricature of her younger self, but model it into a subtly improved and more youthful version. Moreover, he could be relied upon to be absolutely discreet: there would never be any leaks to the gossip columnists from his office.

His discretion was, in fact, why she was headed up to Westchester. Like many of Manhattan's celebrity physicians, Dr. Louria had an office on Park Avenue near Lenox Hill, the hospital that catered to the rich and famous, and that was less than twenty blocks from Charlotte's town house in the East Forties. But to avoid having celebrity patients snagged by the press on the way into or out of his office and to spare them the necessity of having to rub shoulders with the common folk, Dr. Louria had set up a satellite office at his home in Westchester County specifically for the likes of Charlotte Graham, four-time Oscar winner and owner of one of the most well-known faces in the history of the cinema. Should Charlotte choose to avail herself of Dr. Louria's services, the operation would, of course, be performed in his surgical suite at his Park Avenue office. But the initial consultation—the artistic planning, as it were—would take place at his office in Westchester, as would the postsurgical checkups (being seen with a face wrapped in bandages not being a pleasant prospect for even the most humble of patients, and especially so for a famous actress). The doctor was already in receipt of a group of color slides of Charlotte's face, taken by a photographer of his recommendation according to his dictates. The slides would somehow be entered into a computer (the wonders of computer technology still being a mystery to Charlotte) and used as the template for the design of her new face.

Just north of Tarrytown, Charlotte exited the Saw Mill River Parkway in order to join up with the old Albany Post Road, the colonial-era continuation of Broadway that followed the east bank of the Hudson north to the capital city. She had always loved this stretch of road, which was lined with the walls of the great estates that dotted the shores of the Hudson, and which in early spring offered peekaboo vistas of the river through the leafless trees. At this time of year, the barren woods were studded with the billowy blooms of the shadbush, which was the first of the woodland trees to flower, and was named after the fish whose annual migration upriver to its spawning grounds in shallow water coincided with its flowering time. The shadbush was Charlotte's favorite among the spring-flowering trees because of the lovely contrast between its pale pink, almost white blossoms and its copper-tinted leaves, and she took great pleasure in seeing the flowers sparkling in the morning sun along the roadside. Besides, the flowering of the shadbush meant that spring had officially arrived. Though she didn't usually mind winter, this last winter had been a hard one, and she was glad spring was finally on the way.

As she drew near the Hudson River Valley town where Dr. Louria's office was located, she started feeling the familiar sensations—a fluttering in the pit of her stomach, a scratchiness at the back of her throat, a weakness in her knees—that she recognized as stage fright. Common perceptions to the contrary, it was a fact of the performing arts that many experienced actors—herself among them—never got over this fear, no matter how long or distinguished their careers. In Charlotte's case, this condition never afflicted her in front of the camera; it was only on stage, and in certain other instances, such as a visit to a cosmetic surgeon (or, for that matter, any other variety of doctor). The only remedy that had ever worked for her had been suggested by her late friend, the actor Larry Olivier. It was to "think of your feet." This worked like a charm. By some mysterious process, the simple act of shifting one's attention to the feet served to root one to the earth, with the result that negative energy was conducted downward, much the way a lightning rod conducts lightning downward through a cable. Charlotte tried this technique now, but found it awkward with one foot resting on the gas pedal and the other on the floorboard. Instead, she resorted to the diversion trick, and turned on the radio. The weatherman was reporting that the unseasonably cool and windy weather that had prevailed for the last couple of weeks would at last give way to more mild conditions.

Being the provident Yankee that she was, Charlotte had developed a fallback strategy in the event that she should decide to up and bolt from Dr. Louria's office. She didn't want to have wasted a day by driving all the way to Westchester for nothing. She had made a lunch appointment with an old friend named Jerry D'Angelo. A lunch would salvage the day. In fact, a lunch could even be viewed as an accomplishment—was, in fact, often the only accomplishment of the day for the phalanxes of ladies in her neighborhood who appeared to do little else. It was to Jerry that her thoughts now turned as she drove through the busy little downtown of Tarrytown.

She had met Jerry D'Angelo nearly ten years ago when she was a guest at the posh upstate mineral water spa run by her old friend, Paulina Langenberg. Like a face-lift, a visit to a spa was a luxury that Charlotte wouldn't ordinarily have indulged in, but Paulina, having heard about Charlotte's success in discovering the identity of the murderer of her costar in a play at Broadway's Morosco Theatre, had invited her to the spa to investigate what she thought was an attempt to sabotage her business. Jerry was then working at the spa as a trainer after being forced to retire on a disability pension from his position as a detective with Manhattan Homicide after losing half an inch from the tip of his trigger finger in a shoot-out. When guests at the spa started mysteriously dying off in the mineral water baths, Jerry had sought Charlotte's assistance in figuring out who the culprit was. Although they saw one another infrequently, Charlotte and Jerry had stayed in touch via telephone. Having tired a number of years ago of serving as majordomo to a bunch of overweight middle-aged women, Jerry had traded in his spa job for a brief stint as a private investigator before getting back into police work, and was now the chief of police in Zion Hill, which also happened to be the town in which Dr. Louria's home and office were located.

Jerry, whose degree of reverence for good food approximated Charlotte's own (his excuse was being Italian; she had none), had promised her a fine meal at a local bistro that had been awarded three stars from a *New York Times* reviewer, and it was on the prospect of a good meal rather than her visit with Dr. Louria that she concentrated her attentions as she passed a sign welcoming her to Zion Hill. A short distance past the sign, she turned left onto the Zion Hill Road and followed it down toward the river through a residential neighborhood of gracious old homes. At the foot of the Zion Hill Road, she turned left onto River Road, which was lined with enormous houses with magnificent views of the river, over which a luminous morning mist still hung. Dr. Louria lived at number 300, a stone mansion in the medieval style, with a massive tower overlooking the river. After parking in a small parking area, she passed through a door in a stone wall that bore a brass plaque with Dr. Louria's name, and walked along a stone-paved path through a shade garden to a smaller building, also in the medieval style. Opening an arched door with a beautiful hand-tooled metal handle, she found herself in a waiting room that was painted off-white and decorated with paintings by well-known abstract expressionists that she recognized, as the result of having once been married to a collector of modern art, as being extremely valuable.

The waiting room was occupied by one other patient, a young woman with long, light brown hair who looked as if she'd been the victim of a beating. Her eyes were blackened and bloodshot, her nose was bandaged, and her lips were swollen and cracked. The color of her mottled skin covered most of the hues in the chartreuse and magenta ranges of the palette.

"He's not here yet," the young woman said with an attempt

at a smile in which only the corners of her eyes crinkled.

"I'm early," she said. Was this what she was in for? Charlotte wondered apprehensively as she took a seat next to the young woman in one of the chrome and leather chairs that were lined up against one wall.

"So am I," the young woman said. Turning toward Charlotte, she stared at her as if she were trying to figure out where it was that she had seen her before. Charlotte didn't bother to assist her memory.

The young woman extended her hand. "I'm Melinda Myer," she said.

Charlotte responded in kind. "Mrs. Lundstrom," she said, using the name of her fourth and last husband, the art collector. She wondered if the young woman was also a celebrity, but doubted it.

"Have you been here before?" the young woman asked.

"No," Charlotte replied.

"You'll like him," the young woman assured her. "He's very nice. And he does wonderful work. Don't be put off by this," she added, waving a hand at her face. "By next week the swelling and bruises will be gone."

Had this young woman been through this more than once? Charlotte wondered. Reserve being the one Yankee characteristic with which she hadn't been endowed, Charlotte asked: "Then this isn't your first operation?"

Melinda shook her head. "My fifth. I have two more to go."

Charlotte wondered why she had been through five cosmetic surgery operations. Surely it couldn't have been just to improve her looks: to put a patient through multiple operations for the sake of vanity struck her as dangerous, even unethical. Perhaps it was on account of an accident.

The forthright young woman was obviously quite willing to confide in Charlotte (therefore obviating the necessity of her asking another prying question), but their conversation was interrupted by the appearance of the doctor at the door to the inner office.

He had a wide face and a thick head of black hair going gray at the temples, and wore wire-rimmed glasses. He wasn't handsome, but he was pleasant-looking. He appeared to be in his mid-forties, though he could have been older had he availed himself of the same surgical skills that he offered to others.

He greeted his young patient, and then turned to Charlotte, who had risen to her feet. "Mrs. Lundstrom," she said.

"Ah, yes, Mrs. Lundstrom," he said, shaking her hand warmly. He spoke with a trace of a Spanish accent. He was not a tall man, no taller than Charlotte's own five foot eight, but he was very lean and fit, with warm brown eyes, and a dark complexion that was emphasized by his white coat.

Charlotte liked him immediately.

"If you don't mind, Mrs. Lundstrom," he said, "I'll see Miss Myer first. She's here for a postoperative checkup; it will only take a few minutes. Then we'll have our consultation."

Charlotte nodded in assent, and the young woman disappeared into the office with the doctor. Charlotte passed her time browsing through a fascinating article in a medical journal about how botulinum toxin was used to control facial tics by paralyzing the muscle.

After ten minutes, Melinda emerged, and the doctor invited Charlotte into the inner office, where he escorted her down a hallway into a large room with a vaulted ceiling and a bank of floor-to-ceiling windows that looked out over the mist-covered waters of the Hudson.

"What a magnificent room!" Charlotte exclaimed.

"Yes," the doctor agreed. "It was once a music studio for the family that originally occupied the house. They were the Archibalds, who founded this community. There were eight children, and they were all musically talented; in fact, the family gave chamber music concerts together."

"Ah," said Charlotte, noticing the frieze of angels playing musical instruments that ran along the upper part of the walls.

"Would you like a cup of coffee?" the doctor asked.

"Thank you," said Charlotte.

While the doctor fetched the coffee, Charlotte examined the contents of the display cases along one wall, which contained a collection of antique prostheses for the face. She gazed with fascination on a case filled with artificial noses made of leather, ivory, gold, and silver. A nose made of papier-mâché had a mustache attached. Another case contained only artificial ears; still another case displayed only eyes, these being exquisitely crafted from glass-enameled gold and silver.

"Ah," said Dr. Louria, returning with two mugs of coffee on a tray. "You're looking at my collection. As you can imagine, my collection might be a bit off-putting to some of my cosmetic surgery patients, which is why I keep it here rather than at my offices in New York. I hope it doesn't disturb you."

"Not at all," she said. "I'm fascinated."

"Making prostheses was once quite an art," he said. "Not surprisingly, in light of the horrible mutilations that used to occur in warfare."

"How far back does the making of prostheses go?" Charlotte asked, removing her mug from the tray that the doctor held out.

"At least to the Egyptians, probably before," he replied. "The Egyptians were quite skilled at it. This is the oldest item in my collection." He set down the tray and led her over to a nose displayed in its own individual case. "It dates back to the First Dynasty, which was before 3,000 B.C."

"The skin tones are created using enamel?" she asked.

He nodded. "Strictly speaking, though, it shouldn't be in my collection because it's the product of the mortician, rather than the prosthetist. The Egyptians believed that only those with intact physical appearances would be allowed to enter the Kingdom of Osiris."

After picking up his own mug of coffee, he led her over to another of the cases. "This is the prize of my collection," he said. "The iron mask."

"From Dumas!" she said, staring at the heavy metal contraption that the text in the case said had once concealed the face of the man in the famous story of *The Man in the Iron Mask*. "It was a true story, then?"

He nodded. "I bought it at auction in London last year. I'd hate to tell you what I paid for it."

"How did you come by your interest in facial prostheses?"

she asked, as she took a sip of the coffee, which was dark and rich.

"It's my specialty. Auricular, or ear, prostheses, to be precise. My practice is divided between prostheses and cosmetic surgery. If it were up to me, I'd do more prosthesis work. It's very rewarding [unlike doing face-lifts on vain women was the unspoken gist of his remark], but there's a limited market."

"But wouldn't a plastic surgeon be more likely to reconstruct an ear than make a prosthesis?" she asked, reminded of the surgically reconstructed ears of a burn victim she had once met.

"I also do ear reconstructions. But they aren't always aesthetically satisfactory. Nor were prostheses, until recently. There was no good way to attach them, as you can see from these examples." Turning back to the display cases, he pointed out an antique ear prosthesis that was attached to a headphone-like wire, and another that was attached to an eyeglass frame.

"In more recent years," he went on, "auricular prostheses have been attached with a liquid adhesive, but they tended to fall off when the adhesive dried out, which could be very embarrassing for the patient. My area is retention. I don't make the prosthesis; I leave that up to the prosthetist. But I have developed a technique for attaching the ear to the skull."

"How do you do it?" she asked.

"I use a titanium fixture that's implanted directly into the mastoid bone." He tapped the bone of the skull at the back of his ear. "The prosthesis simply clips onto the fixture. The technique is called craniofacial osseointegration, and it's the most significant advance in the field in the last twenty-five years."

"If you don't mind saying so yourself," she teased.

He smiled, his teeth white against his dark skin. "I don't mind saying so myself in the least. Of course, the surgeons who do ear reconstructions hate my guts. My technique puts them out of business."

Charlotte looked at him with a new measure of respect, and, as she did so, noticed that the shade of the skin of the ear under the gray-tinged hair of his left temple was almost imperceptibly lighter and pinker than that of the rest of his face, and that it shone with an unnatural gloss.

"Yes," he said, noticing the direction of her glance. "I have an auricular prosthesis. That's how I came by my interest in the subject." He went on to explain: "I was born with no ear, or, to be precise, two small vestigial remnants of the auricular cartilage. It's a congenital condition called microtia; it affects about one in twenty thousand."

"You're very special," she said.

He smiled. "That's what the ancients would have thought. They viewed a facial deformity as a sign of a special liaison with the gods." He smiled ruefully. "But I can assure you that I didn't view it that way as a child. Nor did my family. My father viewed my"—he groped for the right word—"imperfection as a personal failure."

"A personal failure?" she repeated, not understanding. "Why?"

"Shame, embarrassment, loss of prestige. I don't know. I never could understand his attitude. Until I was eight, my parents kept my ear a secret. I had to wear my hair long to cover it up. I was rarely allowed to leave the house, or to play with other children." He paused for a moment, and then said: "It was a miserable childhood."

Charlotte was surprised at the emotion in the voice of a man who had had many years to come to terms with the deficiencies in his upbringing, and who must have told this story many times. It was a measure of how deep the wounds must have cut.

"My father called it my '*orejita mala*.' Bad little ear."

"What happened when you were eight?"

"My parents brought me here to have my ear surgically corrected."

"From?" Charlotte asked.

"Rio de Janeiro," he replied.

So the accent was Portuguese. The doctor's Brazilian origins also explained the coffee, which was of the type that one of her former husbands used to dismiss as "road tar," but that she liked the best.

Dr. Louria continued: "With my new ear, I was finally able to lead a normal life; it was like being let out of jail. That's when I resolved to become a plastic surgeon when I grew up. But when I eventually did, I became conscious of how unsatisfactory my reconstructed ear was. In fact, I have yet to see a decent ear reconstruction.''

"I imagine it's hard to make something out of nothing,'' Charlotte said.

"Exactly,'' he replied. "So I started searching for an alternative. After I developed the osseointegration technique, I replaced my reconstructed ear with a prosthesis. Having a prosthesis comes in very handy when I'm talking with prospective patients. All I have to do is show them my ear.''

Charlotte smiled. "It's a fascinating story,'' she said, finding that she was quite taken by this charming Brazilian.

"Now,'' he said, gesturing toward the cluster of armchairs that were grouped around a coffee table by the windows overlooking the river, "would you like to get down to business?''

For the next half hour, Dr. Louria discussed what he could do for Charlotte, and what it would entail, both financially (a small fortune, paid in advance) and in terms of its effect on her daily life immediately after the operation. He pronounced her face in good condition for a woman of her age. That she had "no advanced facial laxity'' was good news indeed, as was the fact that her excellent bone structure made for a successful outcome. The doctor's assessment was less complimentary when it came to the loose flesh on her neck (though Charlotte had always been careful about protecting her face from the sun, she had been less so about her neck), or the crepy folds around her eyes. The good news was that "an improved neck and jaw contour'' was readily achievable. Also readily correctible was the sagging flesh around her eyes, which would require a separate procedure called a blepharoplasty. After telling her what he could do for her, the doctor went on to warn her about the potential negatives for a woman of her age. It was not uncommon for an older woman to require a secondary lift within a year because of lack of skin elasticity, though he didn't think that would be necessary in her case. Also, the results weren't likely to last as long as for a younger woman. Finally, he warned her about the slight, but nevertheless existent, risks of serious side effects such as scarring, numbness, and hair loss.

Charlotte was beginning to entertain serious doubts about the whole venture when Dr. Louria invited her into a cubicle to view a computer image of her face. Applying a magnetic pen directly to the color image on the computer screen, he proceeded to change her appearance right before her eyes. She watched in amazement as he moved the tiny squares called pixels around the screen. The changes were subtle and artistic; it was like sculpting with flesh instead of with clay. With pen in hand, he magically obliterated wrinkles, lifted sagging flesh, and ironed out the declivity between the nose and the mouth that he referred to as "the dread nasio-labial fold," and which wasn't, she was disappointed to hear, as readily correctible as the labio-mandibular fold between the mouth and the jaw, a.k.a. the jowl line.

An hour after her arrival, Charlotte's consultation was over. If she decided to go ahead with the surgery, the doctor informed her as he escorted her to the door, he could fit her into his schedule as soon as the end of next month. But if she wanted to reserve that time slot, she would have to let him know by the end of next week. He would be sending her a color proof of the "computer enhanced" image of her face to help her make up her mind.

Her theoretical quandary was now complicated by the actual facts of the matter, she thought as she headed back out to her car. One of her concerns had been allayed: she had absolute faith in Dr. Louria's capabilities and trusted him to turn the clock back without dramatically altering her appearance. But the image of her new, surgically improved face raised anew the question of whether she even wanted to turn the clock back. The face that had stared back at her from the computer screen was a face that looked more youthful, more polished, more glowing. But it wasn't *her* face. Moreover, she doubted whether it was even appropriate for a woman of seventy-two to have unlined eyes, smooth cheeks, and a crisp jaw. It struck her as being undignified. Like a septuagenarian in a miniskirt.

"To lift or not to lift" was not an easy question, she thought as she headed out toward the police station to meet her old friend.

The Zion Hill police station was situated on the Albany Post Road just north of the traffic light at the Zion Hill Road intersection. It was located in a building that also housed a two-bay fire station. Like many of the houses she had noticed in her drive through Zion Hill, the police station was in the Tudor style, which struck Charlotte as being incongruously genteel for a public building. The timber-fronted facade looked more like the backdrop for a sleek advertisement than for the two fire trucks that stood out in front, their chrome fittings gleaming in the morning sun. Entering the station, she announced herself to the dispatcher who sat behind the front desk. No sooner had she done so than Jerry came down the stairs, and, after greeting her warmly, invited her up to his office.

He looked older than when she had last seen him—his mat of tight black curls had turned gray and was receding from his temples, and, although he was still very fit, he was a little heavier. But he looked much happier than he used to. In fact, he glowed with excitement. She knew he was glad to be back in police work, but this had to be more than just that.

"Are you hungry?" he asked peremptorily, as he closed his office door behind them. "I mean, would you mind putting off lunch for an hour or so?"

"Not at all," she replied. Dr. Louria's surgical dissection of her face had put a damper on her appetite. Besides, it was still only eleven-thirty, and, like most New Yorkers, she wasn't accustomed to eating lunch before one.

He grinned. He had a wide grin which the dimples in his round cheeks and the slight gap between his front teeth couldn't help but make appealing. "Good. I have something to show you." With that, he opened a metal locker and removed a soccer ball-sized object wrapped in bubble wrap, which he carefully set down in the middle of his desk. As Charlotte looked on, he slowly unwound the bubble wrap, revealing a human skull.

Charlotte raised a dark eyebrow in an expression that was one of her screen trademarks, along with her clipped Yankee accent and her long-legged stride. "A murder victim?" A murder case would explain Jerry's ebullient mood.

Jerry shrugged his broad shoulders, which pulled at the seams of the lightweight cotton sports jacket he wore over a blue chambray shirt. He had once told Charlotte that homicide detectives never wore wool jackets because the fabric absorbed the corpse reek, which would never come out. Though Charlotte didn't imagine that Jerry would have had much contact with corpses here, she supposed he found it hard to give up his old habits.

"I dunno," he said, his Bensonhurst origins still evident in his accent. "But I'm gonna find out."

"Where did it come from?" she asked.

"A woman found it in a local cemetery the day before yesterday when she was walking her dog. It was resting on top of a headstone."

"A grave robber?" she asked.

"Could be. We get that kind of thing around here, especially around Halloween. It's because of our proximity to Sleepy Hollow—the headless horseman and all that. But I doubt it. There weren't any other bones, and no graves had been disturbed. Besides, there was something else."

Charlotte crossed her arms and awaited his explanation.

"A bouquet of lilies of the valley had been placed at the foot of the headstone." He went on: "We had another incident like this late last summer. A skull was found on a headstone in the cemetery at St. James's." He nodded in the direction of the road. "You probably passed it on your way up."

Charlotte nodded. She remembered seeing the Romanesque-style church as she was looking for the turnoff for the Zion Hill Road.

"Also with a fresh bouquet of lilies of the valley," he said.

Charlotte arched an eyebrow.

"The state forensic anthropologist, Leonore Herman, was able to connect that skull to some body parts that washed up by Fort Tryon Park." Jerry sat on the corner of his desk and looked into the empty eye sockets of the skull, as if he hoped it would cooperate by providing him with its full name and address.

"Any identification in that case?" prompted Charlotte.

Jerry looked up. "Caucasian female; twenty-five to thirty years old; five foot six inches tall, plus or minus an inch; and weighing approximately a hundred and twenty pounds."

"Any missing persons fitting that description?"

"Several hundred in the metropolitan area. Thousands if you take in the whole country. There were—and I quote Leonore—'no other pathological or anomalous features.' The county boys checked the description against the missing persons reports for Westchester County, but there wasn't any point in taking it any farther than that."

"And what about the body parts this time?"

He nodded. "We have body parts. We always have body parts. The Hudson is very good at turning up body parts. In fact, we have a partially decomposed lower torso—what Leonore calls a 'butt'—of a Caucasian female, twenty-five to thirty years old; approximately five foot six inches tall; and weighing approximately one hundred and twenty pounds— that some shad fishermen netted near the municipal park early last week."

Charlotte grimaced. "I bet that was the end of their shad fishing days."

"I hope not," Jerry said. "I'm fond of shad. To say nothing of shad roe."

A pause followed this comment, during which Charlotte suspected that Jerry's thoughts had drifted to the same subject as hers: a plate of shad roe sautéed in butter and served on toast points.

Jerry continued in a more serious vein: "A matching lower arm minus the hand turned up a couple of days later below the high tide line at the local yacht club. We think the butt and lower arm go with this skull, but there's no way to prove it. Leonore estimated in both cases that the victims had been murdered ten days to two weeks beforehand."

"How did you prove the skull went with the body parts in the other case?"

Jerry smiled. "I thought this would be right up your alley." He went on to answer her question: "By the pattern of the cuts left on the tissue and the bone by the cutting instrument that was used.''

"What kind of cutting instrument?" Charlotte asked.

"A meat cleaver," he replied. "In the other case, some of the cervical vertebrae were still attached to the skull, so we could match the patterns of the cuts. The head had been cut off just below the Adam's apple. But this time, there aren't any cervical vertebrae."

Charlotte looked down again at the skull, which was neckless. "No suspicious characters hanging around the graveyard?"

Jerry shook his head. "We don't even know how long it was there. In the other case, we had a rough idea because the maintenance men had been mowing in the vicinity the day before the skull appeared. But this skull could have been there for weeks. The cemetery where it was found is off the beaten track."

"It couldn't have been there for weeks if it belongs to the body parts that turned up at the town park a couple of weeks ago," she said. "Were the flowers fresh?" she asked.

Jerry nodded.

"Was the pattern of the cuts on the"—she paused—"the butt, and the—what was it, the lower arm?—that were recently found the same as the pattern of the cuts on the body parts that went with the other skull?" she asked.

He nodded again, and looked up at Charlotte with the kind of anticipatory smile that one reserves for another who shares one's enthusiasms, and with whom one is about to indulge them. "What's your schedule like? The county boys are tied up with that sensational murder case down in Yonkers, which leaves me pretty much on my own."

"What about your men?" Charlotte asked.

Jerry rolled his eyes. "In the first place, I don't have that many. It's a small department. In the second place, I can't talk to the ones I have. My so-called right-hand man has been here for twenty-seven years, and hasn't had an original thought in the last twenty-six. I could use some help."

Charlotte smiled. "I think I could manage to fit in a few trips to Westchester," she said. "What do we do now?"

"You and I and our mysterious young lady here"—he looked down again at the skull resting on his desk—"at least I think she's a young lady—are going to pay a visit to a friend of mine." With that, he rewrapped the skull and tucked it under his arm like a running back breaking for a run. Then he headed for the office door.

"And, if I may be so bold as to ask, who might that be?" Charlotte inquired, as Jerry held the office door open for her.

"A man named Jack Lister. Who happens to be one of the world's foremost forensic sculptors. And who also happens to live just a mile from here."

"Aha," said Charlotte. This was getting interesting.

3

THEY HEADED BACK the way Charlotte had just come: down the Zion Hill Road, and left onto River Road. Instead of stopping at the parking area just before Dr. Louria's house, however, they continued on. Seeing Dr. Louria's house, which Jerry informed her was called Archfield Hall, straight on, Charlotte was impressed at how big it was: a magnificent stone mansion in the Romanesque style. It was by far the largest of the large houses that lined this stretch of the river. Continuing on, they arrived five minutes later at the end of River Road, where a winding access road marked by entrance gates led up a hill to yet another remarkable house. This house was perched on a knoll high above the river, a wedding-cake affair of five stories, each story slightly smaller in diameter than the one beneath it, and each taking the shape of an octagon. The portion of the roof of each story not occupied by the story immediately above it was taken up by a balustraded balcony, and on the fifth and top story, where, were it actually a cake, a spun-sugar bride and groom might have stood hand in hand, stood a glass-walled belvedere crowned by a gilded onion dome, and surrounded by yet another balustraded balcony. The walls were made of stucco on which columns of ivy had firmly established themselves, and the entrance was via a columned portico facing a circular gravel driveway. Huge old black locust trees, their branches still bare, surrounded the house.

"The Octagon House," said Jerry as they passed through the gates. "It was built by a follower of a man named Orson

26

Fowler, who launched a fad for octagon houses in the mid-nineteenth century. He maintained that the octagon was the truest building form because it enclosed the most amount of space in the least amount of wall. No space was wasted in the corners.''

"A nineteenth-century version of Buckminster Fuller and the geodesic dome," Charlotte commented, as she craned her neck to get a better view.

"Yeah," said Jerry. "I guess he was. Fowler lived in Fishkill, which is just up the river, so we have quite a few octagon houses still surviving in this area. But I understand this is the best example."

"The name sounds familiar. I must have read about him somewhere."

"Probably in connection with phrenology. In addition to starting the octagon fad, he also started the fad for phrenology, which was the science of determining character from the shape and position of the bumps on the head."

Charlotte nodded. She had seen plaster phrenological busts in antique shops, with sections of the skull marked off for such attributes as friendship, sympathy, and self-esteem.

"Got very rich on it too, from what I understand," Jerry continued. "But Lister can tell you more about it. He has a little museum inside. I'm sure he'll be happy to show it to you. He bought the house lock, stock, and barrel from the heirs of Fowler's follower, and it was crammed with stuff."

They had come to the circular driveway at the front of the house, where they were greeted by a sign which read: "Omega Studios: Sculpture and Ecclesiastical Monuments in Marble and Granite." Above the words was the horseshoe-shaped symbol for the last letter in the Greek alphabet.

"Lister has a business making gravestones and the like," Jerry explained. "It's called Omega Studios, for 'the alpha and the omega.' "

"Very cute," said Charlotte.

As they got out of the car, the proprietor of the studios emerged from the house, and stood waiting for them under the portico.

"I'm very pleased to meet you, Miss Graham," Lister said,

once they had joined him at the front door. "I've always been a great fan of yours. Still am, for that matter. I watched a videotape of *The Scarlet Lady* just last night."

"I've been meaning to watch that one myself," she said. Even the most obscure of her old movies were slowly being transferred to videotape, and the opportunity to see them again gave her great pleasure.

Lister, as Jerry referred to him, was a short, lithe man of about fifty whose jutting jaw; long, sharply ridged nose; and deep-set gray eyes overset with flaring eyebrows gave his face a devilish aspect, which was heightened by the fact that his scalp was clean-shaven, giving him a strong resemblance to Vladimir Lenin. In fact, had the original owner of his house been present, he would not have needed to feel the bumps on Lister's head to determine his character: a glance alone would have been sufficient, so prominent were the various protuberances on his shiny skull.

With the introductions complete, Lister's sharp-eyed glance fell on the bubble-wrapped bundle that Jerry carried in a shopping bag. "I hear you have another specimen for me," he said eagerly.

"Another Jane Doe," Jerry said. "At least, I think she's a Jane Doe. Leonore hasn't had a chance to look at her yet. But I wonder if you'd show Miss Graham around first. I think she'd be interested in seeing your collection."

"But of course," Lister replied, bowing slightly as he bade them to enter. "Are you familiar with Orson Fowler?" he asked.

"A little," Charlotte replied as she stepped into a paneled entrance foyer in which a phrenological bust was displayed on a pedestal.

"I bought this house in 1966 from a descendant of a follower of Fowler's. It had been vacant for thirty-one years." He clapped a palm to his shiny foreskull. "Mama mia, what a mess. Nobody had bothered to drain the pipes, and there was water damage everywhere."

"It's a wonder you were able to restore it," said Charlotte, looking at the walls, which appeared to be in excellent shape.

"It's taken me almost thirty years," he said. "Fortunately,

the phrenological collection had been stored in the garden house, so it was spared the water damage. It's also taken thirty years to catalogue everything.''

''There were—what was it. Jack?—something like thirty thousand documents alone,'' said Jerry. He turned to address Charlotte: ''Most of them went to the Museum of the City of New York.''

Lister corrected him: ''Thirty-three thousand documents, and''—he paused, one hand resting on the knob of the inner door—''five hundred and two skulls.''

As Lister opened the door, Charlotte stepped across the threshold into her second bizarre museum of the morning. The museum was set in a large, high-ceilinged room that appeared to comprise half of the first story of the eight-sided building. Directly ahead was a door that opened onto the stairwell of a spiral staircase that was illuminated by sunlight from the glass-walled belvedere overhead. A sentence had been painted on the wall above this door in gold lettering: ''In this museum of skull and race; a grand bazaar of head and face.'' The displays were arranged on shelves lining the diagonal walls that comprised four sides of the octagon. They consisted of shelf after shelf of human skulls, punctuated only by the tall windows that illuminated the room. Looking around, Charlotte had the feeling of being in a Roman catacomb that had become so overcrowded that every inch of wall space was taken up by skulls. Seeing them, the thought struck her that the skull in the cemetery might have been stolen from here as a prank, but then she noticed that the skulls on display had yellowed from age, whereas the one Jerry had shown her had been as white as a freshly laundered sheet.

Lister stood with his hands in the pockets of his jeans, surveying the room. ''The phrenologists believed that the shape of the skull reflected the underlying shape of the brain, and that certain parts of the brain represented particular traits, such as piety, sympathy, and leadership. The original owner of this house collected skulls and cranial reproductions in order to study the correlation between skull shape and personality traits. We've got the skulls of presidents, savages, pirates, saints, murderers—you name it. He called his collection his 'Phrenological Cabinet.' '' He led them over to a skull on a lower shelf. ''For instance, the phrenologists believed in studying the skulls of criminals in order to identify the cranial characteristics of the criminal personality.'' He nodded at a skull on the shelf directly in front of them. ''This is a reproduction of the skull of Dr. Harvey Crippen. He was a doctor who poisoned his wife, dismembered her body, and buried her under his cellar floor. It was the most famous murder case of the day.''

Charlotte and Jerry looked at Dr. Crippen's skull, which to Charlotte's untutored eye gave no hint of the murderous propensities of its former owner, and then followed Lister to another shelf.

''And here we have the devices that phrenologists used to take their measurements: craniometers, cephalometers, callipers, measuring frames, et cetera,'' Lister went on. ''For each skull reading, the phrenologist would measure sixteen different skull dimensions.''

''I understand the Nazis did the same thing,'' said Jerry.

''Exactly,'' said Lister. ''To determine who was an Aryan and who wasn't. They even used some of the same instruments.''

''That's what doesn't make sense to me about it,'' Charlotte said. ''Isn't it terribly deterministic? I mean: what about the poor bloke who was born with bumps indicating a criminal personality? Was there any hope for him?''

''Fowler would have said not, although people did try to alter their skulls,'' Lister said. He led them to yet another shelf. ''This is a display of the special hats and lotions that were used to develop the desirable parts of the brain, and hence the cranial contours.'' Lister bowed again, this time to Charlotte. ''Forgive me, Miss Graham,'' he said. ''But you speak as if we view things differently today. I would argue that physiognomy is just as much destiny now as it was then, perhaps even more so.''

''What do you mean?'' Jerry asked.

''Only that we're just as likely to judge a person by appearances now as we were then, except that instead of using cranial protuberances as our measure, we judge people by youthfulness of appearance, or amount of hair.''

"By that measure, I'm losing ground quickly, and you're out of the game altogether," said Jerry.

Lister smiled.

He was perfectly right, Charlotte thought. Why else was she here in the first place than to improve her chances of success by improving her appearance?

"The standards by which people are judged may change, but the need to judge remains the same. Take the nose, for instance: Roman, aquiline, turned-up—all have been in fashion at one time or another. Case in point," he said, heading toward a door to the right of the stairwell.

"Where to now?" asked Jerry.

"My sculpture gallery," he replied. Opening a set of double doors, he led them into the room that comprised the third quadrant of the ground floor, the most striking feature of which was a larger-than-life marble statue of a beautiful angel with long, flowing hair and outstretched wings.

"Here we have the late nineteenth-century ideal of feminine beauty: low forehead; level eyebrows; wide, almond-shaped eyes; high cheekbones; long nose; strong jaw. I think she's gorgeous, but that's because, being a sculptor, I like strong features. I don't think most people today would think so.''

Charlotte looked up at the statue, which loomed over the room like the Nike of Samothrace over the stairwell in the Louvre. The face was curiously androgynous—it could have belonged to a man or a woman—but it had a heroic beauty. "Were you the sculptor?" she asked.

"No. My father was. But I've carved seven exactly like her." He explained: "The plans for the Zion Hill Church call for twenty-four identical angels to be mounted above the nave arcade. But my father had only carved six when he died. I picked up where he left off.''

"That means you still have eleven to go," Jerry said.

He nodded. "I do them when I have the time." He looked up at the angel's face. "I keep her here as my model. The real model was Lillian Archibald, who was one of the daughters of the founder of Zion Hill. She was a famous beauty of her day. My father was in love with this face. As, I think, am I.''

"She's exquisite," Charlotte said.

"Yes," Lister agreed, staring up at the statue. "Look at that jaw! Society doesn't have the same appreciation for beauty that it once did. The face that's considered beautiful today is too perfect. No one part stands out more than any other. In my opinion, the result is bland, bland, bland."

Charlotte had to agree. She couldn't see the appeal of the models who were being held up as today's great beauties.

"Now Lillian's era!" Lister continued. "That was an era in which beauty was appreciated. Crawford: what a face. Bacall. Graham." His devilish eyes twinkled at Charlotte. "If I may be permitted, Miss Graham: none of the faces I've mentioned would be considered classically beautiful."

Jerry looked over at Charlotte as if he were studying her face.

"The jawline might be too strong, the lips too full"—Lister's glance fell once again on Charlotte—"the eyebrows too heavy."

She smiled. He was referring to the famous incident in Hollywood history when, as a young starlet, she had caused a minor scandal by refusing to let the studio's makeup men pluck her eyebrows to the pencil-line thinness that was then in fashion.

He continued: "But it is faces like these that are the great faces, because it is these defects, if I may call them that, that lend a face interest and mystery." He held up a forefinger. "I quote Francis Bacon: 'There is no excellent beauty that hath not some strangeness in the proportion.' "

"Well said!" Charlotte remarked, and thought again of the unnatural perfection of the computer image of her surgically improved face.

Passing through the sculpture gallery, Lister explained that although the four rooms on the first floor had originally been designated as living room, dining room, parlor, and music room, the house had been designed so that they could be opened into one large hall, which was used for the display of the Phrenological Cabinet, and as an examining room for phrenological readings. Opening the double doors on the far wall of the gallery, he revealed a room identical to the one they had just left. Like the Phrenological Cabinet, this room also displayed a collection of skulls, this time on worktables lined up on either side. Actually, as Lister explained, they were not real skulls, but plaster casts of original skulls. Each rested on a cork collar to keep it in place. And next to each skull was Lister's reconstruction of the face of the person to whom the skull had belonged. Each of the skulls had belonged to someone who had been murdered. Their skulls had been found months, even years later, and taken to Lister by the police for the faces to be reconstructed in hopes that someone would come forward to identify them. There were dozens of them.

"Jack calls himself the 'Recomposer of the Decomposed,' " said Jerry as Charlotte wandered from one reconstruction to the next, marveling at the detail. Each face was painted in an extraordinarily lifelike manner, and each bore its own individual expression. Some seemed to be pining after the life they had left behind; others wore beatific expressions, as if they'd at last found peace of mind. Still others looked angry or bored or sad.

"How do you do it?" she asked.

"It's not as hard as it might seem," Lister replied. "The differences between one person's face and another's are largely the result of differences in the shape of the skull. The skull is the armature of the face. In fact, the shape of the skull is so close to the shape of the face that it almost has its own personality. To say nothing of its own individual beauty, or ugliness."

As he spoke, Charlotte looked at his own hairless head, which offered a living example of his point. She was no connoisseur of beauty in skulls, but she was certain that Lister must have thought of his skull as being quite beautiful to have displayed it so boldly.

Lister continued: "Any artist who does portraits will tell you that after a while you're able to see the facial skeleton through the skin. What I do is the same idea, but in reverse. I work from the facial skeleton out. A lot of it is scientific," he went on. "The depth of the soft tissue varies according to where it's located on the skull, so that you can fit the pieces of the face together as if they were the pieces of a puzzle.''

"But you must take a lot of artistic license, as well," Charlotte said. "After all, you can't determine facial expression scientifically."

"True. Science can only take you so far. The rest is intuition." He picked up the skull of a young girl and ran his thumb across the cheekbone. "If you spend enough time studying a skull—turning it over in your hands, running your fingers over its surfaces, feeling its bumps—you begin to get a sense of what the person was like."

"Shades of Fowler again," said Jerry.

"Maybe," he said. "Maybe Fowler and I are just coming at the same concept from different angles. Although it isn't so much a person's character I sense as their soul. I know it sounds crazy, but . . ."

"They say a good portraitist can sense the same thing," Charlotte interjected, thinking of Oskar Kokoschka, the German expressionist who was one of her fourth husband's favorite painters, and who was said to have painted his subjects as they would look twenty years into the future.

"There you go," said Lister. "I also sometimes have other information—jewelry, bits of clothing—that gives me a feeling for what the person was like. My reconstructions often turn out to be uncannily accurate. Again and again the families tell me that I've gotten the victim's expression exactly right. Like that one you're standing next to, Jerry."

Jerry turned to look at a sculpture of a teenaged girl with long brown hair, her face turned wistfully upward.

"The family identified her from a photo of my reconstruction that was published in the newspapers in the area where her skull was found. They said she always held her head up like that, as if she were searching for hope."

"Searching for hope," Jerry repeated ironically as he looked down into the upturned eyes of the murdered girl.

"She took me the longest to complete," Lister said. "Over four months. She'd been hit over the head with a sledge-hammer, and her skull was broken into a hundred and thirty-two pieces."

"Do police departments pay you to do this?" Charlotte asked.

"No," he said. "I do it as a public service." He smiled. "I guess you could say that recomposing the decomposed is my hobby."

"How did you get into this line of work?"

"My father started the business," Lister replied. "He was a sculptor who was hired by Edward Archibald to sculpt the angels for Zion Hill Church, as I mentioned. People liked his angels so much, they wanted them for their graves. Non-Swedenborgians, that is. Swedenborgians don't make a big deal out of their graves. From there, he branched out into headstones, cinerary urns, obelisks, even mausoleums." He took a seat on the corner of one of the worktables. "During his later years, the business languished. People weren't into elaborate monuments. But it's recently picked up again. People are asking for custom-made monuments that reflect their personal interests. In the past year, I've done monuments featuring a Corvette, a speedboat, and a Welsh corgi."

"No kidding!" said Jerry.

"People are strange," Lister said. "Anyway, to answer your question: I developed a specialty in death masks of the rich and famous. I work primarily with Frank B. Sutherland, which is a funeral home for rich people on the Upper East Side. I'm sure you're familiar with it, Miss Graham."

Charlotte nodded. She had been to many funerals there, especially so in recent years, and, although she had made no plans for the ultimate disposal of her own remains, viewed it as well within the realm of possibility that she would end up there herself in the not-too-distant future.

"What's a death mask?" Jerry asked.

"It's a cast that's made from an impression that's taken of the deceased person's face immediately after death. It's a memento of the dead person, like a lock of their hair." He proceeded to name some of the rich and famous people he'd done death masks of, including a dead president, a famous playwright, and a mobster who'd been gunned down at a clam house on Mulberry Street.

"The wife ordered the death mask in the mobster case," he

said. "But the police insisted on being there when I took the impression. They didn't want the body disappearing. The police officer who was assigned to stay with the body had been trying to identify the skull of a young boy, and asked me if I wanted to try doing a reconstruction of the face from the skull."

"I guess it must have seemed like a natural progression: death mask to soft tissue reconstruction," Jerry commented.

"To him, it did. I confess that it didn't seem like such a natural progression to me, at first. I'd never done anything like that before." He led them back to the reconstruction at the beginning of the display, which was that of a young black boy. "This was the boy. The family identified him from the reconstruction. They were so grateful: it gave them such relief to know for sure what had happened to him. After that, I was hooked."

"Where's your reconstruction of our first Jane Doe?" Jerry asked. "I'd like to show her to Miss Graham." He turned to Charlotte. "She's the one whose skull was found last summer on top of the gravestone at St. James's."

Charlotte nodded.

"Down here," said Lister, leading them down to the other end. "I've arranged them chronologically." At the end of the row of tables, he paused before a sculpture of a beautiful young blond woman, with clear blue eyes fringed with dark, thick lashes, and an enigmatic smile.

"She looks a bit like the angel statue," said Charlotte.

"Yes, she does," Lister agreed. "I was surprised that she came out that way. I wondered if I might be doing too many angels. But if that's the way she came out, that's the way she came out." His glance shifted to the package in Jerry's shopping bag. "And now," he said, "what have you got to show *me*?"

Jerry set the shopping bag down on the table and removed the bubble-wrapped package. Then he peeled back the tape and lifted the skull from its plastic nest. "Here she is," he said as he handed the skull to Lister. "Jane Doe the second. Also found on a gravestone in a local cemetery."

Lister carefully lowered the skull into an unoccupied cork

collar next to the sculpture of the first Jane Doe. Then he leaned over to study the skull, examining it from all angles. "It's a she, all right," he said. "You can tell from the smoothness of the brow ridge. Caucasian, mid-twenties."

"Like our other young lady," said Jerry.

"Yes," Lister concurred as he ran his fingers over the skull's surfaces, caressing each bump and fissure as if he were a blind man trying to get a sense of a new acquaintance, or a phrenologist doing a reading. "She's lovely," he said. "Which cemetery did you find her in?"

"Zion Hill," said Jerry. "A woman found her the day before yesterday while she was walking her dog. That's the cemetery that's right over there," nodding toward one of the tall windows. He walked over to the window and looked out. "I understand it was once all one tract of church property."

"Yes, it was," said Lister, who was still studying the skull. "From Zion Hill right down to the river." He looked up at Jerry. "Was it the fat, blond woman with the frisky black and white dog?"

"Mrs. Snyder," said Jerry, with surprise. "How did you know?"

"I see her walking that dog on the tracks practically every morning," Lister replied. "Any body parts turn up recently?"

Jerry nodded. "What Leonore calls a butt, and a lower arm. The butt turned up in a shad net; the lower arm washed up at the yacht club. But since there's no neck, we can't match the cut marks. The cut marks on the body parts did match those on the body parts of the other victim, though."

"Where were the other body parts found?"

"Fort Tryon Park," Jerry replied, naming the park that fronted on the river just north of the George Washington Bridge. "But that doesn't necessarily mean that the bodies weren't dumped in the river at the same place."

Charlotte knew the Hudson was famous for its eccentric currents. A tidal river almost to Albany, the current could flow either north or south, depending on the tides. The Indians had called it "the river that flows both ways."

"How much did the butt weigh?" asked Lister.

"About ten pounds," Jerry answered.

"Then it probably went in somewhere close to where it was found," Lister said. "A body part weighing that much wouldn't have traveled far."

As he spoke, a thought suddenly struck Charlotte. "I assume the butt, as you call it, must have had flesh on it to weigh that much," she said.

Jerry nodded.

She looked down at the gleaming skull. "But the skull's bare."

Jerry nodded again. "The killer must have macerated the skull."

"Macerated it?" she said.

"Boiled it to remove the flesh," Lister explained. "Usually you throw in a little detergent to help dissolve the fat and get rid of the smell," he added with a little grin. "Tide is good; Fab, anything with enzymes."

"To get your wash whiter than white," said Jerry.

Charlotte shuddered.

Lister was still bent over the skull. "I think your killer used something more than just detergent, though. This skull is like the other one in that it's unnaturally white. I would bet that both of them were bleached."

"But why would somebody bother?" Charlotte asked. To say nothing of bothering to leave it in a cemetery with a bouquet of lilies of the valley, she thought.

Lister shrugged. "That's not my department. I leave that up to the shrinks. But skulls *are* my department, and I think we may be in luck here."

"What do you mean?" Jerry asked.

"If you can't match the skull to the body parts, the next best thing is to have a skull with some unique identifying feature," he said. "I call your attention to the victim's chin."

Charlotte and Jerry bent down to look at the skull.

"The underside," Lister added.

At first Charlotte didn't see anything, but as she tilted her head to get a better look at the underside of the chin, she noticed a faint rectangle etched into the bone. "I see some lines," she said. "What are they from?"

"A surgeon's knife," he replied. "She's had plastic surgery. A complete facial reconstruction, I would venture to guess. The rectangle on her chin is from a chin reconstruction.''

"No kidding!'' Jerry exclaimed as he leaned over to take another look.

"I'm guessing here—you'll have to confirm this with Leonore—but it looks like a wedge-shaped section has been added to the chin, which would have had the effect of making it longer. But that's not all.''

"What else?'' Jerry asked.

"See this abraded area?'' He pointed to an area under the eye socket where the surface of the bone was rougher than elsewhere. "Again, I'm guessing. But I think there was an implant here. To build up the zygomatic bone.''

Jerry whistled softly.

"It's the prominence of the zygomatic bone, or cheekbone, that gives a woman that high-cheekboned look that is so desirable,'' he said. Then he pointed to the ridges above the eye sockets. "Same thing here. Brow implants on the superorbital ridges.''

"That would explain why the flesh was removed,'' Charlotte observed. "The murderer may have been worried that the victims could be identified through the facial implants.''

"Exactly,'' said Lister. "Only a trained eye would notice that the implants had left their mark on the bone. Now for the most interesting part.'' He slid the cast of the first victim's skull over next to the skull that had just been found. "Look at this,'' he said, pointing at the cheekbones.

Charlotte and Jerry leaned over again to look at the first victim's skull. The surface of the cheekbones was rough, exactly as with the second skull.

"Same thing,'' Jerry said.

Lister nodded. "I had noticed the abrasions before, of course, but I wrote them off to some natural anomaly. You often find unusual surface patterns on skull bone. But to find it in a second skull can't be dismissed so easily. Especially with the additional evidence of the chin implant.''

"And especially in the case of a second skull that's been found under identical circumstances,'' Jerry said.

Lister nodded. "Now it's back to the drawing board. I'm

going to have to do another reconstruction for our first young lady. Build up her cheekbones.'' He looked over at Jerry. ''Have I given you something to run with?''

''I'll say,'' Jerry said.

Lister had given them something to run with, all right. But where did they start? Having spent most of her life in Hollywood, Charlotte's first thought was that the victims had undergone cosmetic surgery in order to alter their identities. She thought of it as the *Dark Passage* scenario, after the movie that had starred Humphrey Bogart. But Bogart had played a criminal who wanted to elude the law, which would hardly seem likely in the case of two young women in their twenties. The only reasonable explanation she could come up with was that the young women had been patients of the same plastic surgeon, and that he had killed them because he had botched their surgery: a homicidal variation on the old saw that doctors bury their mistakes. In her research on plastic surgeons, Charlotte had come across an interview with the angry patient of a California plastic surgeon who had used liquid silicone injections, which were now against the law, to reconstruct her face. The silicone had migrated from the places where it had been injected to other parts of her face, turning her into a hideous monster. Half a dozen corrective operations had not solved the problem, and she and the other patients whose surgery the plastic surgeon had botched were suing him for malpractice. She knew of several cases of botched plastic surgery herself. She remembered in particular a beautiful woman who thought her nose (which Charlotte considered flawless) needed to be more fashionably retroussé. As a result of her own vanity (or perhaps insecurity), she had ended up with a nose that squiggled down the front of her face, and through which she had trouble breathing. The botched nose job was a constant reminder to herself and others of the folly of tampering with nature, especially when nature had been more than generous to begin with.

Her point to Jerry was that a few irate patients could jeopardize a plastic surgeon's reputation. And any threat to a reputation that brought in an annual income that could run into seven figures would be motive enough for murdering one's dissatisfied patients.

Then there was the possibility that the dead young women hadn't been mistakes, but experiments that hadn't lived up to their creator's expectations: the Mr. Hyde scenario. The converse of the premise that a plastic surgeon whose reputation was damaged would stand to lose millions was that a plastic surgeon with a reputation for working miracles could stand to *gain* millions. Charlotte knew for a fact that the California plastic surgeons, in particular, were on the cutting edge of the profession, so to speak, and had been known to employ techniques that were considered experimental by the more conservative element of their profession. Charlotte herself would have considered a botched experiment an argument for killing her plastic surgeon, but the argument was just as strong for having it the other way around.

Although Charlotte and Jerry discussed all this on the drive back to the police station, they accomplished little else that day. More time than Charlotte had expected had been taken up by their visit with Lister, as a result of which she had to forego their lunch in order to make it back to the city in time for an afternoon appointment with her agent.

But she promised Jerry that she would be back to take him up on his lunch invitation, and to do what she could to help him out.

As she repeated the drive up the Saw Mill River Parkway two days later, Charlotte found herself pondering the face-lift question once again. The reason she had even considered a face-lift in the first place was that she was worried that she wouldn't get work if she looked too old. But if her meeting with her agent was any indicator, she needn't have worried. The offers were pouring in: movie scripts, television specials, regional theater. She seemed to be in greater demand than ever before. It wasn't youth that was the issue anyway, she decided. It was vitality. Women sought out that taut look because they wanted to convey the impression of energy, of being able to compete. It wasn't the fact that their faces had aged that was the issue, but that they looked weary and careworn. And just

as being told that she's beautiful can make a woman feel
beautiful, altering a woman's appearance to make her look
younger could no doubt help her feel more energetic. But not
having enough energy had never been a problem for Charlotte.
It was her energy that had propelled her to the top of her
profession, and had kept her there for nearly fifty years. And
it was her energy that would keep her going for another ten—
would it be importunate of her to ask for another fifteen?—
despite the crepy folds around her eyes, despite the fatty deposits under her chin, despite the scars that life had inflicted
on her skin and on her psyche. As Francis Bacon had said:
"There is no excellent beauty that hath not some strangeness
in the proportion."

    She still hadn't made up her mind. The jury on the "to lift
or not to lift" question was still out. But the scales were no
longer as balanced as they were when she'd first reconsidered
the question.

4

CHARLOTTE ARRIVED AT the Zion Hill police station at eleven-thirty, ready for Jerry to put her to work (to say nothing of being ready for a good meal). She found Jerry on the verge of calling Leonore Herman, the state forensic anthropologist, whose offices were located in Albany. Jerry had asked Lister to send her the skull of the second victim via Emergency Medical Services after he had finished making his cast. Lister was an experienced student of the configuration of skulls, but he wasn't a forensic anthropologist, and Jerry wanted to confirm Lister's conclusions about the cosmetic surgery before going any further with that aspect of the investigation. In his telephone conversation with Dr. Herman, Jerry had also suggested that she take another look at the skull of the first victim, which was stored with the remains of other unidentified murder victims at the offices of the state medical examiner.

"She should have had enough time to look at them by now," Jerry had said impatiently shortly after Charlotte's arrival. The fact that he was willing to postpone a meal to call someone who probably would have called him as soon as she had finished her report was a sign that the case had gotten hold of Jerry. After two years of stolen bicycles and speeding tickets, he was a man with a mission.

He got through to Dr. Herman right away, and Charlotte could tell from the expression on his face, as well as from the general drift of his side of the conversation, which was lib-

erally sprinkled with words like "rhinoplasty," that he'd
struck pay dirt.

"Lister was right," he said after hanging up. "Both victims
had had plastic surgery. Leonore had noticed the abrasions on
the cheekbones of the first skull, just as Lister had, but she
also wrote them off to a natural anomaly. But the evidence of
plastic surgery on the second skull is clear-cut."

"So," said Charlotte. "Cheek implants for the first victim . . ."

"And a chin implant, posterior mandible implants, cheek
implants, and brow implants for the second victim. Leonore
said that one, if not both, had probably had nose jobs too,
given the extensive nature of the other surgery, but without
the nasal cartilage, there was no way to tell that for sure."

Charlotte sat pensively for a moment in the chair facing
Jerry's desk, and then said: "I've had a night to sleep on this."

"And?"

"I see two problems with the plastic surgeon scenario. First,
why would a plastic surgeon have used a meat cleaver to dismember the bodies? You said it was a meat cleaver, right?"

Jerry nodded. "No question about that, according to Leonore."

"It seems to me that a plastic surgeon would have much
more sophisticated and efficient instruments—surgical saws
and the like—at his disposal."

"Good point," said Jerry. "Unless he didn't want to draw
attention to himself as a member of the surgical profession.
What's number two?"

"Wouldn't a plastic surgeon have been aware that the skulls
would reveal that the victims had undergone plastic surgery?
Especially the skull with the chin implant. And if that were
the case, why would he have deposited the skulls in cemeteries
for anyone to find?"

"Why kill his patients in the first place? If criminals were
rational, they wouldn't be criminals," Jerry said. He went on:
"Maybe he thought nobody would notice. Or maybe he didn't
care. The fact that we suspect a plastic surgeon of being the
murderer doesn't make us that much the wiser."

"What do you mean?"

"I did some calling around this morning. There are over five thousand plastic surgeons in the United States, and nearly three hundred in the greater New York metropolitan area alone." He picked up an accordion-folded computer printout that was four inches thick. "Here are their names and addresses."

Charlotte picked up the stack of papers. "Do you want me to start calling?" she asked, eager to make herself useful.

Jerry threw up his hands. "What would you ask them?"

Their dilemma about what to do next was alleviated, for the moment at any rate, by the buzzing of Jerry's intercom. The dispatcher was on the line. "There's a woman down here who insists that she has to see you," the dispatcher said. "I'm sorry, Chief," she added. "She won't take no for an answer."

Jerry pressed the intercom button. "Who is she?" he asked.

"Lothian Archibald," she replied.

At the mention of the name, Jerry looked exasperated. "Okay," he said resignedly. "Send her up." He looked at Charlotte. "Edward Archibald was the founder of Zion Hill," he said.

"I remember Lister saying that," Charlotte said. "He commissioned the angel statues for the church."

"He also built the church and virtually every other public building in town. The Archibald name still carries a lot of weight around here. To a certain extent, this place is still an Archibald fiefdom."

"And you're one of the serfs?"

"You've got it. She's one of Edward Archibald's daughters." There was a knock at the door, and Jerry rose to answer it. A moment later, he admitted a woman in her sixties with a round, pleasant-looking face, and close-cropped gray hair going to white.

"I'm very sorry to interrupt you, Chief D'Angelo, but this will only take a minute. It's very important."

Jerry made a point of looking at his watch, and then invited her to sit down next to Charlotte, whom he introduced as his old friend, Mrs. Lundstrom. "Let me guess," he said. "You've seen her again."

"How did you know?" she said, oblivious to the sarcasm in Jerry's voice. "I know you didn't believe me before," she went on. "To tell you the truth, I wasn't sure I believed myself. I could have been making a mistake; it was from such a distance. But this time I'm absolutely sure."

"Where?" Jerry asked.

"It was at the drugstore—the one on the corner of Main Street and the Albany Post Road in Tarrytown. Last Tuesday."

"If you were so sure, why didn't you say anything to her?"

She stammered. "I was so shocked, I guess; the idea didn't even occur to me. Also, I wondered if she would respond. If it really *was* her, why hasn't she come forward? It's been nine months since the first time I saw her. But I did speak to her later. After I bought the camera."

"After you what?"

"I was worried that you wouldn't believe me. So I bought one of those disposable cameras and took a picture of her. She was browsing in the hair products aisle. She didn't even notice. Then I went up to her and asked her if she knew someone named Lily Louria."

"Any relation to the cosmetic surgeon?" Charlotte interjected.

"His late wife," Jerry responded. "She died two and a half years ago in a drowning accident in Cozumel, Mexico. Her body was never recovered."

Charlotte was beginning to get the picture. This woman apparently thought the cosmetic surgeon's wife had come back from the dead. Judging from Jerry's attitude, he thought she was a nut case.

"Why?" he asked. "Do you know him?"

Charlotte nodded.

Jerry gave her an appraising look, and then turned back to the Archibald woman. "And?" he prompted.

"When I got up closer to her, I could smell her perfume," Miss Archibald continued. "Then I was absolutely sure. She always wore the same perfume: Muguet. She ordered it from Grasse, France. Her mother always wore that scent too."

"What did she say?" Jerry asked.

"It was very odd." A puzzled look came over the woman's face. "I'm positive she recognized her name. But she pretended not to. Or maybe it wasn't a conscious recognition." She paused for a moment, and then announced: "I think she's a victim of amnesia."

Jerry completed her thought: "Who was miraculously washed ashore in some Mexican seacoast village, and then lost her memory. Miss Archibald, this is real life, not the movies."

"It would explain why she hasn't identified herself," she said. "It would also explain why she seemed to only vaguely recognize the name."

"If she were a victim of amnesia, why would she be here?" Jerry asked.

"Maybe she was subconsciously drawn back here by some kind of homing instinct, but couldn't remember enough to know why. I have the photograph here," the woman continued. Reaching into her handbag, she pulled out an envelope, and passed it across the desk to Jerry.

Jerry pulled the photo out of the envelope and studied it for a moment. "This woman has brown hair. Your niece had red hair."

"She could have dyed it," the woman protested. "Besides, Lily always wore sunglasses like that, and she often wore a scarf."

Jerry passed the photograph to Charlotte. It showed a young woman wearing oversized sunglasses and a silk scarf tied under her chin. All that showed of her hair was her dark brown bangs. She was holding a container of some kind of beauty product, and reading the directions.

Charlotte passed the photograph back to Jerry.

"Do you still have the photo of her I gave you?" the woman asked.

Jerry swiveled his chair around to face the filing cabinet behind his desk. Then he opened a drawer and pulled a photograph out of a file. Holding it in one hand and the snapshot in the other, he compared the two.

"See?" the woman said.

After studying the photographs for a minute, Jerry handed

the first one back to Miss Archibald. "To tell you the truth, Miss Archibald, I can't make anything out of this photograph." His glance shifted to Charlotte. "This woman could be anyone from Jackie Kennedy to Charlotte Graham."

Charlotte struggled to suppress a smile.

"Maybe *you* can't tell, but I can tell," Miss Archibald objected, her chest puffed out with self-righteousness. "I raised Lily. She was like my own daughter. I would recognize her anywhere."

Charlotte studied the photograph that Jerry had passed to her. It showed a stunningly beautiful young woman with a flawless complexion; long, wavy, red hair; and large, dreamy, green eyes. She was sitting on a lounge chair. "She looks like a statue of an angel that we saw at Omega Studios," Charlotte said.

Miss Archibald looked at Charlotte, seeming to notice her for the first time. "The model for that statue was Lillian Archibald, who was Lily's mother and my sister," she explained. "Lily was the spitting image of her mother. In fact, I've never seen a mother and daughter who looked so much alike."

Jerry leaned forward in his chair and looked Miss Archibald in the eye. "You say that she may have recognized the name. But what about you? You raised her as if you were her mother. She might not have rushed into your arms, but don't you think she would have shown a glimmer of recognition?"

Miss Archibald slumped back in her plastic chair.

"Ergo, she is not your niece," Jerry said.

"Please, Chief D'Angelo," she begged.

"Miss Archibald," Jerry said, his patience fraying, "what is it, exactly, that you would like me to do?"

"I followed her home."

"You followed her home," Jerry repeated with a look of annoyance.

Miss Archibald ignored him. "She lives in a two-family house at 33 Liberty Street in Corinth, and her name is Doreen Mileski. I got her last name from the mailbox," she added.

Jerry ripped off a sheet of paper from a memo pad and wrote down the name and address. "And her first name from the mail in the mailbox," he said.

Miss Archibald nodded.

"Do you know that tampering with the mail is a federal offense?"

The woman sat there, implacable.

"I repeat my question. What would you like me to do?"

"Find out more about her," she replied. "Where she came from. I know the police can get previous addresses. How she ended up here."

"Miss Archibald," Jerry continued, his tone more gentle now, "even if I had the resources to do what you ask, I wouldn't pursue this. A snapshot of a woman whose face is almost fully concealed is not enough evidence to prove that your niece did not drown in Cozumel two and a half years ago."

Miss Archibald pursed her lips.

"Also, I cannot go around spying on private citizens for no good reason other than a remote resemblance to a dead person."

"What about the perfume?" she asked.

Jerry shrugged. "Coincidence," he said. "A vivid imagination."

"I was debating whether I should come here," Miss Archibald said. "That's why I waited over a week." Picking up the photograph, she put it back into her handbag, and then rose to leave. "I guess it was a waste of time."

The hope had drained from her face, leaving her looking old and pale.

Coming out from behind his desk, Jerry steered her gently toward the door. "I'm very sorry," he said as he showed her out.

"This is the third time she's been in," Jerry said after she had gone. "The first time was last August; the second was last month. Plus, she keeps calling. She's an annoyance, but I can't be too hard on her. I feel sorry for her. She raised the girl and her brother after their parents were killed in an airplane crash. She devoted her life to them. It's hard to let go."

Charlotte was sympathetic too. She remembered how she used to see Linc Crawford, the only man she had ever loved, after he died. She'd be walking along, and there he would be. Her heart would do a loop-de-loop in her chest and then she'd realize with a pang that it was only someone who looked like him. After more than thirty years, it still happened from time to time.

"It's especially hard to let go when you believe in angels."

"What?" Charlotte asked.

"Have I told you about this community?" Jerry asked.

"No. Though you did mention that most of the inhabitants were members of some sort of religious sect."

"Swedenborgians," he said, and proceeded to tell Charlotte about the history of the community, and the Swedenborgian belief in a heaven populated by various hierarchies of angels.

"Then this Lily Louria is a relative of the founder."

"The granddaughter," Jerry said. He continued: "By and large, the Swedenborgians believe that it's dangerous to try to see over to the other side, as they call the afterworld. But they admit that the barrier is sometimes lowered, allowing people to communicate with the angels."

"And is this what Miss Archibald thinks happened to her?" Charlotte asked. "That her niece appeared to her as an angel?"

"At first, she did. Or, I should say, she was confused. She wasn't sure if the young woman she saw was an angel, or a real person. If she had believed wholeheartedly that the young woman she saw was an angel, she wouldn't have bothered coming to me. I don't deal with angels," he added.

"I would think that real people would be hard enough," Charlotte said. "I wonder if you can photograph an angel?" she mused.

Jerry continued: "But after the second sighting, she was convinced she was a real person. And now, of course, she's come up with the amnesia scenario."

"How exactly did the niece die?" Charlotte asked.

"She was on vacation with her husband, Dr. Louria."

"Is he a Swedenborgian?" Charlotte asked, thinking it must be hard to reconcile a belief in angels with a career in medicine.

"No. They met when he moved here. Most of the houses

on the river side of River Road have been bought up by non-Swedenborgians. They've become too expensive for the locals.''

Charlotte nodded.

"The accident happened on the last day of their vacation, just before they were due to head out to the airport," Jerry continued. "They had decided to take a last swim on a deserted beach, not realizing that it was infamous for its riptides. She was carried off by the undertow."

"What about Dr. Louria?" she asked.

"He tried to save her, but he couldn't reach her in time. He got caught in the current and nearly drowned himself. I suspect that Miss Archibald's delusions, if you want to call them that, have been fostered somewhat by Dr. Louria's actions after his wife's death."

"What do you mean?"

"From what I understand, he had a difficult time accepting the fact that his wife was dead. He made a number of trips to Mexico to make inquiries in the villages on Cozumel and along the coast of Yucatán about a missing gringa with red hair who might have washed ashore."

But Charlotte was still thinking about the girl's broken-hearted aunt. "Getting back to Miss Archibald . . ."

He nodded.

"Are you going to do anything about her request?"

Jerry picked up the piece of paper on which he had written down the name and address and looked at it for a moment. Then he stuffed it into his pants pocket. "I don't know. If I have some spare time, I might make a few inquiries, just to get her off my back."

Charlotte had picked up the photograph from Jerry's files again. "She was a beautiful girl."

"Gorgeous, from what everyone says," Jerry said. He looked at his watch. "How about lunch? I'd still like to take you to Sebastian's."

"Sounds good to me," Charlotte replied.

Sebastian's restaurant was situated a mile or so to the north in a charming hamlet of dollhouse-like Victorian homes that

Jerry said had been built to house the hundreds of artisans that Edward Archibald had imported from Europe to build his utopian community. The hamlet, which was named Corinth, was the same place that Mrs. Archibald had given as the address for the Lily Louria look-alike. It was situated on a steep bank overlooking the Hudson, and, according to Jerry, had in recent years undergone a renaissance at the hands of yuppie defectors from urban life. Lured by the charm and low cost of the housing stock, the outstanding reputation of the local schools, and the magnificent river vistas, they had renovated the houses one by one, slowly turning what had been a down-at-the-heels blue-collar town into one of the most desirable communities on the east bank of the Hudson.

The restaurant was situated in one of these Victorian houses. Like most of the other houses lining the street that sloped steeply down to the river, it was small, close to the curb, and surrounded by big old trees and a cast-iron fence. But it stood out by virtue of the fact that it was painted a dark purple, trimmed with fuchsia and lavender. The windows were over-hung with fringed purple awnings. It looked more as if it belonged on a Caribbean island than on the banks of the Hudson.

After parking in front, they walked up a brick path to the lavender door, where they were greeted by a tall, slimly muscular young man in chef's whites, whose striking bone structure and slanting green eyes were accentuated by the lavender (to match the door) bandanna he wore tied pirate-style around his head, blond curls peeking out from the edges, and the gold hoop he wore in one ear.

He was dashing, romantic, and breathtakingly handsome, with tawny skin and a wide smile with perfect teeth. He reminded Charlotte of a young Tyrone Power, and . . . someone else, but she couldn't think of who.

"Are you the maître d' today?" Jerry asked.

"Only for fifteen minutes," he said. "Larry's late, and I'm filling in until he gets here. The usual table, Chief?" he asked.

Jerry nodded, and they followed him to a table by a window with a peekaboo vista of the sparkling waters of the Hudson over the roofs of the old houses that led like stepping stones down to the river.

Inside, the restaurant was airy and spacious, with mauve-colored walls and a long mahogany bar at the back. The wall around the mirror at the rear of the bar was painted with a mural of fat-cheeked angels carrying cornucopias of flowers, vegetables, and fruits.

After they had taken their seats, the young man handed them their menus, whose covers were decorated with a reproduction of a Renaissance painting of an angel. Paintings of angels also hung on the walls.

"Is it my imagination," asked Charlotte as she considered the angel theme, "or does the maître d' look just like the picture of Miss Archibald's niece?"

"Her brother," Jerry said. "Sebastian Archibald. I think the mother's married name was Griffith, but they took the Archibald name when they were adopted by Lothian. It gets you farther in Zion Hill."

"It's a small world up here, isn't it?"

"It's not midtown Manhattan, that's for sure."

"They look very much alike," she said, remembering her observation about the androgynous face of the angel for whom their mother was the model. "Even down to the cleft chin. What does he think about his aunt's delusions?"

"He's sympathetic," Jerry replied. "He went to angel school."

"Angel school?"

"The Zion Hill School," he explained. "It's a parochial school for the Swedenborgian community. You probably passed it on your way up. It's on the Albany Post Road, just before the Zion Hill Road intersection."

Charlotte remembered passing the gracious, white-columned building.

"Built by Edward Archibald, of course, for the education of his own children. All the local children go there. From there, they can go on to a Swedenborgian college in Pennsylvania. They call it angel school because angels play a big part in the curriculum."

Charlotte gave him a skeptical expression. She didn't have much tolerance for religious fanaticism.

"It's easy to make fun of the angel business, but angels are only one aspect of their beliefs, which are actually very complex," Jerry said. "The religious focus is what makes this community unique. They view their religion as something you live, not just something you believe in."

"You're making Zion Hill sound very appealing," Charlotte said.

"Actually, it is," he replied, surprising her. "It's a little paradise, to tell you the truth. Because they live their religion on a day-to-day basis, they're extremely nice people." He smiled. "A lot of what I do is PR for the community; their beliefs aren't very well understood."

"I should imagine that their belief in the afterlife would free them from a lot of the doubt and insecurity that plague the rest of us," she said.

"Exactly. That and the Doctrine of Uses, which holds that everyone is put on earth for a specific purpose: that the individual fulfills a function for the community and the community for the individual. Between those two ideas alone, members of the New Church get a pretty heavy dose of peace of mind."

Following Jerry's lead, Charlotte opened her menu and scanned the listings under the appetizer column. She had just decided on seared foie gras with honey roasted onions when the daily appetizer special caught her eye. "Sing Sing ravioli?" she said, looking up at Jerry.

"Sing Sing Prison, now known as the Ossining Correctional Facility, is just up the river," he explained. "The ravioli is Sebastian's takeoff on the local specialty. It's striped, black and white. The black part is made from shiitake mushrooms. It comes with a smothered leek sauce."

"A gourmet menu with a sense of humor," Charlotte said. "I love it." She continued studying the menu. "Jerry, this place looks wonderful."

"I thought you'd like it. Sebastian is a culinary genius. As a child, he watched cooking shows instead of cartoons, and was whipping up sauces in the kitchen when he was six. He opened Sebastian's right after his graduation from the Culinary Institute of America in Hyde Park."

"I noticed the three-star review from the *Times*," Charlotte said. She looked around at the roomful of ladies wearing pearls and hats, and drinking Manhattans; the clientele reminded her of that of Schrafft's in the 1950's.

"Hilltoppers," Jerry explained in response to Charlotte's survey of the dining room. "That's what I call them: the people who live in the mansions that are tucked away in the hills of Westchester. They live in a time warp."

"A good market for an upscale restaurant though," Charlotte said.

Jerry nodded. "It's a bit off the beaten track. But there's a need. The only other decent place to eat in the immediate area is the country club, and you have to be a member to eat there."

Sebastian returned momentarily to take their cocktail order, prompting Jerry to remark on the fact that he was filling the roles of both maître d' and cocktail waiter, in addition to that of chef.

"Two people are late today," Sebastian complained, with a disgusted shake of his head. "You just can't get any decent help these days." He smiled his breathtaking smile. "What can I get for you?" he asked.

Jerry ordered a Manhattan for Charlotte and a Campari for himself.

"It looks as if Sebastian's is doing very well," Charlotte commented after Sebastian had finished taking their orders.

"It is," Jerry said. "Sebastian was rated Chef of the Year by his peers. But he won't be here long. His ambition is to open a first-class restaurant in Manhattan, but you can't just start off that way. You have to establish your reputation before you can get backers."

"Of course," Charlotte said.

"He's looking for a suitable property now. He's already raised most of the money he'll need, and he's borrowing the rest against an inheritance. It's going to take three million."

"That's a lot of risk," Charlotte said.

Jerry nodded. "He wants to compete with the best—Lutèce, the Four Seasons, Le Bernardin," Jerry explained, "and that takes money. I have no doubt he'll succeed. He's a very ambitious guy, in addition to being very hardworking and very talented. And I speak from firsthand knowledge."

"As an eater," she said.

"Not as an eater," he said. "As a *stagier*."

"What's that?"

"Someone who visits a restaurant kitchen and helps out the chef: a working visit. I come in to help sometimes on my days off. Sebastian puts me to work: chopping the vegetables, pounding the fillets, taking out the garbage. Whatever he needs."

"I guess you could say that I'm a *stagier* in the police department then," Charlotte said with a smile.

"Exactly," Jerry agreed. "I'm a frustrated chef, just like you're a frustrated detective. If I had it to do over again, I would have enrolled at the Culinary Institute of America instead of the criminal justice academy. Besides," he added, "eating is important to me."

"No kidding," Charlotte said. No sooner did Jerry finish one meal then he started thinking about the next.

"That's another reason why I wanted to get out of the spa work. Who wants to eat cuisine *minceur* all the time?"

Charlotte smiled. They were kindred souls, at least as far as their appreciation of good food went—though Charlotte was perfectly willing to leave the actual preparation to someone else.

Sebastian was back in a minute with their drinks. "I hear Aunt Lothian was in to see you again," he said, as he set the drinks down.

"How'd you know?" Jerry asked.

"One of the waiters"—he nodded at a young man on the other side of the dining room—"saw her going in. Was it because she had seen Lily again?"

Jerry nodded, and Sebastian looked concerned.

"I'm worried about her," he said. "Believing that she was seeing an angel was bad enough, but believing that she's seeing Lily herself is even worse. Anyway, I just wanted to say that I'm sorry if she's being a nuisance. I'm going to try to get her some psychiatric help."

Jerry nodded. "If she'll accept it," he said. "She doesn't strike me as the type to be amenable to that suggestion."

"No," said Sebastian. "It's going to be tough." He pulled

out an order pad and asked them what they would like.

Jerry inquired of Charlotte what she wanted, and then passed the order along to Sebastian: "The lady will have the foie gras and the lamb," he said. He also suggested that she try a glass of the house cabernet sauvignon—a suggestion with which Charlotte was happy to comply.

After Sebastian had left, Charlotte settled back with her Manhattan. She was just thinking how much at home she felt with the hilltoppers—after all, she lived in a time warp too—when it struck her that Jerry hadn't ordered anything. "What about you?" she said. "I can't believe you're not hungry."

"I'm just not ordering," he said. He explained: "It's Sebastian's fantasy to be the kind of restaurateur in whom the guests have such faith that they trust him to send out exactly what they want. It's what they do at his favorite inn in France. To keep him happy, I indulge him from time to time."

"And does he always bring exactly what you want?"

"Always," Jerry said.

Their appetizers arrived a few minutes later, served by a pretty waitress named Connie, who wore a short black skirt and a white button-down shirt, and whom Jerry appeared to know. To Charlotte's astonishment, she brought Jerry an order of shad roe sautéed in butter and served on toast points, prompting her to wonder if it was her mind and not Jerry's that the chef had read. "Is that exactly what you wanted?" she asked, wishing that she had had the foresight to follow Jerry's lead. "Exactly," he replied. As Charlotte had suspected, their minds were on the same track, as regarded food anyway and probably most other things as well. "How did he know?" she asked. "Experience," Jerry replied. He explained: "I eat here often enough that he has a pretty good idea of what I like. Which is almost everything."

But Charlotte didn't regret ordering the foie gras, which was delicious. The conversation, which before the arrival of the food had centered on the topic of Jerry's four daughters and their various careers, became more intermittent as their appreciation for the food wrestled with that for the conversation, and then died out altogether as appreciation for the food gained the upper hand. Nor would either of them have dared to break the spell of the eating experience by commenting on how good the food was. They were like concertgoers rapt in the spell of the performance.

At last their plates were empty. "Did you say you knew this Dr. Louria?" Jerry asked as the waitress cleared their places.

"Yes," she replied. "I met him when I was up here on Wednesday. That's why I came up here: for a consultation with him about a face-lift." She went on to explain her theory about a face-lift being the ante that she needed to stay in the game for another ten years.

"No!" said Jerry, incredulous. (He was one of her biggest fans.) "Why? You've still got a pile of chips to ante up with; you look fifty if you look a day. Don't do it," he added. "You know what my sergeant says about these hilltopper ladies who've had face-lifts?"

"What?" Charlotte said.

"That they don't look lifted, they just look surprised."

Charlotte smiled. It was true: something about a face-lift—the widened eyes, the taut cheeks—gave the recipients a startled look. She wondered how a face-lift would affect her acting. How was a woman who always looks surprised supposed to show other emotions? "I think I've decided against it," she said.

"Good. But before you go telling him that, I'd like to use you as my entrée. I'd like to talk to him about the skulls. Maybe he could tell us something that would help us narrow down the field. For instance, maybe the technique used for the chin implant is only used by certain surgeons."

"I think that's a very good idea," Charlotte said.

He shrugged. "It's a place to start anyway. I thought we might go over to Lister's after lunch and pick up the casts of the two skulls. Then maybe we could take them over to Dr. Louria's."

"I'm not sure he'll be there," Charlotte said. "He might be at his office in the city. But we could call and check."

"Good," said Jerry.

The conversation ceased. Their entrées had arrived.

On their way over to the Octagon House after lunch, Jerry said that Lister might even have finished the soft tissue reconstructions of the face of the second victim. He often worked into the wee hours of the morning when he was on a case. When he did finish, photographs of the sculptures (he was doing reconstructions of the victim's face before and after cosmetic surgery), would be published in area newspapers, and flyers would be sent out to area police departments as well as to missing persons bureaus around the country. In the case of the first victim, these efforts had yielded nothing, but they now knew that Lister's reconstruction of the first victim's face had showed her as she had looked prior to the cosmetic surgery. Maybe if the reconstruction had showed her as she had looked after the cosmetic surgery, they would have had better luck. In any case, Jerry noted, they would have the opportunity to try these routes again when Lister finished the "after" reconstruction of the face of the first victim.

Jerry had called ahead to tell Lister they would be coming. As they drove up the driveway, they could see him waiting as before on his colonnaded porch.

As they walked up the front path after parking the car, Charlotte noticed that the sharp gray eyes under Lister's shining foreskull appeared unusually intense. He didn't smile as he greeted them.

"You look tired," Jerry said, noting the mug of coffee in his hand.

"I've been up all night," he said. "I finished the 'before' and 'after' reconstructions of the face of the second victim, and I did an 'after' reconstruction of the face of the first victim."

His manner was nervous and agitated.

"What is it?" asked Jerry.

"I think you'd better see for yourself," he said. Turning on his heel, he led them through the Phrenological Cabinet and down the spiral staircase to a large basement studio filled with half-completed monuments in marble and granite. Then he passed through this studio to a door on the far wall.

"I have to have a separate studio for the forensic sculpture,'' he explained as he opened the door. ''Because of the dust from the marble and granite. If I worked in here, it would get into the paint.''

The door opened onto a small room in the middle of which stood a worktable. The carefully painted soft tissue reconstructions rested in their cork collars on the worktable: two heads with long, wavy, dark red hair; dreamy green eyes; level brows; long, delicate noses; and jutting jaws.

They were identical.

As Charlotte and Jerry stared, Lister stood by with his arms crossed.

''The one on the left is the new 'after' reconstruction of the face of the first victim,'' he said. ''I had to build up the cheeks to reflect the cosmetic effects of the cheek implants. The one on the right is the reconstruction of the face of the second victim after the plastic surgery.''

Jerry was moving his head from one to the other, as if he were watching a tennis match. ''It's the face of the Archibald woman who was used as the model for the statue you have upstairs,'' he said.

Charlotte agreed. The face of the first victim, which before had borne a slight resemblance to that of the statue, now looked exactly like it, as did the face of the second victim.

And her dead daughter, Charlotte thought.

''Yes,'' said Lister. ''It is. The face of an angel.''

5

THEY RODE BACK down the long, winding access road in silence. Charlotte sat on the passenger's side of the car, holding the shopping bag with the bubble-wrapped casts of the two skulls safely in her lap. As she rode, she reviewed the case in her mind: a few hours ago, they hadn't had anything to go on but two baffling skulls. Now they knew that the skulls belonged to two young women—both between twenty-five and thirty years old; both standing five feet six inches tall, give or take an inch—who looked exactly like a young woman who had supposedly drowned two and a half years before. But what to make of it? Her first thought was that Lister's self-confessed artistic obsession with the face of the dead girl's look-alike mother—the face of the white marble angel—had led him to reconstruct the faces of the victims to look like her. But then, why wouldn't he have done this for the first reconstruction of the face of the first victim, the reconstruction that had borne only a faint resemblance to the doctor's dead wife and her mother? And, if he had felt a compulsion to make his facial reconstructions look like the face of his artistic muse, why wasn't that true of at least some of the dozens of other murder victims whose faces he had reconstructed, some of whom also must have been young women?

Dismissing that theory, she turned her attention to Aunt Lothian's claim that her niece had been a victim of amnesia. Had the amnesiac young woman found her way back to her hometown, only to be brutally murdered? But that would ex-

plain one skull, not two. And what about the cosmetic surgery
angle? Both Lister and Aunt Lothian had said that Lily had
looked just like her mother, which meant that her face must
always have looked as it did in the photograph. Ergo: she
couldn't have had plastic surgery, which meant that she was
not one of the victims. Charlotte's old friend Tom Plummer,
the journalist who had secured her reputation as an amateur
sleuth by writing about her role in solving the murder at the
Morosco case, was fond of quoting a Latin proverb called
"Occam's Razor": "*Entia non sunt multiplicanda praeter ne-
cessitatem,*" which meant "All unnecessary facts in the subject being analyzed should be eliminated." She was always
teasing Tom about his penchant for quoting Latin proverbs
being the only use he could find for his undergraduate degree
in classics, but this was one proverb that she found useful to
keep in mind. The unnecessary fact to be eliminated here was
the possibility that Lily Louria was the murder victim. Which
left her with two young women who *looked* like Lily Louria.
Then she remembered what Jerry had said about Dr. Louria's
unwillingness to accept his wife's death. Could it be that the
skulls belonged to recreations of her carried out by her husband, the cosmetic surgeon? Was it possible that his love for
her was so great that he had felt compelled to bring her back?
He was one of the country's foremost cosmetic surgeons. If
anyone was capable of creating a clone of his dead wife, it
was he.

She turned to Jerry: "Do you think Dr. Louria could have
been creating clones of his dead wife, and then killing them?"

He nodded. "That's the only explanation I've been able to
come up with. But why would he kill them?"

"Because they weren't perfect reproductions," she said.
"Instead of killing his technical mistakes, which is what we
thought earlier, maybe he was killing his artistic mistakes, just
as a writer discards an early draft, or a painter paints over a
canvas he's dissatisfied with."

"But to what end?" Jerry asked.

"Simply to gaze on his creation, like Pygmalion gazed on
Galatea," she said. "He must have been working on more
than one at a time," she continued, thinking aloud. "Aunt

Lothian supposedly saw her niece last Tuesday, but that was about the time the butt and lower arm were found, wasn't it?''

Jerry nodded. "The butt was netted on Monday, and the lower arm washed up at the yacht club on Wednesday."

"Which means that the second victim had already been dead for ten days to two weeks when Aunt Lothian saw her niece in the drugstore. I suppose it's possible that Aunt Lothian saw the look-alikes on the earlier occasions, but made a mistake when it came to this most recent sighting, but I doubt it.''

Jerry thought about this for a moment. Then he changed the subject: "Speaking of Aunt Lothian," he said. "We owe her an apology.''

"That's right. I guess Sebastian doesn't have to start looking for psychiatric help for her either," she added.

"No. In fact, I think that before we go to see Dr. Louria, we should pay a little visit to Aunt Lothian."

He pulled the police cruiser into a driveway on River Road. Then he backed out and headed back the way they had come.

At the end of River Road, they turned left and entered a quiet residential area of winding streets lined by drifts of naturalized daffodils, which were just starting to bloom. In another week, they would be magnificent. Charlotte had seen these plantings of daffodils along the roadsides elsewhere in Zion Hill, and now asked Jerry about them. "The residents planted them," he said. "They're part of an attempt to make the community more"—he groped for a word—"welcoming." He went on to explain: "The people in the surrounding communities have always had a lot of false conceptions about Zion Hill: that it's filled with religious fanatics. The daffodils were part of a public relations campaign that also included posting 'Welcome to Zion Hill' signs out on the Albany Post Road, with a brief explanation of Swedenborgianism. The community also started giving tours of the Zion Hill Church, which include a basic explanation of what the church is all about.''

"I remember passing one of the signs on my way up," she said. "Has the public relations campaign worked?"

Jerry shrugged. "I don't think outsiders are quite as likely as they used to be to think that the residents of Zion Hill have five fingers and a dead body stowed away in the attic, as they put it." He looked over at Charlotte.

"But that may change," she said.

The houses in this neighborhood were smaller versions of the mansions that lined River Road. The architecture of the houses in Zion Hill, even the smallest of them, was unusual. No two were alike, and they were exceptionally quaint, with gables, mullioned windows, and picturesque porches and balconies. Adding to the fairy-tale quality of the houses was the fact that, almost without exception, the properties were unkempt, at least by the usual standards of a New York bedroom community. Part of this was due to the fact that, being as old as the community was, the trees and shrubs had grown to the point where they needed constant cutting back not to look overgrown. Old ivy vines with stems six inches in diameter grew up the chimneys of the houses and around the trunks of the big old trees, and the foundation plantings of rhododendrons grew up to the eaves of the houses. But even areas that didn't require an unusual amount of attention had been let go. The shady lawns looked like meadows, and features of the yard that in another community would have been relegated to a hidden corner if they were tolerated at all—things like chicken wire compost bins, unsightly treehouses made out of scrap lumber, and vegetable gardens still bearing the dead carcasses of last summer's tomato plants—here were allowed places of prominence in full view of passing motorists.

She wondered if this apparent disdain for the usual standards of suburban grooming was a measure of the community's spiritual faith: that the need to create a Garden of Eden on earth was less pressing if you knew you were destined for the gardens of heaven.

She was ruminating on the subject of landscaping as a measure of spiritual faith—what did this theory then say about the residents of places like Forest Hills, where there wasn't a blade of grass out of place?—when they pulled into a forsythia-lined driveway of a stone Tudor cottage that looked as if it could have come from a page in *Grimm's Fairy Tales*.

After getting out of the car, they walked up a winding flag-stone path to the front door, which was made out of planked oak and featured a stained-glass window with a design of a white steed.

Standing at the door, Charlotte inhaled the air, fragrant with that wonderful spring smell of damp earth, and felt the wind off the river against her cheek. The sound of bird song was deafening.

The door was answered immediately by Lothian Archibald, who was wearing a blue-and-white-striped cotton duck apron. The interior of the house smelled like chocolate chip cookies.

"Oh, hello, Chief D'Angelo," she said. Catching sight of Charlotte, she added, "Hello, Mrs. Lundstrom." After wiping her hands on her apron, she held out a hand. "Excuse me," she said. "I was just baking cookies for the church concert. I'm doing it in advance, and freezing them."

Jerry explained: "The annual church concert is one of the big events of the year in Zion Hill. The entire community comes out for a picnic on the lawn of the church, and all the church windows are lit. I believe we're having a boys' choir from England this year."

Miss Archibald nodded. "People come from all around for it," she said. "Won't you come in?" she added, ushering them into a small but charming living room, with a fireplace at one end and a low, beamed ceiling.

Like the design of the house, the furnishings showed an unusual aesthetic sensibility. The furniture was dark and heavy, and medieval in character. Above the fireplace hung a tapestry of a woman, a woman with a jutting jaw, dreamy green eyes, and long, flowing red hair.

There was that face again, Charlotte thought as they sat down on a couch facing the fireplace.

Miss Archibald had taken a seat in a Gothic-style armchair. "The cookies are actually for the pastor's reception," she said. "He always has a little sherry reception before the concert for people who are especially active in the church. I'm the bell ringer," she added proudly.

Charlotte remembered what Dr. Louria had said about the

entire family being musically gifted.

Miss Archibald turned to Jerry. "Do you know the pastor?"

"I've met him," he said.

"He used to be Lily and Sebastian's teacher at the Zion Hill School. I think he's the best pastor we've ever had. He delivers the most intelligent sermons, and he never even uses notes." Having satisfied the social requirement for small talk, she then asked: "What can I do for you, Chief D'Angelo?"

"I have a question to ask about your niece."

"Anything I can do to help," she replied, snapping to attention.

"My question is this: did your niece ever have any cosmetic surgery? Perhaps because she was married to a plastic surgeon, he might have had occasion to improve upon her appearance."

"There was no need to improve upon her appearance," she said huffily. "She was a beautiful girl."

"Yes, she was," Jerry agreed. "Then she never had any plastic surgery?"

She shook her head. "Why do you ask?"

"I have an apology to make," Jerry said.

Miss Archibald looked at him expectantly.

"Frankly, I thought when you told me that you'd seen your niece that you were imagining things," he said. "It's not unusual for someone who's lost a loved one to imagine that they've seen them."

The expression on Miss Archibald's face changed from one of polite hospitality to one of avid interest.

Jerry raised a hand. "No," he said. "I'm sorry to say that the young woman you saw is not your niece. At least, we don't believe she's your niece. But we *do* think you saw a young woman who looks very much like her. In fact, we think you may have seen three different young women who look very much like her."

She looked confused. "Just like her?" she repeated.

Jerry went on to explain about the skulls that had been found in the cemeteries, and about the facial reconstructions that had borne a striking resemblance to her dead niece. For the moment, he left out the part about the body parts that had been found in the river.

She threw up her hands. "I'm sorry," she said. "You've lost me."

Jerry explained: "Both of the skulls we found bore evidence of cosmetic surgery. If your niece never had cosmetic surgery, that means that neither skull belongs to her. We think the skulls belong to young women whose faces were remodeled by a plastic surgeon to look like hers."

"But why?" she asked. Then she said softly: "Victor Louria."

He nodded. "Exactly," he said.

"Actually, I'm relieved," she said. "I was beginning to think I was losing my mind. But then, who would have killed them?"

"Perhaps your niece's husband. He's the most obvious suspect, anyway."

She stared at him, wide-eyed. "But . . . why?" she repeated.

"One theory is that he killed the ones who weren't perfect reproductions of your niece. Another is that murdering these young women was a way of exerting control over your niece. A need for control is often a motive for men who murder women, particularly if they've been rejected."

Charlotte hadn't thought of the latter explanation: murder as the ultimate form of control. But it made sense—more sense than the killing-the-ones-who-don't-measure-up theory.

"That's why we're here," Jerry continued. "We were wondering if you could tell us a little bit about their relationship."

"Where do I begin?" she asked.

"You could start by telling us how they met," Jerry replied. He took a notepad out of his breast pocket and flipped it open.

She shook her head. "Victor," she said. "I can't believe it."

"You don't have to believe it, Miss Archibald. It's just a theory—the first one we've managed to come up with. By the way, we would appreciate your not discussing this with anyone else."

"I understand," she said. "They met the summer after Lily graduated from college. At the restaurant—Sebastian had just opened it the month before. Lily was working there as a waitress. She was planning to go to Europe in the fall, and it was a way of occupying her time until then.''

"That would have been 1985, then," Jerry said.

"Yes," she said. "Late June, maybe July. They were married two years later. When he and Lily met, he had just purchased Archfield Hall, which, as you know, was built by my father."

Jerry nodded.

"I grew up there, as did Lily's mother. In fact"—she waved an arm at her surroundings—"most of the things in this room came from there. We had to sell it to pay the inheritance taxes. The price of riverfront property had climbed so high that none of the children could afford to buy it."

Charlotte nodded at the tapestry that hung over the fireplace. "I notice that the figure in the tapestry bears a strong resemblance to the statue of the angel we saw at Omega Studios," she said. "Was Lily's mother the model for the woman in the tapestry too?"

Miss Archibald nodded, and turned to look at the tapestry. "That used to hang in the dining room at Archfield Hall. Lily's mother was the favorite model of the craftsmen that my father imported from Europe to work in Zion Hill. Her face had that transcendent quality that was in fashion at the time."

"Angelic," said Charlotte.

"Yes," she said. "She *was* an angel too. But her daughter . . ." She shook her head, and smiled. "Her daughter was something else again."

"How old was she when her parents died?" Jerry asked.

"Four. She had red hair and the temper to go with it. She would scream for hours to get what she wanted. Everyone always said that she looked like a little angel—they were thinking of her mother, you see—but I knew better. I loved her, but she could try my patience to the breaking point."

"Did her behavior improve as she got older?" Jerry asked. "Kids do have a way of growing up."

"She only got more sophisticated in the ways in which she manipulated people," she said. "Don't get me wrong. I loved her very much. She had enormous charm. Everyone loved her—especially men. From the time she was a baby, she could wrap any man around her finger, starting with her brother."

"But she was difficult," Jerry said.

Miss Archibald nodded.

"I have a daughter who's like that myself," Jerry said. "Only one out of four, thank God. I assume, then," he went on, "that she had Dr. Louria wrapped around her finger as well."

"Yes. Lapping at her feet would be a better way of putting it. The way she treated him was abominable. It seemed as if the more abominably she treated him, the more he liked it. The things she said to him . . ."

"Did she love him?"

She shook her head. "I doubt it."

"Then why did she marry him?"

"I'm not a psychologist," she said simply.

"But you must have a theory," Jerry prompted.

She nodded. "Two theories, in fact." She thought for a moment. "Actually, three. The first is the simplest: that she married him for his money. Lily was a creature of luxury. Not that she liked *things*—she wasn't a material girl. She'd wear the same pair of jeans all week long, but she liked excitement."

"She liked the high life," Jerry said.

"Yes. Victor has friends in influential places. She liked the balls at Buckingham Palace, the hiking treks in Nepal, the weekends at the French baron's country estate in Burgundy. But, as I said, she could have charmed any number of rich men into marrying her . . ."

"Why him, you mean?" asked Jerry.

"Yes. Which brings me to theory number two. Which is that by marrying him she could reclaim her ancestral home. Have you ever been in Archfield Hall?"

Jerry shook his head.

"Magnificent is the only word for it. My father lavished his fortune on two things: his home, and the church. No expense was spared. When we realized we couldn't keep it in the family, we tried at least to keep it in the community. We wanted to make it into a community museum."

"I understand that you couldn't raise the money," Jerry said.

Miss Archibald nodded. "We had just raised seven million dollars for a new Swedenborgian library. To have asked the town for money for a museum on top of that would have been too much. It broke our hearts to have to sell it to an outsider, but . . ." She shrugged. "Life goes on, doesn't it?"

Jerry nodded. "Yes, it does," he agreed. Then he continued: "So your niece liked the idea of being the princess of her grandfather's castle."

Miss Archibald nodded. "That was part of it. But she also had dreams of restoring it to the community. She had talked about setting up a foundation in their wills to fund a museum."

"And what did Dr. Louria think of this?"

"He would have done anything she asked him to do."

"And theory number three?"

Miss Archibald nodded. "Theory number three isn't so much a theory as it is a fact. I don't know if you know that Victor has a condition called microtia."

"What's that?"

"He was born without an ear. He was drawn to a career in plastic surgery because he had his ear reconstructed as a child. Anyway, my theory is that he was attracted to Lily's beauty—to her physical perfection, if you will—because of his own physical deformity."

"Beauty and the beast," said Jerry.

She nodded. "He's the first to admit that he loved her because of her beauty. He certainly didn't love her because of how kind she was to him. She, in turn, thrived on that feeling of power that came from being able to manipulate him. He was insanely jealous."

Though it was common enough, Charlotte always found it hard to understand men who could be in total control of every aspect of their professional lives but allow their personal lives to be dominated by women.

"She loved to test his limits," Miss Archibald continued. "It was a game for her to see just how much she could provoke him, especially by flirting with other men." She shook her head. "To call it an unhealthy relationship would be an understatement, to say the least."

"Then it fits the picture that he could be so obsessed with her that he would remodel the faces of young women to look like her," Jerry said.

"Yes," she said quietly. "It does."

"And murdering them . . ."

"He's a very kind and generous man," she said. "He operates for free through the World Health Organization on children from around the world who are born with no ears."

"That doesn't answer my question," Jerry said.

She paused for a moment to think. "If it's true that he was creating these clones of Lily because he was obsessed by her memory, and if it's true that murder is a means of exerting control over what you can't have . . ."

Jerry nodded.

"Then, yes. I think he would have felt a need to control her."

Charlotte had called Dr. Louria's office from Sebastian's and been told by his secretary that she could stop by any time that afternoon. They were in luck that it was a Friday: Dr. Louria had left his New York office to return to Zion Hill at midday. Jerry wasn't planning to confront him now—only to present him with the skulls, and ask his opinion. Surely the doctor would expect to be consulted on a murder in his community that involved cosmetic surgery. As they headed back toward Archfield Hall, Charlotte found herself again considering Dr. Louria as a murder suspect. The fact that the skulls had been left in cemeteries, especially cemeteries in his own community, was the most puzzling aspect of the case. Why wouldn't he have just chucked the skulls into the river with the other body parts? Then she answered her own question: because the skull was what he had made, and what he had fallen in love with. By killing it, he had possessed it. But then, what to do with the material evidence of this possession? She considered the other possibilities. Toss it into the river with the other body parts to decompose? Bury it in an unmarked grave? Consign it to the city dump? None of these options would have been acceptable to a man who had created perfection. But to reduce it to its purest essence, to cleanse it of

its last remnant of earthly flesh, and then to bleach it white;
to exalt it by placing it on a pedestal, just as Pygmalion had
placed his Galatea on a pedestal for all men to see what a
perfect woman he had created? *That* made sense. She was
reminded of the bouquets of lilies of the valley that the murderer had placed at the foot of the headstones: put her on a
pedestal and bring her gifts. Had he caressed her too, as Pygmalion had caressed his creation? Had he kissed her fleshless
lips? She shuddered at the thought.

A few minutes later they were walking down the path to
Dr. Louria's office in the old music studio at Archfield Hall,
where Lily's mother had played with her family, and her aunt
Lothian as well.

This time there were two other patients in the waiting room:
the young woman, Melinda, whom Charlotte had met before,
and whose nose bandage had now been removed, though her
face was still blotchy from the surgery, and an older woman,
who also appeared to recently have had a nose job.

With a start, Charlotte recognized the older woman as a
comedienne who was a frequent guest—and a sometime sub-
stitute host—on one of the popular late night television talk
shows. They nodded at one another in mutual recognition.
Then the door opened, and Dr. Louria invited Charlotte in.

Charlotte followed him into the inner office, with Jerry right
behind her. Once Jerry had closed the door, Charlotte introduced him to Dr. Louria.

"I'm afraid I'm taking advantage of my connection with
you to help Chief D'Angelo, who's an old friend of mine, on
some police matters," she told the doctor. "He'd like to ask
you some questions on technical matters pertaining to cosmetic surgery. Would you mind?"

"Not at all," said Dr. Louria, ushering them over to the
cluster of chairs by the windows overlooking the river, which
glowed like polished brass in the afternoon sun. "What can I
do for you?" he asked, once they were seated.

Leaning over, Jerry pulled the first skull cast out of the
shopping bag, unwrapped the bubble wrap, and set it on the
coffee table in a cork collar that he had borrowed from Jack
Lister.

"This skull was found in a local cemetery," he said. "It's been identified by the state forensic anthropologist through the body parts that go with it as belonging to a woman of between twenty-five and thirty years of age, and standing about five feet six inches tall."

Dr. Louria leaned over to look at the skull, and nodded.

Charlotte could detect no unusual reaction, but then the evidence of the plastic surgery on this skull was subtle. Even the forensic anthropologist had missed it the first time around. Maybe Dr. Louria too had overlooked the evidence of his own handiwork. If, indeed, it *was* his handiwork.

Then Jerry took the second skull cast out of the bag, unwrapped it, and set it in a cork collar on the coffee table next to the first.

Charlotte watched closely as the doctor leaned over to get a better look at the skull. There was no mistaking the signs of plastic surgery on the chin; they were apparent even to Charlotte's untutored eye.

The doctor's face was expressionless as he took in the skull's general appearance. But when, upon closer inspection, he noticed the evidence of the implants, the color slowly drained out of his face.

"This skull also belongs to a young woman between the ages of twenty-five and thirty, and standing about five feet six inches tall," Jerry said. "Like the first skull, it was found in a local cemetery."

"A cemetery," the doctor whispered softly as he fought to maintain a facade of professional decorum.

"We'd like you to confirm the observation of the state forensic anthropologist that these two murder victims"—he emphasized the words *murder victims*—"have undergone cosmetic surgery. Also, we'd like to know anything specific you can tell us about the surgery."

"Yes," the doctor said authoritatively, having regained his composure. "Both victims have undergone cosmetic surgery. The first appears to have had cheek implants, and the second to have had cheek, chin, brow, and posterior mandible implants."

"How can you tell?" Jerry asked, obviously hoping that the

doctor would say something that would give away the fact that he had been the surgeon.

"The chin implant is readily visible," he said, pointing it out to them. "The other implants have left their marks on the bone. The implants rest directly on the bone, which has to be devoid of tissue before the device is inserted in order to provide a stable seal."

"Is there anything specific about the technique that might help us identify who performed the surgery?" Jerry asked.

The surgeon shook his head. "I can't tell much from the first skull, but in the case of the second skull, the technique that was used is standard: the surgery could have been performed by any cosmetic surgeon."

"Is there anything else you can tell us?" Jerry asked.

The surgeon shook his head.

"Thank you," said Jerry, as he proceeded to rewrap the skull casts and put them back in the shopping bag. "It helps to have a prominent cosmetic surgeon in the community to assist us with these matters."

"May I ask a question?" the doctor asked. "You've got my curiosity aroused, you see. When were these skulls found?"

"The first one was found late last summer," Jerry said. "The state forensic anthropologist didn't recognize until we found the second skull that the first one also bore evidence of cosmetic surgery."

The doctor nodded. "I wouldn't have either," he said.

"The second was found this past Monday."

"I see," the doctor said. A mask of profound sadness had fallen over his face. Suddenly he looked old and weary.

After thanking the doctor, Charlotte and Jerry took their leave. As they were going out, the comedienne rose to enter. This time, she ignored Charlotte: "I won't tell if you won't tell," was the implication of her attitude.

As they were leaving, Dr. Louria's secretary emerged from an office off of the waiting room and held out a manila envelope to Charlotte. "I was going to mail this to you, but as long as you're here . . ."

While Jerry rearranged the skulls in the shopping bag, Charlotte slid the contents out of the envelope for a surreptitious look. As she expected, it was the computer-generated portrait of her reincarnated face. Though she had seen the same image on the computer screen, the "hard copy" was much more impressive. Without the magnetic pen, the thousands of tiny pixels no longer carried the potential of flux, lending a new authority to the final product.

And there she was: looking younger, more vibrant, and more glamorous than she had in thirty years. She felt a surge of youthful energy. If looking *at* the picture made her feel like this, she wondered, what would looking *like* the picture make her feel like?

She had thought she had her mind almost made up. Now she was waffling.

On the way back to the police station, Charlotte once again found herself pondering the credibility of Dr. Louria as a murder suspect. After their interview with him, she had no doubt that he had performed the surgery. That much was clearly apparent from his reaction to the cast of the second skull. But she didn't think he had murdered the young women. It was his sadness that had convinced her. She was sure that, until Jerry had unwrapped the skulls, he hadn't realized that the young women were dead.

"What do you think?" she asked Jerry as they made the left-hand turn onto the Albany Post Road.

"I think he operated on the victims. But I don't think he killed them."

"That was my impression too. Why don't you think he killed them?" she asked, curious as to his reasons.

"Because he wouldn't have had to ask when the skulls were found," he said. "Also, his comment about the cemetery. He wouldn't have been surprised that the skulls were found in cemeteries if he was the one who put them there."

"This is true," said Charlotte. Though as she was well aware, people could dissimulate. "Let's say for the sake of argument that we're right," she said. "That he didn't kill them, but that he did create them, so to speak."

Jerry nodded.

"If he didn't create them in order to kill them, and thereby exert his contol over them—I thought that was a very good theory, by the way—then why did he create them?"

"Remember what Aunt Lothian said about the amnesia?" Charlotte nodded.

"Maybe he wanted to bring his wife back. Maybe his plan was to create a new Lily: school her in Lily's habits, speech patterns, manner of dress, and so on. Then he would announce to the world that she'd been the victim of amnesia and set her up in Archfield Hall as his wife."

Charlotte thought about it for a moment, and then said: "Any discrepancies would be written off to the amnesia."

Jerry nodded.

"I seem to remember Aunt Lothian posing a similar scenario, and I seem to remember you telling her something to the effect that this was real life, not the movies," Charlotte commented. "But I'll play along for the sake of argument. What would be in it for the Lily clone?"

"Money, position, glamour."

"Yes," Charlotte agreed. It was a preposterous scheme, but not outside the realm of possibility. She remembered a young friend of her stepdaughter's—a French major in college—who had been paid by a wealthy family to pose as the deceased French wife of an elderly member of the family who had lost his mind. For many years, this young woman had lived in luxury as the deceased Marie-Claire, benevolently shepherding the doddering millionaire around the world according to the dictates of the social season. She had thought it a wonderful job, and had stayed in it for a number of years before marrying an heir to a great fortune whom she'd met through her putative husband's social connections.

A girl could do worse, she thought. Particularly one who didn't have anything to begin with. "Why more than one?" she asked.

"For the reason you gave earlier: that the first ones didn't work out. They didn't look right, or they couldn't learn to hold their fork in the proper way."

"Where did he find these girls, do you suppose?" she asked.

"We're going to have to find that out."

For a moment, Charlotte leaned back and imagined the doctor, like some latter-day Henry Higgins, teaching the young women to speak like Lily, to walk like Lily, to dress like Lily. Hadn't Aunt Lothian said the young woman in the drugstore had been wearing sunglasses just like those Lily always wore. The Henry Higgins scenario would also explain why the girl in the drugstore had worn the same perfume Lily always wore. Suddenly, Charlotte sat straight up in her seat. "Jerry!" she said.

"What?" He looked over at her.

"The girl in the drugstore!" she said. "If Aunt Lothian was right that she looked like Lily, she might be the next victim."

"Jesus!" Jerry said. "You're right." Instead of turning into the police station, he passed it by, and then turned left onto the road leading to Sebastian's. "Lothian said she lived in Corinth," he said. He looked over at Charlotte. "I hope you don't have to get right back."

Charlotte shook her head as Jerry felt around in his pockets. "Where'd I put that slip of paper—the one that I wrote the name and address that she gave me down on?" he asked himself.

"Doreen Mileski," Charlotte said. "Thirty-three Liberty Street. It's in your right pants pocket." It was too bad she had never managed to stay married—she'd been widowed once and divorced three times—because she possessed a number of wifely skills that were going to waste.

Jerry shot her a look. "I thought you weren't supposed to be able to remember anything once you got to be over seventy," he said as he leaned back to extract the slip of paper from his pocket.

"My short-term memory's still pretty good," Charlotte replied. "From what I understand, though, I'm supposed to start losing it as I get older. Then I'll only be able to remember what happened in 1942."

"That's the point I'm at now," Jerry said as he opened the piece of paper against the steering wheel.

"Obviously," Charlotte said.

"Doreen Mileski," he read. "Thirty-three Liberty Street."

6

It took only a few minutes to get to 33 Liberty Street. The house was located right down the street from Sebastian's, which wasn't much of a surprise, since everything in this little village was located within a stone's throw of everything else. It was a small two-story colonial, painted white, as most of the houses in Corinth were, with black shutters and a front door of Chinese red. Next to the front door were two black wrought-iron mailboxes, one each for the upstairs and downstairs tenants. The label on the mailbox for the downstairs tenant read: D. Mileski.

Jerry climbed the steps to the small front porch and rang the buzzer for the downstairs tenant.

As they waited for an answer, Charlotte gazed out at the river, which was just visible over the roofs of the houses that stepped down to the riverbank, and which looked as smooth and peaceful as a lake. A riverboat was plying its way back downstream on the Manhattan-to-West-Point-and-back cruise that, along with the cruise that circled Manhattan Island, was a favorite attraction for tourists to the New York area.

When no one answered, Jerry tried the buzzer for the upstairs tenant, whose name was C. Wald. Judging by the muffled sounds of children playing, the upstairs tenant, at least, was home.

The buzzer was answered by the noise of someone thumping down the stairs in what sounded like wooden clogs. A moment later, the door was opened by a young woman with a pockmarked complexion and stringy brown hair pulled back in a ponytail. A child clung to her leg, and behind her the entrance hallway was cluttered with balls, bats, and assorted kiddie vehicles.

"Mrs. Wald?" Jerry asked.

"Ms. Wald," she replied tersely.

He showed her his badge. "We're looking for the downstairs tenant, who I understand is a young woman named Doreen Mileski. She didn't answer the buzzer, and I wondered if by any chance you knew where she was."

"I don't know," she replied. "I haven't seen her in a while."

"When was the last time you saw her?"

She thought. "I guess it was a week ago last Monday. She was just going out walking. She liked to walk on the golf course early in the morning. I thought she might have gone on a trip, but her car's still here." She nodded at the tan Honda that was parked in front of a small barn at the back.

Jerry pulled out his pad and made a notation of the make and model of the car, and the number of the New York State license plate.

"How long has she lived here?" he asked.

"Since last fall," she replied.

"This might seem like a peculiar question, Ms. Wald," Jerry continued. "But it's important to us. Did you ever notice any evidence that she'd recently had an operation? Any bandages, that sort of thing? Particularly on her face."

She shook her head.

"Bruises?"

For the first time, the young woman appeared to take an interest in the line of questioning. "Why, yes, I did notice bruises around her eyes a couple of times. She would wear sunglasses and a scarf, but I could see the bruises through the sides of the sunglasses."

Jerry nodded.

"I thought maybe her boyfriend had beaten her up," she added. She said this as if it were a fact of life that women had to put up with.

"Any sign of a boyfriend?" he asked. "Or any other visitors?"

She shook her head. "Not that I noticed," she said. "But I'm usually at work during the day. Has anything happened to her?" she asked.

"That's what we're trying to find out. Did she have a job?"

"I don't know," Ms. Wald replied. "She went out every day. But she wasn't regular about it. One day she'd go out for an hour, the next for a whole afternoon. I don't know much about her," she added. "She wasn't very friendly."

The little girl tugged at her mother's sweatpants. "Ma, can I have my dinner now?" she asked.

"Just a minute, Jenny," her mother replied.

"Just one more question," Jerry said. "Do you know anything about her background? Where she originally came from? Where she lived before she came here? Her interests, and so on?"

She shook her head again.

"Ma," the girl implored.

"Why don't you try the landlord?" she suggested. "The question about previous residences is on the rental application. He would probably know if she had a job or not too. She had to be able to show she could pay the rent."

"What's his name?"

She gave Jerry the landlord's name, which was Peter De Vries, and told him that he could usually be found at the Zion Hill Church, where he worked as the sexton. He lived in rooms at the back of the Parish Hall.

Then they thanked her and left.

When they got back to the police car, Jerry radioed headquarters and asked the dispatcher to find out who the Honda was registered to. Then they headed back out to the Albany Post Road. At the intersection with the Zion Hill Road, they turned left and followed the road up what Charlotte presumed was Zion Hill to the church, which was set on a high lawn overlooking the town. At the sign for the church, they pulled into a driveway lined with old yews and holly trees that led to a parking lot. After parking the car, they climbed a set of stone stairs that led up to the lawn of the church. At the top of the stairs, they paused at the balustrade at the foot of the lawn to admire the view, which was magnificent. Charlotte guessed that the panorama extended for twenty-five miles in either direction: the New York skyline could be seen to the south, and the distant domes of the rugged Hudson Highlands to the north. In front of them, the waters of the Hudson spread out to fill the basins of the Tappan Zee and Haverstraw Bay, and on the western horizon, beyond the hills on the opposite shore, the distant ridge of the Catskill Mountains stood out against the western sky. Immediately below, the misty greens and fairways of the local country club stretched down to the Albany Post Road, and beyond the road, the hamlet of Zion Hill clung to the riverbank.

From their vantage point, Charlotte could see the tower of Archfield Hall, and the Octagon House sitting primly on its little green knob of a hill overlooking the river. "What a view!" she exclaimed.

"Yes," Jerry agreed. "My grandfather thought it was the finest view he had ever seen outside of the Bay of Naples."

"Your grandfather?" she said.

"Yes," said Jerry. "He was also an Archibald serf. It's an old family tradition. He was a stonemason who came here to work on the New Croton Dam and ended up working for Edward Archibald. He helped build this church. As well as the dry walls along the Albany Post Road."

"I thought you were from Bensonhurst."

"I moved there with my parents when I was ten," he said. "But until then, we lived with my grandparents in Corinth."

"Corinth!" she said.

"Right around the corner from Sebastian's, as a matter of fact," he said. "Though there wasn't anything chic about Corinth in those days. That's why I decided to take the job here— it certainly wasn't because of the pay," he added. "Some of my happiest memories are of growing up in this area."

For a moment, they leaned on the balustrade, gazing out at the view.

"My grandfather died just after we moved to Bensonhurst," Jerry continued after a while. "But I still remember driving with him along the Albany Post Road. He was so proud of those dry walls. He used to say, 'A full-grown man can jump up and down on top of them, and they won't budge an inch.' ''

"I've always admired those walls," she said. "Nobody can do that kind of work anymore. It's a lost art."

"It certainly is," he agreed.

"Jerry," Charlotte asked, "why are all the roofs blue?" Though she hadn't noticed it from ground level, it was readily apparent from their vantage point high above the town that the roofs of half the houses in Zion Hill were shingled with unusual blue roofing tiles.

"They took their cue from the church, I guess," Jerry said. Turning, he pointed out the blue tiles on the roof of the picturesque stone church.

The effect was lovely; it was like the varying shades of blue of the mountains on the distant horizon.

"Edward Archibald had the tiles specially made," he explained. "There are sixteen different shades of blue, applied in specific percentages. The idea was to simulate the heavenly empyrean. The architecture in Zion Hill is very symbolic, though in most cases I couldn't tell you of what."

"It's a beautiful place," Charlotte commented.

"Yes, it is," Jerry agreed. "Edward Archibald wanted to make this the most beautiful spot on earth, and I think he did a pretty good job of it."

As they stood there, they could hear another person trudging up the stairs, and in a moment, a gray head appeared on the stairs just below them. It was Lothian Archibald, who was there, she explained when she joined them at the top, for her daily bell-ringing duties.

Together, they headed across the lawn to the church, which stood on the brow of the hill. It was in the Gothic Revival style, with narrow lancet windows, and heavy stone buttresses supporting the exterior walls. A crenelated bell tower stood to the south of the entrance.

As they walked, they asked Miss Archibald where they could find Peter. When they arrived at the church, she led them around to the south side, where a cloister connected the transept to the neighboring Parish Hall.

"There he is," she said. She pointed to a man with long blond hair who was working on a platform that had been erected over the door to the south transept. Then she excused herself and headed back in the direction of the door at the foot of the soaring bell tower.

A moment later, they had entered the cloister. At closer hand, they could see that Peter was installing a plastic sheet over the opening for the center window of a stained-glass triplet. The window had been removed, and lay on the bed of an old red pickup that was backed up to the other side of the cloister.

Jerry walked up to the foot of the scaffolding. "Hello," he called up to the man. "We're looking for Peter De Vries."

The man turned around. "That's me," he said, and proceeded to start down the ladder that was affixed to the scaffolding.

As he did so, Charlotte noticed that he had only one arm.

"Hello," he said, as he dismounted the ladder. He extended his right hand. "Peter De Vries." The left sleeve of his plaid flannel shirt, which was pinned up where the elbow should have been, swung free. "What can I do for you?"

He was a thickset man in his late twenties—handsome in a rough-hewn sort of way—with a lantern jaw and dark blue eyes that were set close together in his face. He wore a full-length leather apron over his jeans and shirt, the pockets of which were stuffed with tools.

Jerry returned his handshake. "Hello," he said. "I'm Jerry D'Angelo, chief of the Zion Hill Police Department, and this is my friend, Mrs. Lundstrom, who's visiting from New York."

Charlotte stepped forward to shake his hand.

"So you came for the tour," he said.

Jerry paused for a moment, undecided about whether to take Peter up on his offer of a tour or get right down to business. He checked his watch. "We only have a few minutes," he said. "Could you give us an abbreviated version?"

"Sure," Peter said.

"I was just telling Mrs. Lundstrom that much of the architecture of Zion Hill is symbolic, though I'm not sure of what."

Peter nodded. He led them back out to the south side of the church and looked up at the bell tower. "We can start with the symbolism of the church bells," he said, looking up at the bells that hung in the open belfry. "These bells have a very profound symbolic significance."

He paused, and Jerry and Charlotte patiently awaited his explanation. He had a very slow, distracted manner of speaking, almost as if he had forgotten what it was that he was about to say next.

Finally, he spoke: "The church bells ring every evening at six o'clock, signaling to the inhabitants of Zion Hill that it is time to participate in one of the most important religious rituals of the day."

"And what is that?" asked Charlotte.

"The cocktail hour," Peter responded with a deadpan delivery.

Charlotte and Jerry smiled.

"I speak only partly in jest," he continued. "The residents of Zion Hill take their cocktail hour very seriously."

"As well they should," said Charlotte, for whom the sanctity of the cocktail hour was also inviolable.

"On a more serious note," Peter continued, "the church was built from 1909 to 1911 by Edward Archibald. The model was a thirteenth-century English parish church. Archibald chose a preindustrial model because he believed that a house of God should express the artistry of men, not machines."

"It seems like an odd attitude for someone who made his fortune in railroads to take," Charlotte commented.

"Yes," he agreed. "But not an uncommon one for that period. The arts and crafts movement, which advocated a return to craftsmanship in design, was very influential, and Archibald subscribed to their ideas. He insisted that his workmen use only preindustrial tools, but I suspect they cheated."

"I know they cheated," Jerry said. "My grandfather was a stonemason who came here to work for Edward Archibald."

"Actually, I know they cheated too," he said. "I used to be apprenticed to a glassblower who came from England to work for Archibald. That's where I learned about stained glass. He came from Stourbridge, England, which was famous for its glassworks. Now I take care of all the stained glass.''

"And he admitted to cheating?'' Jerry asked.

"Not so much him, because the glassblowing art wasn't amenable to twentieth-century techniques. But he told me that others did. Anyway, the end product was preindustrial, even if the workmen sometimes did use modern tools.'' He continued with his lecture: "Archibald also felt the Gothic model was the best expression of Swedenborg's Doctrine of Uses, which holds that each man is put on earth to play an individual role, but that the role of the individual should be subservient to the harmony of the whole.''

Jerry looked over at Charlotte, reminding her of their discussion earlier that day about this aspect of the New Church's beliefs.

"The idea was that the work of no one individual would stand out from that of any other; it was a communal undertaking. Which is not to say that individual contributions weren't recognized. They were, and the way they were recognized was through the concept of freedom in variety.''

At their puzzled expressions, he led them back through the cloister into the Parish Hall, where he paused before a large glass-fronted armoire. A quote from Isaiah was carved along the top: "And the key of the house of David will I lay upon his shoulder.''

Then he opened the door of the armoire, which contained a display of large, hand-tooled metal keys hanging on hooks mounted on a background of purple velvet. Each key was a work of art, and each one was different.

"This is our key cabinet,'' he said, "which I always show to visitors to illustrate the concept of freedom in variety. No two details of this church are the same. No two windows are exactly alike, no two doors, no two keys. Even the length of each individual pew varies slightly.''

Leaning forward for a better look, Charlotte could see keys with heads in the shape of a castle turret, a rosette, a Gothic trefoil, a Celtic cross, a Star of David, and ornamental knot.

"This one is modeled after the key to the great west door of Notre Dame Cathedral in Paris,'' Peter said, pointing out one of the larger keys.

"They're beautiful," Charlotte said.

"We have twenty-two doors, and each one is different: different shapes, different latches, and different keys. Freedom in variety. In the case of the doors, the differences also have another symbolic meaning," he went on. "They also symbolize the many ways to the divine truth."

"Fascinating," said Jerry, who was studying the keys.

Peter went on: "The New Church is unusual in that it believes that all world religions have their own validity."

"What's the metal?" Charlotte asked, admiring the silvery white sheen of the heads of the keys on display.

"It's called monel," he replied. "It's a natural alloy of nickel and copper. It's used throughout the church. It's very difficult to work with, but its virtue is that it doesn't rust, and, as you can see from the heads of the keys, it develops this lovely patina where it's been touched."

"It's very beautiful," she said.

"Would you like to go into the church now?" he asked.

As he spoke, the church bells overhead started to peal. Charlotte recognized the melody as that of a lovely old English hymn.

"It's the cocktail hour!" Jerry announced. Then he addressed Peter: "I think we'd better skip it. Maybe we could come back another time. We actually came here on another mission, and our time is running out. Thank you, though. I think Mrs. Lundstrom enjoyed the tour very much," he said. "As did I."

Charlotte nodded in agreement.

"We came here to ask you about one of your tenants," Jerry continued. "A young woman named Doreen Mileski, who resides in a two-family house that you own at 33 Liberty Street in Corinth."

"What would you like to know?" Peter asked.

"Anything you can tell us," Jerry said.

"I'll have to get my files," he said. "They're inside." He nodded toward his rooms at the back. "Would you like to take a seat?" he asked, gesturing toward the Gothic-style chairs that flanked a large table displaying a collection of Swedenborgian literature.

Charlotte and Jerry sat down, and Peter disappeared down a hallway at the back of the Parish Hall.

As they awaited his return, Charlotte scanned the titles of the booklets: *Our Eternal Home, Through the Valley of Death, Hell: Its Origins and Nature*, and *The Presence of Spirits in Madness*. She would have liked to look at some of them, but Peter was back momentarily with his files.

Pulling up another chair, he sat down and opened the file folder. "She moved in last November. Her full name is Doreen Marie Mileski. Birth date: April 16, 1967. Birthplace: Detroit, Michigan."

"Place of employment?" asked Jerry, who was making notes.

"She wasn't employed," he said.

Jerry looked up at him. "How'd she pay the rent if she wasn't employed?"

"She didn't pay the rent. It was paid for her."

"By whom?" Jerry asked.

"Dr. Victor Louria," he said. He held up the file folder for them to see. The tab was labeled "Dr. Louria." "He rented the apartment; he even filled out the rental application, for that matter. Hey," he said, clapping a palm to his broad chest, "who am I to ask questions?"

"You figured he'd be good for the rent," Jerry said.

"You're darned right I did," Peter said. "He's probably got an annual income of a million dollars."

"Do you have any idea why he rented the apartment for her?"

Charlotte wondered too. Why wouldn't he have put her up at Archfield Hall? Then she answered her own question: he would have wanted to keep her a secret, and if he'd put her up at his house, people would have seen her coming and going, and become curious.

Peter shook his head. "As I said, I didn't ask any questions. Why do you want to know, anyway?"

"She's been missing since a week ago last Monday," Jerry replied. "She probably went on a trip, but we thought we'd check it out."

Peter nodded.

"You wouldn't happen to know if she had any friends or relatives in this area, would you?"

Peter shook his head. "I have fourteen properties in Corinth," he said. "I can't keep track of the personal lives of all of my tenants."

"Fourteen!" said Jerry.

"Yeah," he replied. "I bought the first one eight years ago. Fixed it up and rented it. I'm pretty handy," he said, "despite this." He looked down at his empty sleeve. "Then I bought another, and another . . ."

"A one-man gentrification movement," Charlotte commented.

"I guess you could say that," he said.

"Has Dr. Louria ever rented any other apartments from you?" Jerry asked as they were getting up to leave.

"Yes, as a matter of fact," he said.

Jerry's head swiveled sharply around, his throwaway question having yielded an unexpected payoff.

"He had two other girls in another one of my apartments; it's on Hudson Street, down by the river."

"Names?" Jerry shot out the question.

"I don't remember," he said. He leafed through the file folder in his lap. "Here it is," he said. "The first one was Kimberly Ferguson." He gave an address on upper Broadway, near Columbia. "She moved in last May."

"When did she move out?" Jerry asked.

"She never did move out. She just took off. I still have her stuff stored in the attic over there. The furniture stayed for the next tenant; it was all Dr. Louria's. He had furnished the apartment for her."

"When did she take off, then?" Jerry asked.

"Early September," he said.

Which was when the skull of the first victim was found, Charlotte thought.

"The second one was Liliana Doyle. Born October 12, 1966, which would have made her twenty-six. She moved in late last September."

"After Kimberly had disappeared," Jerry said.

He nodded.

"Last address?"

"Let's see," he said, studying the form. He pushed his long blond hair out of his face with his one hand. "Here it is. In the city, again. In the East Village." He gave an address on East Fourth Street.

"What happened to her?" Jerry asked.

"Same thing," he said. "She up and left. At the beginning of last month."

"Didn't you think it unusual that three young women occupying apartments rented on their behalf by Dr. Louria disappeared?" Jerry looked over at Peter, awaiting his explanation.

He shrugged. "Now I see that it's unusual, yes. But I was only aware of two. I didn't know about this last one until just now. To tell you the truth, I didn't think much about it. It happens all the time."

"It does?" Jerry said.

"Yeah," he said. "You'd be surprised. People just take off. Especially these young women. They meet a guy, and— poof!—they're gone. In this case, the furniture didn't even belong to them, anyway. I'm not dealing with the most stable class of people."

"Did Liliana take her personal belongings?"

Peter shook his head. "They're in the attic of the house on Hudson Street with the first one's stuff."

"We'll probably want to take a look," Jerry said. "Would you be able to let us in there sometime?"

"Sure," he said. Reaching into one of the pockets in his leather apron, he pulled out a business card and passed it to Jerry. "This is my number here. If you can't reach me here, you can try my beeper number. I'm always out and about fixing toilets and the like."

Jerry stood to leave. "Thanks," he said, holding out his hand. "You've been an enormous help."

"Anything I can do," Peter said.

They had written Dr. Louria off as a suspect because of his reaction at seeing the skulls, but maybe they had done so prematurely, Charlotte thought as they drove back down the hill.

She was reconsidering Jerry's theory that Dr. Louria had created the young women in his dead wife's image, and then
killed them out of a need to exert the control over his dead
wife that had eluded him when she was alive. The fact that
he had set them up in Peter's apartments as if they were kept
women would seem to point to such a need. It struck her as
unlikely that a man with such a solid public persona would
harbor a homicidal obsession, but then she remembered what
he had said about being forced to keep his "bad little ear" a
secret until he was eight years old. To a person schooled in
secrecy as he must have been, the ability to conceal such an
obsession didn't seem so farfetched. It was quite possible that
he went through life wearing an invisible mask that concealed
his dark side as thoroughly as the iron mask he displayed in
his office had concealed the face of the French nobleman who
had worn it for so many years.

Charlotte wondered what to do about her own surgery. She
was supposed to let him know by next week if she wanted to
go ahead with it, but she sure as hell wasn't going to sign on
with a surgeon who might be a homicidal maniac.

They had reached the bottom of the hill before either of
them spoke. "What do you think?" Charlotte asked as they
pulled out onto the highway.

"I think we're in business," said Jerry. "We know who
the victims are. At least, I think we know who they are. That's
half the battle . . . " He was interrupted by the crackle of the
police radio.

"I've got the registration on that Honda," the dispatcher
said. "It's registered to Dr. Louria. The plastic surgeon on
River Road."

Charlotte and Jerry exchanged looks.

"There's something else too, Chief," she said. "We just
got a call from the Corinth P.D. They've got a thirty-seven at
the municipal park at the foot of Hudson Street. It's in the
water," she added.

"Shit!" Jerry muttered. Then he picked up the microphone
and spoke to the dispatcher: "Tell them I'll be right over."
He thanked her and returned the microphone to its cradle with
an angry thunk.

"What's a thirty-seven?" Charlotte asked.

"A dead body," he said.

A few minutes later, they turned off the Albany Post Road onto Hudson Street, a road that pitched steeply down to the shore of the river. The river's mood had changed once again. A stiff breeze had come up at the close of the day, and the surface of the water, which had been so placid only a few hours before, was now choppy again. Sea gulls wheeled and dove for their dinner against a sky that was tinted orange by the setting sun. The water, which had looked blue-gray earlier in the day, now looked emerald-green against the diminishing light of the sky. At the foot of the road, a small postage-stamp shaped park jutted out into the water. Half a dozen police cars were parked at the base of the footbridge that led over the railroad tracks to the park, and policemen were strung out along the shore of the park like fishermen at the edge of a trout stream on the opening day of fishing season.

As they parked, one of the policemen drew away from the cluster gathered around the police cars and came over to speak to them. He was dressed in plain clothes. Jerry introduced him as his captain, Harry Crosby.

He was a tall man with stooped shoulders, a big belly, and a long, lugubrious-looking face that was heavily lined.

"I hear we've got another body," Jerry said.

"Not a body," Captain Crosby said. "An arm bone." He turned to nod at a group of picnic tables under a small grove of willows whose branches were just beginning to bud. "A young couple spotted it while they were having a picnic."

Charlotte grimaced at the thought.

"Any other body parts?" Jerry asked.

"That's what we're looking for," Crosby said, nodding at the policemen who were spread out along the shore. "The county guys came right over."

As he spoke, one of the policemen who was searching the shoreline at the far side of the park let out a shout. "I've found something," he yelled, signaling for the others to join him.

A few minutes later, Charlotte and Jerry were heading toward the policemen who had gathered at the water's edge.

"Are you sure you want to see this?" Jerry asked.

Charlotte nodded.

The latest find was floating between the rotted pilings in the water and the algae-coated boulders that buttressed the shore. It was a woman's foot, neatly severed at the ankle. A size eight, Charlotte guessed.

The little group stood staring at the foot, which rocked gently in its watery pen on waves driven inland by the stiff breeze. No one spoke: it was as if they were mesmerized by its perfection.

There were no corns or calluses, no twisted toes or bunions. Only a dead-white foot, its toenails perfectly painted with red polish.

Charlotte couldn't get the image of the foot, with its perfect pedicure, out of her head. She thought about it all the way back to New York, all the way through her dinner at her favorite neighborhood bistro, and, afterwards, as she sat in an armchair in the living room of her town house in Turtle Bay. Like the twisted nose on the woman she had met at the Hollywood party, the dismembered foot seemed to symbolize a quest for physical perfection that had gone awry, in this case horribly awry. Doreen Mileski, like Kimberly Ferguson and Liliana Doyle before her, had sought out cosmetic surgery to improve her appearance, and had lost her life as a result. Who were these young women who had been willing to undergo operation after operation in order to look more beautiful? Presumably, Dr. Louria had operated on them free of charge, paying their rent and probably their other living expenses as well. Maybe he had even paid them a salary. If so, it meant that they must have been young women in need of money, who didn't have educations, or good jobs, or middle-class parents holding out a financial safety net. Were they prostitutes, perhaps? she asked herself, and then dismissed that idea on the basis that they wouldn't offer pristine enough working material for Dr. Louria. Runaways from the Midwest? But how would Dr. Louria have established contact with them? Then she thought of a possible answer to her question: aspiring actresses.

Aspiring actresses would fit all the requirements. With the exception of models, there were probably few categories of young women who were more concerned about their looks. They were also accustomed to a transient way of life, and were always in need of money. The addresses confirmed that: Morningside Heights, the East Village. They were the kinds of neighborhoods where young aspirants to the stage might share a low-rent apartment. Also, their acting talents would come in useful, if, as they suspected, Dr. Louria's ultimate intention was to have them take over the role of his dead wife. And there would be a large pool to draw from. New York was a mecca for aspiring actresses. How would he have recruited them? she wondered. Then she thought of the answer: an ad in *Backstage*, the periodical that was the equivalent of the daily newspaper for every young aspiring actress, or maybe *Variety*, which served a similar purpose.

Though Charlotte didn't subscribe to *Backstage*, which was virtually all casting calls, she did get *Variety*. She liked to keep up with what was opening, what was closing, who was making what movie. Getting up, she went into her library, where her housekeeper, Julie, stored the old issues, presumably because she was saving them for recycling, though they seemed to accumulate until they were eventually thrown away. A three-foot stack stood behind one of the chairs in the corner. Where should she start? she asked herself.

She had no idea how long the process of facial reconstruction took: how many operations were needed, how far apart the operations could be spaced. So she took a wild guess—half a dozen operations, spaced a month apart. Presuming that Dr. Louria wouldn't have killed the most recent victim, Doreen Mileski, before her course of surgery was completed, she counted back six months, which brought her to November. Which sounded about right: Peter had said that Doreen had moved in in November. Searching through the stack of back issues, she located the October issues near the bottom—thank God they hadn't been thrown out already—and pulled them out. Taking a seat, she started leafing through them one by one. But a review of the month of October turned up nothing.

Going back to the stack behind the chair, she pulled out the September issues.

She found it in the issue for the second week of September. It was in the "Health and Fitness" column of the classified section:

COSMETIC SURGERY—FREE!

Seeking to improve your appearance? Highly respected board-certified plastic surgeon seeks young women between the ages of twenty-five and thirty to serve as models for the demonstration of new techniques of facial reconstruction. Must be five foot six inches tall, and of normal weight. Safe, effective. Excellent results.

The ad didn't say that the recruits would serve as experimental subjects, Charlotte noted, but rather as "models": a term that was guaranteed to appeal to those with image problems. It was a new twist on the old ruse of offering modeling assignments or posing as a talent scout in order to lure young women to a particular location for nefarious purposes. The ad gave a telephone number with a Westchester area code. Going over to her telephone, Charlotte dialed the number, and received a recorded message saying that the number was no longer in service. Then she called the operator and asked what town the exchange was for.

"Zion Hill," was the operator's reply.

Next she called Jerry. As she suspected, he was still at the office. "Do you have one of those telephone books in which you can look up a telephone number and find the address of the person it belongs to?"

"A reverse directory," he said. "I have one for Westchester County. What's this about, anyway?"

"Westchester County's what I need. I'll tell you what it's about when you find the number." She gave him the number, and waited. She could hear the sound of the pages being flipped.

"Here it is," he said finally. And then: "The address is a residence at 300 River Road, Zion Hill."

"Archfield Hall," she said.

7

CHARLOTTE HAD BEEN right: all three young women had been aspiring actresses working marginal jobs—two as waitresses, the third as a part-time salesclerk in a SoHo boutique—while waiting for the big break. Jerry had spent the next two days tracking them down. He had also sifted through their belongings, which, as Peter had predicted, didn't amount to much. One had originally been from Arkansas, one from Florida, and one from Detroit. All three had been five feet six inches tall, with blue or blue-gray eyes. Two had been blondes, and one a brunette. The first two victims, Kimberly Ferguson and Liliana Doyle, had been matched through their dental records to the skulls that had been found in the cemeteries; the third victim, Doreen Mileski, had been identified through X-ray records of an arm broken in an ice-skating accident, which matched X-rays of the forearm that had washed up in Corinth. No skull had yet been found for Doreen Mileski, though the county police had instituted round-the-clock surveillance at local cemeteries in anticipation that the killer would leave his latest victim's skull on a gravestone, as he had the skulls of his first two victims. Friends and associates of all three victims had been questioned. A former roommate of Doreen Mileski's remembered Doreen talking about her intention to answer Dr. Louria's ad. She had taken off not long afterward, and they hadn't heard anything more from her. In the transient world of the city's aspiring actresses, roommates were always coming and going. Nor had the suspicions of the families of the

victims been aroused when they didn't hear from their daughters; in all three cases, communication had been intermittent
at best, and relations between the girls and their families—or
rather, their mothers, since in all three cases, the fathers were
absent—had not been good. Perhaps weak family relations
was one reason Dr. Louria had chosen these women over the
other respondents to his ad. In addition, of course, to a basic
resemblance to his dead wife.

In any case, the time had come to confront Dr. Louria.

Charlotte and Jerry arrived at Archfield Hall at ten the next
morning, after having called first to make sure that Dr. Louria
would be in. Though Charlotte had now visited Dr. Louria at
his office in the former music studio on two occasions, this
would be her first visit to Archfield Hall, and she was eager
to see the inside of the fabled former residence of the founder
of Zion Hill. After pulling into the circular driveway, which
surrounded a pool with a fountain in the shape of a medieval
gryphon, they parked the car, and mounted the stone steps to
the front door, which was covered by a columned portico.
If the front door was any indication, Archfield Hall was indeed
the architectural masterpiece that Lothian Archibald had described. The double door was crowned by an arch on which
was carved a series of ten sheep: a ram and a ewe with their
heads intertwined, and four lambs on either side. The names
Edward and Ruth were inscribed above the ram and the ewe,
and the names of the Archibald children, including Lillian and
Lothian, above each of the lambs. The door, which stood ten
feet high, was made of glass set in a frame of ornamental metal
in the form of a soaring tree. The monel handles were wrought
in the shape of birds, whose heads had turned a silvery white
from the touch of human hands.

The door was answered by a short, sweet-faced Hispanic
housekeeper, who admitted them into an entrance foyer with
a richly paneled ceiling. The walls were sheathed in glittering
mosaics dotted with medallions illustrating scenes from the
Bible. But the entrance hall was nothing compared to the Great
Hall into which the housekeeper then led them. It was a huge
room, baronial in scale, with a vaulted ceiling and a fireplace

on the river wall that was big enough to stand up in. A second-story balcony made of the same beautiful hand-carved wood that paneled the entrance foyer ran around the other three walls. The furniture was in the heavy Gothic style—suitable for your typical Westchester castle—and the stone floor was covered with exquisite Oriental carpets.

But the feature of the room that captured Charlotte's attention was the magnificent mosaic above the fireplace. It depicted a heavenly chorus of angels surrounding a central angel with a familiar face. It was a face with wide green eyes, a jutting jaw, and long, flowing red hair. It was the face of the marble angel in Jack Lister's gallery, and of the tapestry angel in Lothian Archibald's living room. It was the face of Lillian Archibald, and of her dead daughter, Lily Louria.

Leaving them at the door to the Great Hall, the housekeeper excused herself to summon the doctor, who appeared momentarily. He was casually dressed in a dark-patterned sports shirt and gray flannel slacks.

"What a majestic room!" Charlotte said as the doctor showed them to a cluster of furniture by a floor-to-ceiling window with a view of the river.

"Majestic, but comfortable at the same time, which is what I like about it," the doctor said. "Edward Archibald built it to be the center of family life for the Archibald family."

He indicated that Charlotte and Jerry should be seated in an oversized couch upholstered in a tapestry fabric, and then he sat down in a navy blue Queen Anne-style wing chair.

"Would you like a cup of coffee?" he asked, which reminded Charlotte of the delicious Brazilian coffee he had served at his office.

Much to Charlotte's disappointment, Jerry declined the doctor's offer, and Dr. Louria dismissed the hovering housekeeper with a nod of his head.

"I think you know why we're here," Jerry said. He nodded at Charlotte, who reached into her tote bag for the copy of *Variety* she had brought along. She set it on the coffee table. The ad was circled in red.

The doctor nodded resignedly.

It struck Charlotte that he didn't look nervous, only exhausted: as if he had been through a long ordeal that was finally coming to an end.

"We know that you placed this ad," said Jerry. "We also know that you set up the young women who responded to this ad and the others like it in apartments in Corinth, and we know that you operated on them." Reaching into his briefcase, Jerry pulled out a clasp envelope and withdrew four five-by-seven color prints. "These are photographs of the soft tissue reconstructions that were made from the skulls that we showed you the other day. They were done by a local forensic sculptor named Jack Lister. You've probably heard of him."

The doctor nodded in recognition of the name.

"He did two facial reconstructions for each skull. The first represents what he thought the victims looked like before their cosmetic surgery, and the second represents what he thought they looked like after their cosmetic surgery." He spread the photos out on the coffee table next to the copy of *Variety*: the two "befores" on one side, and the two "afters" on the other. "And this"—he reached into his briefcase again and pulled out another envelope—"is a photograph of your late wife, which was given to us by her aunt." He removed the photograph and set it down above the two "after" photographs. "What these photographs tell us is that you were trying to re-create the face of your late wife," Jerry said. He studied the photographs for a moment, and then looked back at Dr. Louria. "Would you like to explain?" he asked.

The doctor sat with his head down and his hands clasped between his knees. For a moment he was silent, and then he spoke: "When I first saw Lily, it was as if I'd been hit over the head with a two-by-four. I'd never had that feeling before. Suddenly I knew what the lyrics meant in the love songs: walking on air, head over heels. Before that, I'd always thought they made them up. I didn't know you could feel that way. I couldn't eat, I couldn't sleep."

Jerry nodded solicitously. He was a good listener.

"Despite my profession, I had always felt intimidated by beautiful women. It was because of this." He touched a hand to his artificial ear. "I always thought that women would be revolted, as in fact they had been in the past. But I was determined to have Lily. She was the ideal of feminine beauty that I had been seeking for years to create in my patients. I pursued her with a vengeance. I sent her flowers. I wrote her love letters. I bought her jewelry. I thought that if I could possess someone as beautiful as Lily, it would be a refutation of this.'' He touched his hand to his ear again. ''I was amazed when she didn't reject me, and even more amazed when, in time, she consented to marry me. I knew that she didn't love me, that she wanted to marry me for all this''—he glanced around the room—''but I don't think I'm flattering myself if I say that I think she had some regard for me.

''Anyway, the fact that she didn't return my love didn't matter to me. I possessed the most beautiful woman in the world. For two and a half years, I was the happiest man alive. I was married to an angel.''

Charlotte looked up at the mosaic over the fireplace.

''Her mother,'' the doctor said, following Charlotte's glance. ''They could have been twin sisters.'' He continued: ''Then came that afternoon in Cozumel.''

''Tell us about that,'' Jerry said.

''She had been captivated by the beauty of a secluded beach we had seen on one of those Robinson Crusoe tours we had taken of the island. The boat had stopped there for lunch. It was on the southern shore, nestled in a half-moon shaped cove tucked into the cliff: a little jewel of a beach. It was our last day—our last afternoon, in fact. We had a few hours to kill before our flight, and Lily suggested that we go back there for a swim. She liked to swim in the buff.''

There was a pause as he delved into his memory. Then he continued: ''I still don't know how it happened. One minute we were swimming in the turquoise waters, the next she was slowly being carried away from me. It was as if she'd boarded a train that was pulling out of the station.'' He clenched his fists, and his face became twisted with the pain of the memory. ''Then I got caught up in the current too. I don't remember much after that. Fighting to stay afloat, seeing her in the distance, struggling to make it back to shore. Finally, crawling back up on the beach, and finding that she was . . . gone. I still have nightmares about her beach towel—it was striped, red and white. Her beach bag, her sunglasses, her container of sun block. All just sitting there, as if she would be back any minute.''

He shut his eyes and massaged his brow. After a moment, he lifted his head and went on with his story: "I blamed myself, of course. I'd play the 'if only' game for hours on end: if only I'd taken a different flight, left earlier for the airport, paid attention to the warnings in the guidebooks about swimming at unsupervised beaches. If only I'd been in better physical shape . . . '' He continued: "I came back here. I went back to work. I went through the days like an automaton. And at night, I would dream of her being swept away in the current, and of her red-and-white-striped towel lying there on the sand. I spent the hours between work and sleep sitting in this chair, looking out at the river.'' He stared out at the river, which sparkled in the morning sun. "I called it my chair of inertia,'' he said. "Once I sat down in it, it was impossible to get back up again.''

"I have one like that in my house too,'' Jerry joked.

The doctor made a feeble attempt at a smile, and then continued: "On a couple of occasions, I had experienced the illusion that I could see her out there on the river, being carried downstream by the current. I would sit here for hours with my binoculars''—he nodded at the binoculars that rested on a table next to the chair—"looking out at the river in hopes that I would catch another glimpse of her. I would be just about to give up, and then I'd see her head bobbing out there among the whitecaps again.'' Shifting position, he turned away from the river, as if he couldn't bear to gaze upon the entity that had been so parsimonious with its offerings.

Charlotte was reminded again of the severed foot bobbing in the water, with its painted toenails. If Dr. Louria was the murderer, his identification with the river—with the current that had taken his wife away—might explain why he had disposed of the body parts by throwing them in the river.

"I sought consolation in religion,'' he continued. "I envied Lothian and Peter their belief in the afterlife. At least they had the comfort of believing that they would eventually join Lily in heaven. I wanted to believe: I went to discussion groups, I talked with the pastor. But it didn't work for me."

"Who's Peter?" Jerry asked.

"Peter De Vries," Dr. Louria replied, "who owns the rental properties in Corinth. He was a childhood friend of Sebastian and Lily's. They all went to the Zion Hill School together. Peter is Sebastian's best friend, and he and Lily were very close as well."

Jerry nodded, and then said: "You were saying?"

"I was talking about the afterlife. Even the consolation that I might see Lily again in heaven wasn't enough to make me believe in a God who had been cruel enough to take her away from me in the first place. Another reason I found it difficult to develop faith in the afterlife is that I never really believed she was dead. I kept expecting her to come walking in. I had convinced myself that she was a victim of amnesia, that she had washed ashore somewhere. I thought it was only a matter of time before she'd turn up."

"I understand you went to Mexico to look for her," Jerry said.

"Yes," he replied. "I would show her picture around in the villages on Cozumel and along the coast of Yucatán." He nodded at the photograph on the coffee table. "That same picture, as a matter of fact."

Charlotte remembered what Jerry had said about Dr. Louria's refusal to accept Lily's death setting the stage for Lothian Archibald's belief that the young woman she had seen was a victim of amnesia.

"I would go back to that beach with her towel and her beach bag, and spread them out as they had been spread out that day. I thought that if I recreated the same conditions that had existed at the moment we decided to take that swim, that I could turn back the clock. I was mad with grief," he said simply. "I'm still mad with grief," he added. "I'm just mad in a different way. Anyway, I went on like that for over a year. Then one day, a patient came to me wanting a complete facial reconstruction. She was in her late twenties. I did three operations on her. To my surprise, she came out looking like Lily."

"Was that Kimberly Ferguson?" Jerry asked, nodding at

the "after" photo of the reconstructed face of the first murder victim.

"No," the doctor said. "This young woman came before Kimberly. She was the one who gave me the idea of creating a new Lily. During the time I was working on her, I noticed that my mood improved. The world didn't seem as black as it had. I looked forward to getting up in the morning because I had something important to do. That's when I decided that I would try to create the perfect Lily. I placed the first ad in *Variety* that May."

"That would have been May of 1991, then," Jerry said.

He nodded. "I installed a special telephone for taking the calls." He went on: "I was concerned that I wouldn't get enough replies to yield a good pool of candidates, but I needn't have worried."

"How many did you get?" Jerry asked.

"Over seventy, and half a dozen of them met the physical requirements." He continued: "As you know, I chose Kimberly Ferguson. She was from a small town in Arkansas. Grew up in a mobile home, quit high school when she was sixteen, had a baby out of wedlock when she was eighteen. The baby later died, which was when she decided to come to New York to pursue an acting career."

"What made you choose her?"

"Two reasons, apart from the general resemblance to Lily. The first is that she was bright. Some of the young women who responded weren't intelligent enough to have impersonated someone as unique as Lily. I also wanted someone who didn't have connections: no strong family ties, no steady boyfriend, no close friends. Because I had other plans for her."

"To kill her, you mean?" Jerry asked.

He shook his head and smiled ironically. "No," he said. "Why would I have wanted to kill what I had labored so long and hard to achieve?"

"I can think of a number of reasons," Jerry said. "One might be that she didn't measure up, that she wasn't the perfect Lily. That you killed her because you wanted to start with a fresh canvas, so to speak."

"If that were the case, I could simply have advertised again.

I wouldn't have needed to kill her," he said. "But, in fact, she did measure up. She was the most true to Lily of them all. As you can see from Jack Lister's reconstruction. He did an incredible job, by the way."

For a moment, they all looked at the photo of the reconstructed face of Kimberly Ferguson after she had undergone the plastic surgery.

"Kimberly was pretty even before the surgery," said Charlotte as she compared the photo of the "after" reconstruction to the photo of the "before" reconstruction that lay beside it.

"Yes," said Dr. Louria. "She was the prettiest. I wondered why she even wanted the surgery, but she had a poor self-image. Often it's the prettiest women who think they're the most unattractive."

"Is the 'before' reconstruction as accurate as the 'after'?" Jerry asked.

"It's incredible," he replied. "As is the one for Liliana. Kimberly's hair was a little shorter, but he got the style and color exactly right."

"I presume Liliana was the second victim," Jerry said.

The doctor nodded. "I'll get to her. But to continue with Kimberly for a moment: I never would have killed her because she didn't measure up. In a way, she looked more like Lily than Lily herself. Besides, I wouldn't have killed her because, as I said, I had other plans for her."

Jerry looked up at him. "What plans?" he asked.

"I wanted to make her my wife," he replied. "For over a year, I had been married to a corpse. By transforming Kimberly, I could look forward to being married to a real woman. Plastic surgeons talk about the Pygmalion complex: the plastic surgeon who feels as if he has *created* his patient. That was my goal: to bring Lily back to life, to make my creation warm to my touch. The new face was just the beginning. I also was planning to enlarge her breasts, to have her teeth capped, to get her fitted with tinted contact lenses . . ."

"A latter-day Henry Higgins," Charlotte interjected.

"Yes. I did think of myself in those terms," he said. "Creating Lily would be an act of parturition. I knew it wouldn't be easy. Especially with a girl from backwoods Arkansas. She would have to be schooled in Lily's speech, gestures, mannerisms. But I looked forward to the challenge of it.''

"Which is why you chose aspiring actresses," Charlotte said.

He nodded.

"Would you have had her pose as an amnesia victim?" Jerry asked.

"Yes. It's not as farfetched as it sounds. It even happens with some degree of frequency to people who undergo near-death experiences. I had studied the medical literature after Lily's death. I knew enough about the condition that I could have made a very convincing presentation.''

Jerry nodded, and made a notation.

"My plan was to fly Kimberly to Mexico and set her up in a village on the coast of Yucatán, and then to go down there and 'discover' her. Since I'd been there three times already to search for Lily, it wasn't a stretch of the imagination that I might actually find her. Or rather, her stand-in.''

"And Kimberly?" asked Charlotte. "What did she think of this?''

"She liked the idea. It was like a game for her. Of course, she wasn't thinking beyond the immediate future. Nor was I, for that matter. I had no long-term plans. She also liked the money," he said. "I paid her liberally.''

"Then what happened?" Jerry asked.

"She disappeared.''

"When was that?" Jerry asked.

"Just after Labor Day." He continued: "As you know, I had set her up in the apartment on Hudson Street. She would come here every day for Lily lessons. When she didn't show up, I went over to the apartment, and she wasn't there. Our agreement was that she wasn't to see anyone but me until her coming out.''

"At the governor's ball?" asked Charlotte. She explained: "That's where Henry Higgins introduced Eliza Doolittle in Shaw's *Pygmalion*.''

He smiled. "I hadn't decided how I would formally introduce her, but it would be something like that." He continued: "I thought that she'd violated our agreement—gone to the city to visit a friend, perhaps. I kept going back to the apartment to check, but there was no evidence that she'd returned. After a couple of weeks, I concluded that she'd taken advantage of me, that she'd only been staying around for the free surgery."

"Were you upset?" asked Jerry.

The doctor shrugged. "Upset, but not surprised. She wasn't from the most stable of backgrounds."

"Then what?" Jerry prompted.

"I advertised again. The second girl's name was Liliana, as I mentioned. I chose her because of the similarity in the names. Out of sentiment, which was a mistake. Her background was similar to Kimberly's, except that she was originally from Florida, instead of from Arkansas. But she wasn't as smart: she wouldn't have been up to the part. Nor did she have the bone structure. She didn't come out looking as much like Lily as Kimberly had, despite the fact that her surgery was much more extensive."

They looked at the photo of the reconstruction of Liliana's face after she had undergone the cosmetic surgery. Though there was a strong superficial resemblance to Lily, her features were more coarse and leaden.

"In fact," Dr. Louria continued, "I was considering letting her go after she was finished with the series of operations."

"But it wasn't necessary to let her go, because she disappeared too," Jerry said. "When was that, exactly?"

"The end of March."

"Didn't it alarm you when your second Galatea disappeared?"

He shook his head. "She knew I wasn't happy with her. We'd had a number of run-ins. In addition to being stupid, she was unreliable. She wouldn't show up when she was supposed to. She also had a negative attitude. I figured that she'd just walked off the job."

"Then you advertised for the third time."

"Actually, I already had. I was working on two at once. I'd had a sense that Liliana wasn't going to work out, so I advertised again a month later. In fact, I wondered if Liliana took off because she found out that she had a competitor. The third girl's name was Doreen Mileski. She was from Detroit,

had been to college. She would have made the best Lily of
all. She wasn't from a white trash background, like Kimberly
and Liliana. She didn't come out looking as much like Lily
as Kimberly had, but she came out looking very much like
her, and she was a very good actress. She had Lily down pat.
I was upset when she disappeared. She seemed more committed than the other two had been. We also got along well.
No one could ever have replaced Lily for me, but Doreen was
a start. I was even beginning to entertain fantasies that she
would agree to stay permanently with me—that it would be
something more than just a game. And I think she was beginning to entertain the same fantasies." He sighed. "Then you
showed up here with your skulls."

"We've found some of her body parts," Jerry said.

The doctor looked up at Jerry, and then away. As Jerry
continued to speak, he gazed out of the leaded glass windows
at the silver stream of the river.

"A forearm and a foot washed up at the Corinth Municipal
Park on Friday," Jerry said. "We identified them as Doreen's
through a break in the forearm. If the murderer sticks to his
pattern, we can expect to find her skull in a local cemetery
within the next few days."

Removing his glasses, the doctor leaned his head against
the wing of the oversized chair and wiped a tear from the
corner of his eye.

"When was the last time you saw her?" Jerry asked.

"It was on Tuesday, April twenty-first," he said. "She had
gotten some dye for her hair that morning at the drugstore."

That must have been when Aunt Lothian saw her, Charlotte
thought.

"She was a brunette, and Lily, as you know, had red hair.
She was going to dye her hair that afternoon, and come over
here that evening to show me how it turned out. She'd also
gotten fitted for some tinted contact lenses. Lily had green
eyes, and Doreen's were blue-gray. She never showed up. As
I said, it wasn't like her. I kept going over to the apartment
to look for her, as I had done with the others." He sobbed
quietly. "But she never showed up."

"Why didn't you go to the police?"

"I thought about it," he said, regaining his composure. "But that would have meant revealing the nature of my . . . strange obsession, if you will. Anyway, any impulses I might have had of that nature were obviated by your appearance with the skulls. I realized that, if it was discovered that I had performed the surgery on the dead girls, I would be the one accused of the murders."

Jerry nodded. "Which brings me to the question of where you were when these three young women disappeared." He went on: "We don't have any exact times, which means that it's going to be difficult for you to establish an alibi. Unless you were out of the country, or something like that."

Dr. Louria sat up at attention.

"*Were* you out of the country?" Jerry asked.

"Yes, as a matter of fact, I was. Not when Liliana disappeared. But I was out of the country when Kimberly disappeared. I had gone to Rio to visit my mother in the hospital. She'd had a hip replacement operation. I only found out after I got back that Kimberly had taken off."

"Is there any way we can confirm this?"

"Yes, you can call my mother."

Jerry looked skeptical.

"Or call Varig Airlines. They should still have the records. I would have the exact dates and flight numbers in my appointment book."

"I'd appreciate that information," Jerry said.

"If you don't believe that my mother would tell the truth"—he smiled—"and to be perfectly honest, she would say anything to protect me—I have other relatives who'll verify my alibi. You could talk to them. There was a family gettogether at my brother's; there were thirty people there."

"I'd like all the names and telephone numbers," Jerry said. "Also, we'll want to search your house. I could get a search warrant, but it would be easier if you would just offer your consent. We're also going to have to talk with the people you see on a daily basis: the housekeeper, your office help."

"I understand," he said.

"Did anyone else know about the Lily look-alikes?"

"Only my housekeeper, Marta," he said. "Marta Herrera. She lives here."

Jerry wrote down the name. "Did you have a nurse assisting you during the operations?" he asked. "Or an anesthesiologist?"

He shook his head. "I didn't need a nurse, and I used a local anesthetic."

Jerry leaned forward. "Dr. Louria, if it's true that you didn't kill these three young women—and I think it should be fairly simple to verify your alibi—then it means that somebody else did."

Dr. Louria nodded.

"Let's say for the moment that you were successful in your attempt to pass off one of these young women as your wife. Is there anyone you know of who would have a reason for not wanting to see this come about?"

He shook his head.

"Were you your wife's heir?" Jerry asked.

"No," he said. "She thought I had enough money. Which I do. Her heir was her brother, Sebastian Archibald."

Charlotte remembered Jerry saying that Sebastian was borrowing the start-up money for his new restaurant against an inheritance. This must have been the inheritance that he was counting on.

"Then it would be correct to say that Sebastian would have stood to lose his inheritance from his sister if you had been successful in your scheme to resurrect your wife from the dead."

Leave it to Jerry to have a backup theory, Charlotte thought. It was an angle that hadn't even occurred to her.

"I know it sounds farfetched, but I'm grasping at straws," Jerry said.

"I suppose it's correct," Dr. Louria said, "although I imagine he could have tried to prove she was an imposter."

"Did Lily have any money of her own?" Jerry asked.

"Yes, a fair amount," the doctor replied.

"How much is a fair amount?" Jerry asked impatiently. "Two or three million? Or enough to pay next month's bills?"

"The former. Somewhere between a million and a half and two million."

"From Edward Archibald trust funds?"

"She had inherited some money from her grandfather, but much less than you'd expect. Most of his fortune was left to trusts that were set up to benefit the community, as I'm sure you are aware. The rest was divided among his eight children and nineteen grandchildren."

"Then where did her money come from?" Jerry asked.

"She had a small inheritance. Also, the men she kept company with before she married me were very generous with their . . ." He paused for a moment, apparently searching for the right expression, and then said: "Gifts."

Jerry gave him an inquiring look, but said no more.

The doctor's implication was that his late wife had not been above exchanging sexual favors for money. Charlotte remembered what Lothian had said about the balls at Buckingham Palace, the weekends in France. It didn't sound as if Lily Louria had been quite the angel everyone was making her out to be.

"She also invested wisely," he continued. "It seems odd to say of someone like Lily, whose personality was so extravagant, but she was very good with money. She wasn't a spender. Herself, that is. She'd get other people—like me"—he smiled sheepishly—"to spend money on her behalf."

"Where'd she learn how to invest?" Jerry asked, his curiosity piqued. "From reading investor's guides?"

"Lily never read anything," he said. "She'd pump people for information. She had a nose for money: she knew who had it, and who didn't; whose portfolios were doing well, who was living off their capital."

"I wish I had some of that talent," Jerry said. "We'll need the name of the estate lawyer."

Dr. Louria gave him the name.

"Has any of the estate been distributed?"

The doctor shook his head. "The settlement has been held up by the fact that her body was never recovered."

"Any other ideas about who might have wanted to kill the Lily look-alikes?"

The doctor shook his head. "No ideas at all."

8

AFTER THEIR TALK with Dr. Louria, Jerry summoned his troops, and the search of Archfield Hall began. While one of Jerry's men stayed with Dr. Louria in the Great Hall, half a dozen others spread out over the house and grounds in search of evidence that might incriminate the doctor. Jerry himself had chosen to search the library, and Charlotte tagged along. Unlike the rest of the house, which tended toward the monumental, the library was warm and cozy, with a low ceiling and hand-carved wooden bookcases, above which ran a frieze with a quote from Swedenborg: "The doctrine of charity teaches: The common good in a society or kingdom consists of these things: there shall be morality, knowledge, and uprightness. There shall be the necessities of life—occupation, industry, and protection. There shall be justice. There shall be a sufficiency of wealth. There shall be what is divine among them." A round table surrounded by Windsor chairs occupied the center of the room. The fact that its surface was covered with file folders indicated that this was where the doctor spent much of his time. As in the Great Hall, there was a fireplace at one end of the room. The opposite end was taken up by a "media center," which included a large-screen television set and a built-in desk.

They started by scanning the bookshelves, which held mostly medical books and journals. Several of the medical texts were authored or edited by Dr. Louria, including a thick tome with the forbidding title, *Osseointegrated Alloplastic Auricular Reconstruction*. Finding nothing on the bookshelves, they moved on to the media center. It was here that Charlotte made her first discovery: a series of videotapes labeled "Lily I," "Lily II," and "Lily III." They were on a shelf above the television set, sandwiched in among a series of videotapes demonstrating cosmetic surgery techniques.

"I've found something," she said as she pulled them off the shelf.

Jerry was at her side in an instant, and she showed him the labels on the spines of the plastic cases.

"Since they're included with the technical tapes, I presume they're videos of the surgical procedures that were used on the Lily clones," she said.

"There's one way to find out," Jerry said. Taking the tape labeled "Lily I," he turned on the television, inserted the tape into the videocassette recorder, and pushed the "Play" button.

Then they sat down on the couch to await the show.

As it turned out, the tape wasn't a record of the operations, but of the postsurgical "Lily lessons," in which, in the case of Kimberly Ferguson, a poor, uneducated girl from backwoods Arkansas was transformed into the pampered wife of a rich cosmetic surgeon.

The tape started off with several close-ups of Lily, then cut to Kimberly sitting at a dressing table in a bedroom that, judging from the massive hand-carved furniture, was the master bedroom at Archfield Hall. She was wearing a white terry cloth bathrobe and applying makeup. Though they had seen Lister's "after" reconstruction of Kimberly's face, it was nevertheless remarkable to see that face reflected in the mirror of the dressing table, and to see how closely it resembled the original. The only difference was the hair, which was straight and blond and of medium length. Obviously, Kimberly had yet to dye it red.

The date on the videotape said August 15, 1991, which would have been shortly before Kimberly disappeared. It was gruesome to think that the face of this pretty young woman would be nothing but an eyeless skull in only a matter of weeks. The voice of Dr. Louria, with its hint of a Portuguese accent, was giving Kimberly instructions: "After you put on the eyeliner, take the Q-tip and rub it down into the base of the eyelashes. That's how she always did it. First the eyeliner, then the mascara.''

With the video camera recording her every move, the Lily look-alike applied the makeup, removed it, and reapplied it under Dr. Louria's watchful eye until she got it right.

"Weird," said Jerry after Dr. Louria had pronounced the job perfect.

"I'll say," Charlotte agreed.

"Now the perfume," Dr. Louria said.

Kimberly looked down at the array of bottles on the dressing table. "Which one?" she asked with a drawl that would have made Henry Higgins wince.

"The Muguet," said Dr. Louria. "That's what she always wore. She ordered it from Grasse, France.''

Searching among the bottles, Kimberly picked one out and applied it to the skin behind her ears and on the insides of her wrists.

"Now the jewelry," Dr. Louria said. As he gave a voice-over discourse on what type of jewelry Lily had worn (she had been particularly fond of bangle bracelets), Kimberly proceeded to put on the gold hoop earrings and heavy gold bangle bracelets that the doctor had laid out for her on a tray. After she had finished putting on the jewelry, Dr. Louria asked her to put on the dress that he had laid out on the bed. "It was one of Lily's favorites," he said as Kimberly slipped the dress on over her head.

It was a long, snug-fitting sheath of a dark green wool jersey, which was worn with a wide green snakeskin belt and high-heeled green suede boots. Even on Kimberly, with her thin, straight, blond hair, the outfit was stunning; it must have been all the more so on Lily, with her mane of vivid red.

As they might have expected, Dr. Louria then asked her to walk around the room, but it was *how* he asked her to walk that surprised Charlotte. It wasn't with the phony grace of a make-believe princess or the mincing prance of the runway model, but with her chest stuck out and her rear end swaying as if she were a Playboy bunny. Poor Kimberly, who had the lunging stride of the country girl, was obviously finding it rough going, and complained that the high-heeled boots hurt her feet. But Dr. Louria mercilessly made her repeat her circumambulation of the room over and over until he was satisfied.

Charlotte wondered if Lily had really walked like that. The stride struck her as so unnatural and so stereotypically provocative that she wondered if Dr. Louria might be taking liberties with the truth in order to satisfy the demands of his own sexual fantasies.

Throughout it all, the girl had been cooperative, and quick. She had talent, Charlotte thought. She would have made a good actress, though her Arkansas twang would have taken some work.

They were about to look at the tape labeled "Lily II" when they were interrupted by a knock on the door.

A policeman stuck his head through the door opening. "I think we've got something, Chief," he said.

The policeman didn't say what they had found, and Jerry didn't ask. He would see for himself soon enough. With the policeman in the lead, they passed through the house and across the lawn to a patio that was cantilevered out over the railroad embankment. Though it seemed odd to build a recreational structure so close to the railroad tracks, there was no getting away from the tracks if you wanted to take advantage of the view. Charlotte had seen mansions on the Hudson that had the railroad tracks running right past the front door. From the patio, they headed down a path that traversed the embankment. Though it was now overgrown, it was clear that the path had once been beautifully landscaped. The green shoots of garden perennials—Charlotte recognized those of daylilies and Oriental poppies—peeked up through the weeds in the terraced beds, and colonies of lilies of the valley grew among the pachysandra, their buds still only tiny dots on the stems. The path had probably been used for access to the river when it had still been clean enough to swim in. An old canoe lay in the weeds next to railroad tracks below, leading Charlotte to wonder if people still canoed on the Hudson.

At the end of the path, about twenty yards up the embankment from the tracks, was the type of structure that Charlotte had known in her youth as a summer house: a pavilion-like building made of wood, with half-open sides. It was painted dark green. Though it must once have been charming, it had fallen into disrepair: the roof had caved in on one side, and it was overgrown with a tangle of old wisteria vines.

As they approached, they could see a small cluster of policemen inside. The group looked up expectantly as Jerry entered.

"What have we got?" he asked.

The policemen stood aside to reveal a workbench piled with stacks of old clay flowerpots. Charlotte's first thought was that the summer house must have been put to later use as a potting shed, and the workbench as a potting table. But then she noticed the stench that permeated the spring air, and saw that the surface of the workbench had a greasy sheen, and was stained with dark blotches, and that the rough wood bore fresh scars from the blade of a cutting instrument.

His question was answered by Captain Crosby, who nodded at the workbench. "We've found where the doctor cut up the bodies, Chief," he said. Then he nodded at a heap of old burlap bags on the cement floor, which were also stained with dried blood. "We think these are the burlap bags he used to carry the bodies down to the river. We haven't found the cleaver. I figure he probably kept it, or threw it in the river. But Bert's looking for it with the metal detector, anyway."

Jerry nodded and went over to the workbench.

Seeing the gashes in the wood, Charlotte conjured up a mental image of the corpse cutter at work on his grisly task. It must have been hard work carrying the bodies down the path, and then carving them up. Suddenly, she felt her knees begin to buckle. She realized that it was nearly two, and she was hungry. The smell would have been hard to take in any case, but it was even more so on an empty stomach.

Stepping forward, she tapped Jerry on the shoulder. "Jerry," she said, "I'm going to take a little walk down to the river. It's the smell," she explained, and remembered what Jerry had said about wool absorbing the corpse reek. Damn! She had worn a wool jacket.

He nodded. "It takes some getting used to," he said with a grimace. "Some people never get used to it," he added. "Like me, for example."

Leaving the summer house, Charlotte continued on down to the railroad bed, where a policeman was scanning the weeds at the side of the tracks with a metal detector. Crossing the tracks, she stood on the riverbank, and took a deep breath; the air smelled refreshingly of the sea.

Captain Crosby had been quick to jump to the conclusion that Dr. Louria was the murderer, but Charlotte was skeptical. One of Jerry's favorite sayings was that the crime scene was the mirror of the perpetrator. But the summer house hardly struck her as the crime scene of an eminent plastic surgeon. For one thing, why would he have used a summer house that was virtually in his own backyard when he had an operating room at his disposal? If he had arranged to perform cosmetic surgery on the young women in private, surely he could have arranged to cut them up in private, as well.

But even if one conceded that there was a reason behind his use of the summer house—perhaps to mislead the police by making them think that he was too obvious a suspect—it was still difficult for Charlotte to believe that a surgeon would have left the crime scene such a mess. In fact, she guessed it would have been constitutionally impossible. Neatness would have been as intrinsic to his methods as precision for an engineer, or logic for a mathematician. No, she concluded, if Dr. Louria were to have planned a murder, she was sure he was capable of a more elegant, and less incriminating, job.

A far more likely scenario was that the murderer was someone who had wanted to incriminate Dr. Louria. She wondered if the murderer had taken the path down the embankment. If so, he would have had to park on River Road and then carry the body across the Archfield Hall property, a scenario that struck her as unlikely, given the risk of being observed. Which meant that he had probably come from some other direction. She looked up and down the tracks: to the south, there was nothing; to the north was the railroad station.

Since Jerry was still busy, she decided to take a walk. As she headed north, she heard snatches of sound from a distant loudspeaker, and wondered where they were coming from. As a compound on the river shore came into view, however, she realized from the guard towers and the sodium vapor lamps that shone even in the sunshine that the source was the Ossi-ning Correctional Facility, otherwise known as Sing Sing, and, next to Alcatraz, probably the most famous prison in America.

She hoped that its overcrowded cell blocks would soon be accommodating another inmate: one who would be there for the rest of his life.

Six minutes later, she found herself at the south end of the railroad station parking lot, which sat at the foot of a cliff. The station building was located at the other end of the parking lot, a hundred yards away. Moreover, there were no other buildings, and the access road came in from the opposite end. Though there wasn't an empty parking spot in the lot, the station was devoid of people, and she guessed that no one other than an oc-casional teenager would come here in the middle of the night.

The murderer could easily have parked his car at this end of the lot, removed a body from his trunk, and carried it along the tracks to the summer house.

A few minutes later, she hooked up again with Jerry back on the riverbank by the summer house. For a few minutes, they stood looking out at the gray-green water. Then Charlotte said: "It was probably right at this spot that the murderer dumped the bodies into the river."

"Two of them anyway," Jerry concurred. "I think he prob-ably chopped up Kimberly's body somewhere else."

"Why?" Charlotte asked.

"Because the smell would have alerted somebody. The smell isn't bad now because it's only just started to warm up. But it would have been terrible in early September. We always used to get bodies in August and early September that would have gone undiscovered at any other time of year."

"That would also explain why Kimberly's body parts washed up in Manhattan, while the body parts of the others washed up here," Charlotte said. "He probably cut the body up somewhere else, and threw it in there. I wouldn't imagine that the parts turn up very far from where they're thrown in."

"I think you're probably right, Graham," Jerry said. He smiled. "I'm glad we're paying you the big bucks." Then he turned serious: "We're going to have to bring Dr. Louria in for questioning," he said.

The next day was overcast, with intermittent drizzle. But only the worst weather deterred Charlotte from her daily pre-breakfast walk. She was turning the corner onto First Avenue when she noticed the screaming headline on a copy of the *New York Post* displayed in a news kiosk: "WESTCHESTER PLASTIC SURGEON QUESTIONED IN LOOK-ALIKE MURDERS." The headlines in the other newspapers were similar. She immediately bought a copy of the *Post*, and then copies of the *Daily News*, the *New York Times*, and *Newsday*, all of which also contained stories on the murders, although the *Times*, with its typical disdain for any story that smacked of sensationalism, had buried theirs on the fifth page of the metropolitan section. All the stories included photographs of Dr. Louria and descriptions of his career as a cosmetic surgeon and his volunteer work with the World Health Organization. Several also included photographs of the summer house, or, as the *Post* called it, the "Hudson River charnel house." The combination of the fact that the photographs had been taken from some distance (it must have been cordoned off), and that the newspaper reproduction made it look almost black, gave the charming little building a decidedly sinister look—an impression that was enhanced by its sheathing of leafless vines. The *Post* also featured an article on Jerry's career with Manhattan Homicide, which was entitled "One Smart Cop." The photograph must have been an old one from their files: it pictured him with a thinner face and a fuller hairline than Charlotte had ever known him to have, and she had known him for ten years.

As she drank her morning coffee and ate her customary bagel, Charlotte read every last word of every story. It was clear from Jerry's statements that he had gone to great lengths to make the point that Dr. Louria was only being questioned, not accused. She readily understood why he had done so. Dr. Louria as the murderer simply didn't make sense. It was also clear that the questioning of Dr. Louria had been fruitless, as had that of his housekeeper, who hadn't even admitted to knowledge of the Lily look-alikes, though Dr. Louria himself had said that she knew about them.

As she sat there pondering the case, her housekeeper, Julie, came in. Julie and her husband Jim were a Chinese couple who had worked for Charlotte for over thirty years. Her high-brow friends referred to them as Jules and Jim after the French art movie of that title.

"Why so many newspapers?" asked the ever-inquisitive Julie, nodding at the newspapers that were spread out on the counter. "Aha," she said, reading the stories over Charlotte's shoulder. "Westchester. That's why you've been spending so much time up in Westchester lately."

Charlotte looked up at Julie over the tops of her reading glasses—half glasses with tortoiseshell frames. There wasn't much that Julie didn't catch, and what she didn't, Jim did.

"What do you think?" Julie asked. "Did the doctor do it?"

Julie was a great follower of tabloid crime. She also watched the live broadcasts of criminal trials on court television. She had been following the Yonkers murder case for weeks with the avidity that sports fans reserve for the National Football League play-offs.

"I don't think so," Charlotte said.

The phone rang, and Julie answered it. "For you," she said, holding out the phone. "It's Chief D'Angelo," she added. "It must be a new development in the look-alike murder case," she whispered as Charlotte took the phone.

"I thought you might want to come up," Jerry said. "We just got a call from the pastor at Zion Hill Church. Peter De Vries found a skull in the undercroft this morning. The county crime scene guys are coming over here, and then we're all heading up to the church."

"In the undercroft," she repeated. It was a place where bodies were traditionally buried, but it wasn't a cemetery. Very clever of him, she thought. "He outwitted you, didn't he?" she said. The look-alike murderer was beginning to take on his own personality.

"Yeah," Jerry said unhappily. "We had every cemetery in town staked out, and he goes and deposits the skull in the basement of the church."

"It will take me an hour or so to get there," Charlotte said.

"That's okay. We expect to be there for a while."

Though it was still rush hour, Charlotte was going against traffic, and it took her only twenty-five minutes to get to the outskirts of Zion Hill, in spite of the wet weather. At the light at the Zion Hill Road intersection, she turned right and followed the road up the hill to the turnoff for the church parking lot, where she pulled into an empty space at the end of a row of police cars. Then she climbed the stairs to the church lawn. At the top of the stairs, she paused again to take in the view. Though it was only misting in Zion Hill, she could see storm clouds hanging over the Hudson Highlands, and she could feel the wind picking up. The water was already getting choppy: it was only a matter of time before the storm came whipping down the river.

Continuing on to the church, she asked a policeman posted outside the entrance how to get to the undercroft, and was directed to the door at the base of the crenelated bell tower. As a result of their discussion with Peter, she took notice of the door, which was hand-carved of the same rich wood she'd seen at Archfield Hall, and fitted with ornamental hardware that had been wrought of monel in an intricate medieval design.

She opened the door, and was greeted by another policeman, who was sitting on a Gothic-style side chair in what appeared to be the vestibule of the church. Racks for hanging up coats lined the walls.

He stood up. "Mrs. Lundstrom?" he said.

She nodded.

"The chief's in the undercroft," he said. Crossing the vestibule, he opened yet another hand-carved door for her.

She noted that this door was of a different design—another way to God. A spiral stone staircase led downward to the undercroft, and upward, she presumed, to the belfry. From below, she could hear the murmur of men's voices. She followed the steep, narrow stairs around until she came to yet another door, which opened into the undercroft. It was a large room—it presumably ran the length of the church—with a low, vaulted ceiling supported by twisted columns topped by early Gothic capitals.

A simple wooden altar stood at the east end, and on the altar rested Doreen Mileski's skull. The skull was flanked by two tall votive candles in red glass containers, whose dim, flickering light made the setting all the more eerie. Like the other skulls, this one had been bleached white.

Seeing her, Jerry broke away from the cluster of crime scene specialists who were busy measuring, photographing, and dusting for fingerprints. "Hi," he said, a grim expression on his face. He turned to the altar. "We've found Doreen Mileski's skull, as you can see."

As Charlotte looked again at the skull, she noticed the sweet fragrance that perfumed the dank air of the underground room. Then it dawned on her that it came from the fresh bouquet of lilies of the valley that lay on the altar to one side of the skull. "Jerry," she said, "I just realized something."

He gave her an inquiring look.

"*Muguet* is French for lily of the valley. Muguet is also the name of the perfume that Lily Louria always wore. She always ordered it from France. Remember Dr. Louria's comments to Kimberly on the videotape?"

Jerry nodded. "Which means, as we suspected, that the murderer of the Lily look-alikes was someone who knew Lily well enough to know what her favorite perfume was," he said.

Charlotte added: "And still had enough regard for Lily to have buried her look-alikes with her favorite scent."

After Charlotte had taken a closer look at the skull, she and Jerry climbed back up the spiral staircase to the vestibule, where they opened yet another of the church's beautiful doors. This door led into the church proper, where they were to meet with the pastor and the sexton, Peter De Vries. The interior of the church was unusually austere, with an open timber roof, unplastered stone walls, and a simple ceramic tile floor. Despite the spare detailing, however, the intimate beauty of the space and the richness of the materials gave it a feeling of luxurious elegance. The only decorative elements were the stained-glass windows and the statues of angels that were mounted above the arcade of the nave. As Lister had said, there were thirteen of them, six on one side and seven on the other, each with the face of Lily Louria. Or to be precise, her mother Lillian. There were no memorial plaques or statues of the saints, no stations of the cross or banners with liturgical themes. There wasn't even a cross, which was unusual for a Christian church. Instead, the focus of attention was an altar surrounded by tall brass candlesticks. On the altar, a large Bible lay open, its pages illuminated by shafts of soft violet light that streamed down from the stained-glass windows at the sides of the sanctuary.

The effect was moving, and unearthly.

"I remember that light from when I used to come here sometimes as a kid with my friends," said Jerry, as they looked at the Bible on the altar. "I always thought it was very spooky."

"It is," said Charlotte. "And very beautiful."

As they stood there admiring the effect, a tall, thin man emerged from the door to the sacristy and headed down the aisle to join them.

He wore a black clerical shirt with a white collar, and over it, a light blue golf cardigan. An old-fashioned watch chain hung across his midsection. But he might have been wearing a frock coat and a tricorne hat, so closely did he fit the role of the old-fashioned country parson.

"Hello," he said, extending his hand to Jerry. "I'm John Cornwall, the pastor." He had a thick cap of dark brown hair, and a large nose whose profile matched that of the oversized Adam's apple that appeared to be resting uncomfortably atop his clerical collar.

"Jerry D'Angelo," Jerry said, returning his handshake.

"I believe I met you once at the town hall," the pastor said. He gestured toward the door from which he had just emerged. "We can meet in the sacristy," he said, and went on to add that he would be happy to answer any questions Jerry might have about the church.

"We were just admiring the unusual light in the sanctuary," Jerry said as they continued down the aisle.

"Yes. It's very striking. It was the product of a great deal of experimentation. The side windows are made up of red and blue medallions, and it took a while to get the proportions that would produce the right color of light. The church is famous for its stained-glass windows," he added.

"I understand that the windows are the major attraction of the tour, which I regret to say that I have yet to take," Jerry said. "In full, that is," he said, adding, "Peter gave us an abbreviated version on Friday. But I don't think today is the day to take the rest of it."

"No," the pastor agreed as he led them into the sacristy and showed them to two of the chairs that surrounded a table. After a few minutes of conversation about the "unfortunate incident," they were joined by the sexton, Peter De Vries.

Peter explained that he'd discovered the skull at about nine that morning when he'd gone down to the undercroft to get out the folding wooden chairs that would be needed to accommodate the crowds that were expected for the upcoming concert.

"It was quite a shock," he said. "To come upon it in the dark like that. At first I thought it was some kind of prank."

"How often do you go down there?" Jerry asked.

"Not much," he said. "We don't use it much. I only go down there to get out the folding chairs. On big church holidays, and for the concert, basically." He looked over at the pastor, who explained:

"This church is a replica of an early English Gothic church, which had a crypt where a relic of a saint was displayed. A throat bone, I believe it was. But, of course, we don't believe in saints."

Peter explained: "We don't believe it's desirable for personalities to be associated with our worship when our thoughts should be only of the Word, which is what we call the Bible. That's also why we have no cross."

Jerry nodded, then asked: "When was the last time you were down there?"

"Yesterday," Peter replied.

"Yesterday!" Jerry exclaimed.

"Yeah. Yesterday. In the afternoon. Around four, I guess." He looked over at the pastor. "John wanted me to see how many chairs there were. He thought the church might need to buy some more before the concert."

The pastor nodded in confirmation. "We commandeered three or four dozen of them for use in Tina's Kitchen," he said. "It's a meals program for the indigent that we started last year," he explained.

"Was the skull there then?" Jerry asked.

"No," Peter said.

"Then someone must have put the skull there sometime between four p.m. yesterday and nine a.m. this morning," Jerry said. He addressed Peter: "Were you around much during that time?"

Peter shook his head. "I finished work at four-thirty, and then went up to Corinth. I was back by seven, but I just went to my rooms. I started work again at eight this morning, but that leaves a lot of time in between."

"Did you see anyone unusual hanging around?"

He shook his head again. "But that doesn't mean anything. I'm all over the place. Somebody could easily have slipped by me. Also, we have visitors here all the time for the tours. I did give a tour late in the afternoon: a middle-aged couple. Their names would be in the guest book."

Jerry nodded. "And you, Reverend?" he asked, turning to the pastor, who toyed with his old-fashioned watch chain. "Did you see anyone unusual?"

"No," he replied. "But the rectory's out in back."

Jerry nodded. "You mentioned a soup kitchen for the homeless . . ."

"We call it a meals program," the pastor said. "I know it's just a matter of semantics, but somehow it doesn't sound as degrading."

"Sorry," Jerry said. "A meals program. Would you have been serving meals yesterday?" he asked.

"Yes," he replied. "We serve meals every day but Tuesday."

"Would you be able to provide me with the names of the people who participate in the program?"

The pastor shook his head. "It's not that kind of program," he said. "People don't sign up, they just come."

"That's what I was afraid of," Jerry said.

"But Tina—she's the woman who runs it, or, I should say, the saint who runs it—could probably give you a list of names. She knows most of the people who come personally. I'd like to say, however, that just because . . .''

Jerry raised a hand in protest. ''I know what you're going to say.''

The pastor looked at him in surprise.

Jerry continued: ''Just because someone's indigent doesn't mean that person's a murderer. I'm aware of that, Reverend Cornwall. But I have to start somewhere, and there's a good chance that one of these people has a criminal record.''

But there wasn't much chance that any of them would have known that Lily Louria had worn Muguet, Charlotte thought.

The pastor nodded, and then checked the pocket watch that was attached to his watch chain. ''Tina should be here by now,'' he said. ''We can go over to the Parish Hall and talk with her if you like. It's quite an experience.''

''What do you mean?''

''Tina is an original. We think of her as a benevolent dictator, who manages to keep our sometimes less than genteel crowd of patrons in line with little more than a stern glance,'' he said. ''She runs her kitchen with an iron fist.''

Peter stood up to go. ''I was afraid I was going to miss my lunch.''

Led by the pastor, the four of them passed through the cloister into the Parish Hall, where they found Tina in the kitchen, chopping vegetables. She was a short black woman with gray hair covered by a baseball cap and a no-nonsense manner.

''What's for dinner?'' asked Peter, as he lifted the lid of a pot on the stove and peered in.

''It's minestrone soup,'' she replied, adding the chopped vegetables to the pot. ''But it's not for today; it's for tomorrow. Today's is there,'' she said, nodding at another pot. ''Split pea with ham.''

''What else?'' Peter asked, lifting the lid of another pot, an act that earned him a rap on the knuckles with Tina's wooden spoon.

Picking up a plate, Tina proceeded to load it with a huge serving of baked chicken, mashed potatoes, and collard greens. Then she topped it with a slab of buttered corn bread and handed it to Peter. ''Now get out of here,'' she said.

Charlotte's mouth was watering.

"This is Tina Furman," the pastor said after Peter had gone, and proceeded to introduce the cook to Jerry and Charlotte.

"Pleased to meet you," Tina responded with a wide smile. Unlike the pastor, Tina took no offense at their request, and proceeded to provide Jerry with as many names as she could remember. While she talked, she dished out plates of food, which were served by church volunteers.

She had just finished with her list of names, which included thumbnail sketches of each personality, when Peter returned to the kitchen through the swinging door, holding out his empty plate in his one remaining hand.

Tina looked up. "If you think you're getting a second helping, you'd better think again," she said, gesturing with her wooden spoon for emphasis. "I've got other mouths besides yours to feed."

"Don't worry," he said. "You managed to fill me up. I don't know why," he added. "It was a pretty stingy serving." Peter set the plate down on the counter. "I must not be hungry today."

Tina rolled her eyes to the ceiling and went back to her work.

Peter turned to Charlotte and Jerry and the pastor, who was helping to pass the plates to the church volunteers. "I just remembered," he said. "I did notice something unusual."

"What?" Jerry asked.

"When I was giving that tour late in the afternoon, I noticed that there was a key missing from the key cabinet. Now that I think about it, I think it might have been the key to the door of the undercroft."

"What time was that?" Jerry asked.

"Just before I quit."

"But wouldn't you have had the key to the door of the undercroft?" Charlotte asked. "You'd just been down there to count the chairs."

"I have my own set of keys," he said. He reached down to jingle the key ring that hung from his belt loop. "The ones in the key cabinet are just for display. That's why I noticed that one was missing; they're usually all there."

"Is the key still missing?" Jerry asked.

"I have no idea," Peter said.

A few minutes later, they were standing in front of the key cabinet in the Parish Hall foyer. As far as Charlotte could see, none of the keys that were displayed against the background of purple velvet was missing. At least, none of the hooks appeared to be empty.

Holding the handle of the cabinet door with a plastic evidence bag, Jerry proceeded to open it. "They look like they're all here now," he said. He turned to Peter. "Do you remember which one it was?"

Peter stepped forward and pointed to a key in the second row from the bottom. It was one of the smaller keys, with a head in the shape of a diamond. He was about to remove it from its hook when Jerry lightly touched his wrist.

"Allow me," he said. Using the evidence bag as a mitt, he lifted the key off its display hook. Then he closed the door and turned to Peter. "Do you have your key to the undercroft?" he asked.

Reaching down to his key ring, Peter started sorting through the keys, which were like the keys in the cabinet, but without the ornamental heads. When he found the one he was looking for, he held it out.

Moving around next to Peter, Jerry held the post of the key from the cabinet next to the post of Peter's key. They were identical. Jerry turned to the pastor. "Is this cabinet kept locked?" he asked.

The pastor shook his head. "We open it to display the keys almost every day. The key cabinet is one of the first things we show to visitors. To illustrate the point that there are many doors to God," he added.

"So anyone could have taken the key," Jerry said.

The pastor nodded.

"But how would someone have known it was the key to the undercroft?" Charlotte asked. "The keys in the cabinet aren't labeled."

"Good question," the pastor replied. "There's a diagram in here." He reached down to open a drawer at the bottom of the cabinet, and was stopped by Jerry. ''Sorry,'' he said, with a contrite expression.

Opening the drawer with his plastic mitt, Jerry withdrew the diagram, which was sheathed in plastic. It showed the layout of the keys in the cabinet and told which of the church's doors each key opened.

''In order to have known which key to take, the person who took it would have to have known that the diagram was in the drawer,'' Jerry said. ''Which means that he must be associated with the church.''

They all thought about this for a moment.

Then the pastor said: ''I think that's quite likely, although it's possible that someone from outside the church could have assumed there would be a diagram, and gone looking for it. The drawer would be a natural place to look.''

As she studied the diagram, Charlotte noticed that one of the keys was marked ''exterior tower'' and had another thought. ''What about the other doors?'' she asked. ''The door to the bell tower, and the door to the staircase?''

''They would have been locked,'' Peter said. ''We don't want kids climbing up to the belfry. But Lothian Archibald would have unlocked them when she came to ring the bells just before six o'clock.''

''For cocktails,'' Jerry said.

''But only one key was missing—not three,'' Charlotte said. ''Which means that the person who took the key to the undercroft knew that the other doors would be unlocked while Lothian Archibald was ringing the bells.''

''Which points to a member of the church again,'' Jerry said. He turned to Peter. ''Does she always lock the doors when she leaves?''

''Sometimes she forgets, although she didn't forget yesterday,'' Peter replied. ''The doors were locked when I made my rounds at ten.''

Jerry nodded. ''Which means that somebody probably put the skull in the undercroft while she was ringing the bells.'' He went on to ask the pastor who else worked at the church, a list that included half a dozen employees.

Then they thanked Peter and the pastor and left. They still

had to talk with the other church employees, but that could wait until after lunch. As Jerry had said, it was important to keep one's priorities straight.

And eating came first.

9

As THEY DROVE back to the police station, Charlotte and Jerry discussed the developments in the case. Jerry's list of things to look into now extended to two pages: follow up on Dr. Louria's alibi, talk to the lawyers for Lily's estate, interview the other church employees, check to see if the patrons of Tina's Kitchen had criminal records, check for fingerprints on the key to the undercroft and on the key cabinet—the list went on and on. But it seemed to Charlotte that the solution of the case depended on something much more ineffable than what could be offered by these possible clues, and that was the mind of the murderer. The case was like one of Jack Lister's reconstructed faces: you could glue the fractured pieces of the skull back together and you could reconstruct the face according to scientific averages for the depth of the flesh, but without an intuitive sense of what the victim was like, the reconstruction wouldn't come alive. In the case of Lister's reconstructions, it was clues like the circumstances in which the skull was found and the bits of clothing and personal possessions that were found with it that gave him the material on which to set his intuition to work. In this case, there were also such clues in the form of the circumstances in which the skulls had been found, and the things that had been found with them, namely the bouquets of lilies of the valley. However bizarre and illogical the murderer's actions might appear, there was a logic behind what he had done and how he had done it. It was buried in this twisted logic that the key to his identity lay.

Though Jerry didn't discount the value of routine police work—it was through such tedious work that most cases were solved, he pointed out—he agreed that it was important to figure out why the murderer had acted as he had. Why had he preserved only the skulls? Why had he bleached them white? Why had he left them in consecrated places? Why had he left the flowers with them?

A few minutes later, they had arrived at the police station. As they pulled into Jerry's parking spot, which faced the adjacent vacant lot, Charlotte noticed a colony of lilies of the valley growing under an oak tree. Unlike the lilies of the valley that had been growing by the path leading down the embankment, these were already in bloom.

She was thinking about picking some to take home when she was struck by a sudden thought. "Jerry!" she said. She turned to face him. "Where did the murderer get the lilies of the valley for the bouquets?"

Jerry gave her a look, and she realized she was shouting.

She lowered her voice. "This time, he could have picked them. They're in bloom now. But the first skull was found in September, and the second in April. They're not in bloom then. Also, they're not the kind of flower that you can pick up from your local florist."

"They're not?" Jerry said.

"No, they're not. That's why you need woman cops," she teased. "What's a guy from Bensonhurst know from lilies of the valley?"

"I don't have the faintest idea where he might have gotten them." he replied. "But I'll tell you how you can find out, and you can do me the favor of checking it out. Is it a deal?"

"It's a deal," she said.

"Winter Garden Florist," he said. "In Corinth. If you don't succeed there, try Anderson's. Or McNabb's. Corinth used to supply the roses to the New York florist trade; there used to be acres of roses there under glass."

"What happened?" she asked.

"I think they come from overseas now," he said. "But the wholesalers are still located there. I'll have Pat give you a map," he said, referring to the dispatcher. "They're easy enough to find."

"What about lunch?" Charlotte asked.

"You go ahead. I'm going to get a sandwich. You could try the Broadway Diner or Jack's Luncheonette. They're both on the Post Road. The diner's just before Zion Hill, and Jack's is in Corinth."

Charlotte crossed her arms in mock exasperation and gave him a withering look. "I thought we had our priorities straight," she said. "Which means that food is at the top of the list."

"Not all of the time," Jerry said.

After the dispatcher had written down the directions for Charlotte, she set off for Corinth. But as she thought about their morning at the church, she was struck by an idea. She was still nagged by the feeling that she didn't know the victim. She had once heard a homicide detective say that it was as important to figure out what made the victim tick as it was to figure out what made the murderer tick, and in her limited experience she had found that observation to be true. "Victimology," it was called: to find out about the perpetrator through the victim. It was possible, of course, that the victims had been chosen at random: that the killer had favored five-foot-six-inch redheads in the same way that Son of Sam had favored women necking with men in parked cars, or Jack the Ripper had favored prostitutes from London's East End. But Charlotte suspected not. Though the victims had been Kimberly, Liliana, and Doreen, the bouquets that the murderer had left with the skulls led her to believe that the real victim was Lily Louria. It was Lily Louria that someone had been killing over and over and over again.

Charlotte's only sense of Lily was as a beautiful face. Was that all there was to her? It was very possible. There was precious little behind many of the beautiful faces she had known. But whether or not there was much behind the face, something about Lily had provoked the killer to murder her substitutes. Was it jealousy, revenge, greed? Dr. Louria's love-besotted description of his wife wasn't any help. Nor was that of her devoted Aunt Lothian, despite her account of Lily's being difficult as a child. Charlotte needed an assessment of Lily—her loves, her hates, what she liked to eat for breakfast—from a more objective observer. And in that category, a minister who had known her since she was a teenager would serve very well.

She pulled into a gas station, and then turned around and headed back in the direction from which she had come. She arrived at the church a few minutes later. Since it was lunchtime, she decided to try the rectory first, and continued on up the hill. About fifty yards past the church, she came to a sign for "The Manse" and turned into a driveway lined with big old rhododendrons. The driveway ended at a charming house: a gabled, gingerbread-adorned Victorian Gothic confection, which was painted a pale yellow trimmed with white.

After parking at the side of the driveway, she walked up the brick pathway and rang the doorbell. She waited a few minutes, but there was no answer. She had just decided to try the church office when she saw the pastor approaching along the path from the church. He was wearing his white vestments, which billowed in the spring breeze behind his tall, thin figure like a sail from a mast.

"Ah! Mrs. Lundstrom," he exclaimed, upon seeing her waiting at his door. "What a pleasant surprise!" After they had exchanged greetings, he escorted her into a sun-filled center hall, where he proceeded to remove his robes and hang them up in the hall closet.

"Excuse me," he apologized, as he removed the outer vestment, "I just did a baptism—hence the clerical garb." Having removed the outer vestment, he then proceeded to remove the inner vestment. "We wear two robes," he explained, "which makes this process all the more unwieldy."

"Why two?" asked Charlotte.

"Symbolism," he said. "The New Church is rife with it. The outer one stands for the outer man—the public man, if you will—and the inner for the spiritual man." After hanging up the inner robe, he escorted her into a study filled with beautiful antiques and art objects.

"What a charming house!" Charlotte said as she took a

seat on an Empire-style sofa covered in pale green silk damask. He was clearly the kind of bachelor who took great pride in the appearance of his house.

"Thank you," the pastor replied, as he sat down in the armchair opposite her. "It's typical of the Gothic villa style that was in fashion during the 1840's, and which was very popular in the Hudson River Valley. The house antedates the church, of course."

"Is that it there?" she asked, nodding at a framed engraving hanging on the wall that showed the house as it must have looked when it was built.

He nodded. "The property was originally a farm that ran all the way down to the river. I've restored the house to its original condition," he said. "I've also tried to furnish it with pieces that are typical of the period."

"You've done a beautiful job," she said as she looked around at the bookshelves lined with leather-bound copies of Thackeray and Tennyson, and the antique mahogany secretary heaped with papers.

"Thank you," he said with a smile. "This is my favorite room in the house. It makes me feel like a man of letters."

"Aren't you?" she asked.

"Only the church newsletter and the ideas for my weekly sermons. I'm more of a reader than a writer. I'm reading a very interesting book right now," he said. "I think you might be interested in it as well, Mrs. Lundstrom."

Rising from his seat, he lifted a book off the mantelpiece and handed it to Charlotte. The title was *My Story* by Charlotte Graham.

"Aha," she said with a smile. "You're onto me."

"I was onto you from the moment I met you," he said. "I've been a fan since I was a young sprout. It's a great honor to meet you," he added with a deferential nod. "May I offer you a glass of sherry?"

"It's not six o'clock yet," she commented.

"Rules are made to be broken," he said with a smile.

"Yes," she replied. "That would be very nice."

"How did you meet Chief D'Angelo?" he asked, as he

poured the sherry out of a crystal decanter on a mahogany campaign table.

Charlotte explained about helping to solve the murder case at the spa where Jerry had worked, and her reputation as an amateur sleuth that had come out of her solving the murder at the Morosco case.

"You talked about that a bit in the book," he said. He gave her her glass and sat back down in his chair with his own. "Is it about the murder that you've come to see me?" he asked, taking a sip.

"Murders, I'm afraid," she said. She didn't think that she was committing any indiscretions. Anything she might be about to tell him had already been splashed all over the newspapers.

"I've read the newspapers," he said, echoing her thoughts.

Charlotte went on to explain how each of the victims had been a cosmetic surgery patient of Dr. Louria's, and how he had remodeled their faces to resemble that of his dead wife.

"What you're saying is that the real victim was Lily."

"Exactly," she said. "That's why I've come to you. I understand that you knew her since she was a teenager. I'd like to find out more about her."

"What would you like to know?" he asked.

"What she was like," Charlotte replied simply.

"Would you mind if I work while we talk?" he asked.

When Charlotte replied that she wouldn't, he set down his sherry glass and pulled over a low, three-legged stand covered with a linen cloth. "I do Victorian hand braiding," he said as he removed the cloth cover to reveal the donut-shaped cushion that comprised the top of the stand.

"I've never heard of it," Charlotte said.

"I never had either. I found out about it through the Victorian Society, of which I'm a member. I'd always been interested in Victorian decorative arts, but hand braiding was new to me. It was extremely popular during the Victorian era—more popular, in fact, than knitting."

He proceeded to show her how each of the many threads that hung over the sides of the stand was attached to a weight in the center hole. The opposite ends of the threads were held down by wooden bobbins, which hung down from the perimeter of the stand like the fringe on a lamp shade.

He then went on to show her how, by manipulating the threads, each of which was numbered, one could create an intricately patterned braid that could then be molded or woven into various designs.

"How interesting!" Charlotte said.

"My watch chain is braided," he said. He reached down to show her the triple-stranded chain that was attached to his pocket watch. "As is the design on my ring," he added, holding out his long-fingered hand.

"What are you working on now?" she asked.

"This is going to be a part of the design for a wreath, which I'll frame," he said. "I've been working on it for about two weeks."

"How did you get into this?" she asked.

"My sister had introduced me to embroidery when I gave up smoking several years ago. She thought it would help me keep my hands occupied. I found it to be very relaxing," he explained, "but it was a hobby that I didn't like to engage in in public."

"Why not?" Charlotte asked.

"People don't think of it as being very masculine," he said with a rueful little smile. "I liked to do samplers in *point tresse*, which is an especially delicate form." He nodded toward the center hall. "Maybe you noticed some of my samplers hanging in the hall."

Charlotte nodded. She had noticed the framed embroidery work.

"Then I read about the braiding and thought I'd give it a try." He adjusted the bobbins on the braiding stand. "It was a pastime that was engaged in during Victorian times by both men and women."

"So it was socially acceptable," Charlotte said.

He nodded. "I also found it to be a good conversational gambit. People often come here to discuss their personal problems. Talking about the braiding was a good way of getting the conversation rolling. Which brings me back to the reason for your visit."

Charlotte nodded.

"What Lily was like," he repeated. He leaned his head back and looked up at the ceiling. Then he looked back at Charlotte, his deep brown eyes smiling under his shiny cap of dark brown hair. "That's a tall order," he said.

"Why?" she asked.

"I was never able to figure Lily out," he replied. "She was beautiful, of course. She had amazing eyes. They were a very pale green, like a celadon glaze. They were also an unusual shape—cat's eyes, everybody said. She also had that magnificent red hair, of course."

He paused for a moment, deep in thought.

"But in addition to being beautiful, she was also captivating, mysterious, exasperating, electrifying." He threw up his hands. "I could go on, but I think you get the idea."

"It sounds as if you were . . ." She paused to fish for words.

He completed the sentence for her. "A little bit in love with her?" He turned back to his work. "There wasn't a man who wasn't. Just because I wear this"—he lifted a hand to his clerical collar—"doesn't mean that I'm immune to the blandishments of feminine charm."

"Her aunt said that she could wrap any man around her finger."

"I'd say that's a pretty accurate assessment. I managed to tie myself to the mast, but there were many others who couldn't resist."

"She was charming, then?"

"Yes, but not in a demure way. Hypnotic would be a better way of putting it. She was one of those people—not unlike yourself, if I may be so bold—who seem to have an aura. But where your aura is steady, hers was erratic. She'd be shooting sparks one minute, and a black hole the next."

"It sounds frightening."

"It was," he agreed. "She was a bit of a manic-depressive. When she was in her manic phase, there was a reckless quality about her. You never knew what outrageous stunt she was going to pull next. Sebastian used to call her the 'mistress of the gratuitous act.' " He went on: "He has the same reckless quality, though to a lesser extent."

"What kinds of gratuitous acts?" she asked.

"Oh," he said, pausing to think. "I remember her driving down the Storm King Highway once at sixty miles an hour," he said, naming the highway in the Hudson Highlands that was famous for its hairpin turns. "Or swigging vodka from the bottle until she was falling down drunk. Or taking off all her clothes and jumping into the quarry lake."

"Which is what she did in Mexico," Charlotte said.

"Yes. She was one of those people who crave stimulation, who live every moment to its fullest." He thought for a minute, and then continued: "I think it came from losing her parents so young. She had no inner stability. I'm not surprised that she died young."

"Lothian couldn't compensate?"

"She tried, of course. She was genuinely crazy about both of them. But I think they were just too much for her. Even as adults, they'd bully her, so I can imagine what they were like as children. I had a taste of their bullying myself, for that matter. I used to be their teacher."

"At the Zion Hill School?" she asked.

He nodded. "That's where I first met them. I taught religion there when I first came out of theological school."

"How old were they then?"

"Lily was a sophomore, and Sebastian was a freshman. They could be a very intimidating pair. I was new to teaching, and they really had me flummoxed." He chuckled to himself. "It was a very small school—only eight or ten students to a class. The students in Lily and Sebastian's classes did what they said."

"Such as?" Charlotte prompted.

"I remember an incident where I was writing on the blackboard, and when I turned around, there was no one in the classroom except for one very shy girl. Lily and Sebastian had climbed out of the window, and the rest of the class had followed them." He added, "The classroom was on the second floor."

At Charlotte's look of amazement, he explained:

"It turned out that they'd shimmied down the drainpipe. They all came waltzing defiantly back in the door a few minutes later. My point is that if Lily and Sebastian whistled, the rest of them jumped.''

"Literally, it sounds like," Charlotte commented.

"They were hard to resist," he said. "Even at that age, they had that devil-may-care romantic appeal: they were orphans, they were beautiful, they were bold, they were irrepressible.''

"And they were Archibalds.''

"Especially that. They were Archibalds in a town where the face of Lily's mother is as ubiquitous as that of the virgin mother at the Vatican. Their little clique dominated the school. Lily, Sebastian, Connie Teasdale, who was Lily's best friend, and Peter . . .''

"Peter De Vries?" she asked.

He nodded. "He was Sebastian's best friend, and he was mad about Lily. They were high school sweethearts. In fact, they were engaged to be married for a time. Lily broke off the engagement after the accident.''

"The accident in which he lost his arm?" Charlotte asked.

The pastor nodded. "He was up on the church roof, and he lost his footing. He reached out to steady himself on a cable. The cable turned out to be the grounding cable for the lightning rods. He became part of the circuit.''

"He was up on the church roof in a lightning storm?''

"He didn't realize that a storm was brewing," he explained. "There wasn't any thunder until some time after he was hit.''

Charlotte shuddered at the thought. "How horrible," she said.

"Yes, it was. The bolt came, quite literally, out of the blue. He never really got over it. He still carries a newspaper clipping that describes a study in which electromagnetic detectors were used to show that flashes of lightning often occur when no thunder is heard.''

"As if the clipping would help him understand what had happened.''

"Exactly. He shows the clipping to anyone who asks about the accident. Actually, he's very lucky he didn't die from the fall; he was caught in the gutter. Anyway, as I was saying, Lily broke off the engagement. I guess she didn't want to be married to someone who wasn't physically perfect.''

"But Dr. Louria wasn't perfect," Charlotte said, thinking of his ear. "I guess the difference was that he had money and position."

"Yes," he agreed. "He also lived in her grandfather's house. But I often wondered if her feelings of guilt over her rejection of Peter may have played a part in her decision to marry Dr. Louria."

"You mean that she was trying to make up for dumping Peter by marrying someone else with a physical defect?"

"Something like that. Peter was never the same after that."

"Because she jilted him?" Charlotte asked.

"I don't know if it was because she jilted him, or because of the accident itself. People here say that his brains were fried. That may be overstating the case, but he did suffer damage to his nervous system, and psychotic behavior can result from damage to the cerebral cortex."

This description seemed a bit extreme to Charlotte. He had struck her as being eccentric, but not psychotic.

"Do you know the story of the Leatherman?" the pastor asked.

Charlotte shook her head.

"He's our local legend," the pastor said. "The Leatherman is to Zion Hill what Ichabod Crane is to Sleepy Hollow. He was a Frenchman who lived here around the time of the Civil War. I suppose you'd call him a tramp. He had a 365-mile circuit through Westchester, Putnam, and Fairfield counties that took him thirty-four days to complete. The Dutch farmers' wives fed him. They always knew exactly when he would come, and would mark their calendars accordingly."

"Why was he called the Leatherman?" she asked.

"Because he was always dressed from head to foot in old, patched leather. He never spoke, and he never worked. The story went that he was the son of a woodcutter who had been engaged to the daughter of a leather merchant, who jilted him for someone older and wealthier. He supposedly murdered her in a jealous rage, and then fled to America, where he wandered in sorrow, wearing leather and taking a vow of silence as self-imposed penance for his sin."

Charlotte thought back to their meetings with Peter. On both occasions, he had been wearing a full-length leather apron. "And Peter?" she asked.

"Well, he didn't become a tramp. But he did start wearing a leather apron, and he did start carrying a staff, as the Leatherman had. He also started acting peculiarly. One of the local kids started calling him the Leatherman, and the nickname stuck. Everyone knew the story of how Lily Archibald had jilted him after he lost his arm, you see. Come to think of it, he has something else in common with the Leatherman too."

"What's that?" Charlotte asked.

"I never made the connection before, but it was also about that time that he stopped cooking. He cadges his meals wherever he can, just as the Leatherman did. He often eats here, at Tina's Kitchen, as he did yesterday. But he also eats at Sebastian's, at the Broadway Diner, at Jack's Luncheonette."

"They give him free meals too?"

"Yes," he replied. "Of course, you would expect Sebastian to. But the others do too. I guess they feel sorry for him."

"Doesn't he have money?" she asked, thinking of his rental properties.

"I'm sure he does. He must have quite a lot of money, actually. He earns a salary as sexton, plus he has the rental income. But having money doesn't always go along with a middle-class lifestyle."

Charlotte supposed that he had a point.

"I'm sure the people at the Broadway Diner and at Jack's Luncheonette know that he has money. But money isn't the issue. The issue is the romance of the legend. In Peter, they have someone who's willing to keep it alive."

"And if the price is a free lunch now and then, so be it," said Charlotte.

"Exactly. In fact, it used to be considered an honor to feed the Leatherman. The farmers' wives would trade his favorite recipes. Everybody loved him. He was said to be very kind, especially to animals. He would fill in the potholes in the road so the horses wouldn't trip."

"Fascinating," Charlotte said.

"I think I have a pamphlet on the Leatherman here." Setting the braiding stand aside, he rose from his chair and went over to the bookshelves. A moment later, he pulled out a slim pamphlet, which he handed to Charlotte.

The pamphlet was entitled: *The Road Between Heaven and Hell: The Last Circuits of the Leatherman*. The cover showed a photograph of a gravestone with the marker:

Final Resting Place of
JULES BOURGLAY
of Lyons, France,
"The Leatherman"
Who regularly walked a 365-mile route through Westchester and Connecticut from the Connecticut River to the Hudson living in caves in the years
1858–1889

"The local historical society raised the money to erect a marker on his grave at St. James's a few years ago," he said as he sat back down. "His body was found in a cave near Pleasantville. The local people started looking for him when he didn't show up for one of his meals."

Charlotte was still studying the pamphlet, and, intrigued by a quote from a psychiatrist, read it aloud to the pastor: "This says, 'Perhaps our attraction to him reflects the little part in some of us that would like to get away from the constraints of society.' "

"Yes. It's true, isn't it?" the pastor said. "We all have that little strain of wildness. Fortunately for society, it's usually buried a little deeper than it was in the case of the Leatherman."

"Getting back to Lily . . ." Charlotte said. She continued: "As you may know, one of the suspects in the look-alike murders is her husband."

The pastor nodded.

"Can you imagine any reason why he might have wanted to murder her look-alikes? Or why anyone else might have wanted to murder them?"

"I don't know about anyone else," he replied, his long

fingers flying over the bobbins of the braiding stand. "But I do know why Victor Louria might have wanted to murder them. Create them, and then murder them."

"Why?" Charlotte asked.

"Jealous rage," he replied. Charlotte lifted an eyebrow, which produced an amused reaction from the pastor. "I didn't think I would ever see Charlotte Graham raising an eyebrow at me," he said.

"Would you care to elaborate?" she asked.

"Actually, I wouldn't. I hope you understand. Lily was one of my parishioners. I feel as if I've probably already said more than I feel comfortable with. But I'll tell you who you *can* talk to."

"Who's that?" Charlotte asked.

"Her best friend, Connie Teasdale. I don't know where Connie lives, though I suppose you could look her address up in the telephone book. But you can usually find her at Sebastian's. She works there as a waitress."

She must have been the Connie who had been their waitress the other day, Charlotte thought. "A pretty brunette, with long hair and blue eyes?"

He nodded.

"She was part of the clique you mentioned."

"Yes. The four of them practically grew up together: Lily and Sebastian, and Connie and Peter. They were inseparable."

Charlotte thanked him for his help and rose to leave.

"Before you go, I'd like to ask a favor," the pastor said. He handed her a pen that he'd removed from the breast pocket of his clerical shirt, and then picked up her autobiography from the coffee table. "I'd be delighted if you would autograph your book for me."

"Gladly," said Charlotte. Taking the book, she signed it "To the Reverend Cornwall with best wishes" in her bold, round scrawl.

After leaving the Manse, she headed back down the Zion Hill Road, and then turned north toward Corinth. She glanced at the clock on the dashboard: it was now 1:45. If she went to see Connie Teasdale now, she would catch her after the lunchtime rush. Besides, she could kill two birds with one stone: talk to Connie and then eat. As fond as she was of diners, she would take Sebastian's over the Broadway Diner any day of the week, and Jack's Luncheonette, which she remembered having passed on their earlier visit to Corinth, was simply out of the question. She would inquire about the lilies of the valley at the wholesale florist after lunch, she decided as she turned off on the road that led to Sebastian's.

A few minutes later, she was comfortably settled at a small table near the door, pitying Jerry, who was probably eating a submarine sandwich at his desk. She didn't have a view of the Hudson, but there was no view to be had. Though it hadn't yet started to rain, it was still overcast.

Connie appeared momentarily to take her cocktail order. As before, she was wearing a short black skirt and a white button-down shirt.

"Are you Connie Teasdale?" Charlotte asked.

The young woman nodded. She had a flawless complexion, a dimpled smile, and big blue eyes with thick eyelashes. She was very pretty, but in that bland, all-American way that Jack Lister had dismissed.

"Reverend Cornwall said I might find you here." After introducing herself, she went on to say: "I wanted to talk with you about Lily Louria. I'm working with Chief D'Angelo on the look-alike murder case." She might as well use the term that was all over the newspapers.

Connie nodded. "You came in with him the other day," she said. "You ordered the foie gras and the grilled lamb."

Charlotte nodded. It was refreshing to be identified in terms of foie gras and grilled lamb, instead of as an aging grande dame or an Oscar-winning star of stage and screen.

She continued: "As you may know, one of the suspects is Dr. Louria, who admits to refashioning the faces of the dead girls to resemble that of his late wife. Reverend Cornwall said that you might be able to enlighten me as to why he might have killed the look-alikes."

"Cornwall sent you to me?" she said.

Charlotte nodded. "He didn't want to be put in the position of talking about a dead parishioner."

"Gossiping, in other words," she said. "That sounds like Cornwall."

"He said you were Lily's best friend."

"To the extent that a woman could be her best friend," she said.

"What do you mean by that?"

She shrugged. "Lily was one of those women who have no use for other women. Listen," she said. "Do you want to go out to the patio? Sebastian wouldn't approve of me chatting with a customer in the dining room."

"Sure," she said, and followed Connie through the French doors at the side of the dining room onto a brick-paved patio. Though it was cloudy, the air was warm, and it felt good to be outside.

Connie wiped the moisture off the seats of a pair of chairs, and they sat down. "I have about ten minutes," she said. She took a cigarette out of a packet and lit it. Then she leaned back and took a puff, exhaling a stream of smoke into the misty air.

Charlotte looked enviously at the cigarette. She had cut back to only a couple a week as a prelude to stopping completely.

"Would you like one?" Connie asked, noticing her gaze.

"Thank you, I would," Charlotte replied.

"I'm sorry," Connie said as she offered her the packet. "So few people smoke anymore that I rarely bother to ask." She flicked her lighter and held it to the tip of Charlotte's cigarette. "I'm no psychiatrist," she said once Charlotte's cigarette was lit. "But I can speculate."

"Please do," Charlotte said.

"If the girls who were murdered were stand-ins for Lily," she said, "he might have been taking his anger against her out on them."

"That's what the pastor said," Charlotte said. "He didn't elaborate," she added, not wanting to give the impression that he'd been gossiping. "But I'd be delighted if you would. Anger about what?"

"Jealous anger, I'd suppose you'd call it."

Charlotte remembered what Aunt Lothian had said about

the delight Lily had taken in provoking her husband. "She was a flirt, you mean?"

"More than just a flirt," she said. She looked over at Charlotte. "To put it crudely, Mrs. Lundstrom, she was a cock-teaser. She wasn't happy unless every man within a radius of ten miles was chasing after her with his zipper open."

Charlotte was stunned. She'd had the sense that there had been more to Lily than just a pretty face, and this was it.

Connie elaborated: "She liked the power of it. She kept track of her conquests, like the soldiers who notch their belts." She paused, and then said: "She was my friend, but I hated her sometimes. We were friends because we went to angel school together; you come to think of yourself as a special breed."

"Which means that you stick together," Charlotte interjected, "even though you may not always have liked one another."

She nodded. Then she continued: "Anyway, the more righteous and upstanding her quarry, the more intense was her pursuit. She claimed—don't ask me if it's true—but she *claimed* that she'd never had a failure. Some men took longer than others, but eventually they all cracked. Or so she said."

Charlotte remembered the videotape. She had thought that the doctor had been indulging his fantasies in directing Kimberly to parade around the room in such a suggestive way, but that must have been how Lily had really walked.

"It doesn't go with her angelic image, does it?" Connie asked, sensing Charlotte's surprise. "But the image was part of her appeal. Did Hugh Hefner choose women who looked like call girls for his Playboy bunnies? No, he chose women who looked like Kansas cheerleaders."

"Did she really act, or was she just talk?" Charlotte asked.

"She certainly acted before she was married," she said. "She was—to put it crudely again—a slut. After her marriage, I don't know. I do know that she liked to torment Victor with that possibility . . ."

"With what possibility?"

"That she was sleeping with other men. He was insanely jealous. He would check her mileage to see if the distances she traveled squared with her given destination, or he would time how long she was gone. Sometimes he'd even follow her.'' She tilted her head back again to exhale.

"How do you know this?"

"Peter told me," she said. "Peter De Vries," she added. "He's the sexton at the Zion Hill Church."

"I've met him," Charlotte said.

"He and Lily were very close." A shadow slid across her face. "They were engaged to be married at one time. That was before Peter's accident."

"Was Dr. Louria jealous of Peter?"

"No. Peter was the one person he wasn't jealous of. I guess he figured that—having rejected Peter once—Lily wouldn't be attracted to him again. Which she wasn't. In that way, anyway."

"What about Peter?" she asked.

"Peter has always carried the torch for Lily," she said. "Always has, and always will. He never got over her rejection of him. She ruined him," she added bitterly. "He's only a shell of the man he used to be."

Hearing a rap on the pane of the French door, they looked up. Another waitress was standing at the window and pointing at her watch.

Connie stubbed out her cigarette. "I have to go now," she said.

"Thanks," Charlotte said, "I appreciate your help."

10

A FEW MOMENTS later Charlotte was giving her order to Connie. She chose asparagus: cream of asparagus soup followed by an asparagus omelette. She figured that she might as well take advantage of asparagus season, though she wondered if in doing so she would henceforth be identified by Connie as "the asparagus." Actually, it would be a better match than "the grilled lamb." She liked lamb, but she loved asparagus, and the recent scientific finding that it contained a chemical that helped prevent cancer only added to its appeal. With the help of her cook, Julie (Charlotte herself being all but useless in the kitchen), she had once given an asparagus dinner party. She had taken the idea from a "Get Even" dinner she had attended when the movie *Jaws* was released by a studio she was then working for. A publicity stunt to promote the movie, the dinner had consisted of seven courses, all featuring shark. Instead, she had served seven courses of asparagus, from asparagus soup to asparagus soufflé. The dinner party had been a big hit, which, since only asparagus lovers had been invited, was no surprise. The conversation had ranged from the relative merits of thin stalks versus thick to the weighty question of whether asparagus should be eaten tip first or stem first. The latter question, which fell into the same category as that of whether corn on the cob should be eaten in a spiral or back and forth, was one on which her dinner guests had displayed strong opinions, the stem-firsters accusing the tip-firsters of harboring a streak of self-indulgence. As a tip-firster herself,

Charlotte had been shocked that there were stem-firsters in their midst. To her, being anything but a tip-firster implied a certain diffidence in asparagus attitude that made them unworthy of being guests at a dinner party for asparagus lovers.

Sebastian's soup was delicious, a delicate blend of creamed asparagus with fresh herbs. As Charlotte savored it, she thought about what Connie had told her. In considering Dr. Louria as a suspect, they had thought he had murdered the young women because A. they hadn't been perfect renditions of Lily, or B. it was a way of exerting his control over his late wife. Though the second was more plausible than the first, both of these hypotheses struck Charlotte as being weak. Why kill the young women who didn't measure up? Why not just start over, as Dr. Louria himself had pointed out? Or, with regard to the control theory: Why kill the young women as a means of controlling Lily? Hadn't Dr. Louria already controlled her? She had been bought and paid for as surely as he had bought and paid for the iron mask at the London auction. But the jealous rage theory: now *that* was a real motive, a motive that had proven itself over and over again as being sufficient to drive someone to murder. He could have killed the Lily look-alikes because his love had turned to rage. Rage over how she had manipulated him. Rage over how she had humiliated him. Rage over how she had betrayed him with other men. Then she had died, rejecting him again, for wasn't death a form of rejection? With the object of his rage removed, he had simply created new Lilys to replace the fantasy he had lost, Lily voodoo dolls. But instead of sticking pins into them, he'd cut off their heads, and torn them limb from limb, preserving their skulls as trophies of his heinous acts. Then, he'd offered up his trophies. This was the part she still didn't get. Out of guilt: as a form of atonement? That would explain the cemetery, sort of. Out of pride: as a form of showing off? Out of remorse: as a way of getting caught?

She was halfway through the omelette, and was sipping her glass of California chardonnay when she saw a curious figure turn up the brick walk leading to the front door. He had shoulder-length blond hair, and was wearing a full-length leather apron and a peculiar leather hat with a plastic visor to protect his head from the drizzle. In one hand, he carried a tall wooden staff. His other sleeve swung free.

It was Peter De Vries, the Leatherman.

When the pastor had told her the story of how a local boy had christened Peter the Leatherman, it hadn't really made sense to her. His leather apron hadn't seemed that out of place, and he hadn't been wearing the hat or carrying the staff. But seeing him in full regalia, she now understood why his appearance would strike the imagination of a little boy.

Climbing the front steps with the slow, shuffling gait of a man absorbed in his own little world, he opened the door, and was greeted by the maître d', who, after carefully placing his staff in an umbrella stand by the door, escorted him to a bar stool at the back. Though the other diners looked up when he entered, as they might for any new arrival, they barely noticed the bizarre figure who shuffled past their tables. It was clear that they were as accustomed to his presence as they were to that of any of the well-dressed suburbanites who made up the rest of the restaurant's clientele.

Watching as Connie waited on him, Charlotte noted the care with which she set his place and the warmth with which she smiled at him, and thought of what the pastor had said about the high esteem in which the Leatherman had been held. But then it dawned on her that Connie's attitude expressed more than just high esteem. Connie, she realized, was in love with him.

After lunch, Charlotte headed off to talk to the wholesale florists Jerry had referred her to. Following the dispatcher's directions, she arrived at the largest of them a few minutes later. The business was located in a lovely old cast-iron conservatory, which was flanked by two long greenhouses. Behind the conservatory were a number of other greenhouses. A sign over the entrance read: "Winter Garden Florist, Wholesale and Retail Flowers Since 1906." Entering the building, Charlotte passed through an anteroom into a miniature tropical paradise: the conservatory was filled with exotic plants of every description, from calla lilies to moth orchids. It had finally started to rain, and the sound of the raindrops thrumming on the curved glass of the roof added to the air of intimacy. On either side, doors opened into light-filled greenhouses in which baskets of plants and flowers hung from the ceilings, and pots filled with geraniums, impatiens, petunias, and the other bedding plants that were in big demand among home gardeners at this time of year covered the tables.

A young woman behind the counter was taking an order over the telephone. As Charlotte waited for her to finish, she savored the smell. There was nothing like the smell of a greenhouse, with its mixture of damp, moist earth and the sweet fragrance of flowers in bloom.

"What can I do for you?" she asked, once she had hung up the phone. She was a lively-looking young woman with short, curly, black hair, an olive complexion, and a ready smile.

"I'd like to buy some hanging flower baskets," Charlotte said. As long as she was here, she might as well get some flowers for her patio, she thought. She also figured that the clerk would be more likely to answer questions that were put to her by a paying customer.

"Our hanging flower baskets are in this greenhouse," she said, heading off toward the greenhouse on the left. "We have geraniums, lantana, impatiens. What else?" she asked herself. "Petunias, cineraria, blue lace flower."

Charlotte followed her down the center aisle, marveling at the heady riot of color, with its promise of bright summer days, that contrasted so starkly with the grayness of the weather outside.

"Stop me if you see something you like," the girl said. "Also, watch out for the buckets," she said, indicating the buckets that had been placed on the floor to catch the rain from the leaky roof.

"Here," Charlotte replied, stopping at a plant with funnel-shaped flowers of a lovely lemon-yellow color. "Are these hibiscus?"

She nodded. "They're very unusual. We have a lot of unusual plants here." She stopped to wipe a drop of rain from her nose. "We also have a lot of broken glass," she added.

Charlotte looked up at the exposed sky. "So I see," she said.

"We have eleven houses, so it's hard to keep up with the breaks. We get a lot of breakage from kids throwing balls; we have a big housing development next door." She looked up at the broken glass. "This isn't so hard to replace, but the curved glass in the conservatory takes someone with special skills."

"Actually, I'm surprised that these old greenhouses are still standing," Charlotte said. "It seems as if a lot of the older ones have deteriorated to the point where they're beyond repair."

"Those are the wooden ones. Our glazing bars are made of cast iron. The manufacturer was from England. They built a lot of conservatories around here. Iron requires a lot more maintenance than wood, but if you take care of it, it'll last forever." She looked up at the flowers. "How many would you like?"

"Three, please," Charlotte said.

As the girl took down three of the hanging baskets, Charlotte introduced herself and explained that she was helping the local police with their investigation into the look-alike murders.

The young woman in turn gave her name as Lisa Gennaro and explained that she was the daughter of the owner.

Then Charlotte asked her about the lilies of the valley: "I realize that it wouldn't be a problem to get lilies of the valley at this time of year. But I was wondering about the other two incidents. Where would someone have gotten them in September or in April?"

"You've come to the right place," Lisa said. "We specialize in growing lilies of the valley."

Charlotte raised an eyebrow.

"You can get lilies of the valley from any wholesale florist," she explained. "But because they're flown over from Holland, you wouldn't be able to get them right away. You'd have to order a couple of weeks in advance. We have them available all the time. We grow them right here."

"How do you get them to bloom out of season?"

"We dig the pips from our fields, plant them in pots, and set them in bulb crates, which are held in a suspended state in our coolers. After three months, they're ready for forcing. They bloom eighteen to twenty-one days after they come out. We take some out every day, so we always have some in bloom."

"Would you be able to tell me who might have ordered some in September and in April?" she asked. "It was probably someone local," she added.

"That shouldn't be too hard. We're computerized now. I'd be happy to look it up for you." Picking up the hanging baskets, the young woman led Charlotte back to the conservatory, where she set the baskets on the front counter. Then she picked up a brochure and handed it to Charlotte.

The cover of the brochure read: "Lilies of the Valley, From the Finest Imported German Pips." It went on to read: "We offer only 'extra select' grade: strong, twelve- to fifteen-inch stems; ten to fifteen bells to a stem." The rest of the brochure gave price and ordering information.

When Charlotte had finished looking at the brochure, Lisa led her down a hall lined with colorful posters advertising Holland-grown bulbs into an office at the rear and sat down at a computer terminal. As Charlotte looked on, she called up the sales records for the previous month.

"Most of our orders for lilies of the valley are for weddings," she said as she tapped the keys on the keyboard. "So it shouldn't be hard to single out the orders that aren't wedding-connected."

"Do any other local greenhouses grow lilies of the valley?"

"No. We're the only commercial suppliers in the country. We started growing them back in the 1950's for one of Edward Archibald's daughters." She looked up at Charlotte. "Edward Archibald was the founder of Zion Hill. Maybe you've heard of him."

Charlotte nodded. "Which Archibald daughter would that have been?"

"Lillian," she said, as she scrolled through the records. "Lily of the valley was her favorite flower. I suppose it was because of her name. There's a beautiful stained-glass window in the Zion Hill Church that shows her walking through a field of lilies of the valley.''

"I understand the church's stained-glass windows are magnificent,'' Charlotte commented as she peered over Lisa's shoulder.

"They are,'' Lisa agreed. ''People come from all over to see them. Ah, here's April,'' she said. ''Let's see. Wedding, wedding, wedding. I can tell the weddings because they order other flowers too. Lilies of the valley are popular for weddings because they symbolize purity.''

In light of what Connie had just told her, lilies of the valley didn't seem a very appropriate choice for Lily's favorite flower, Charlotte thought.

"We don't get that many non-wedding orders for lilies of the valley because they're very expensive,'' she added. She had stopped scrolling. ''Ah, here we are. April twenty-sixth. A single order for a bouquet of two dozen.'' She leaned back to allow Charlotte a better view of the screen.

The name and address of the buyer were spelled out in glowing green letters next to the date: Victor Louria, M.D., 300 River Road, Zion Hill, N.Y. The evidence was right in front of her eyes, but Charlotte still couldn't believe it. ''Dr. Louria?'' she said stupidly.

The girl nodded. ''He used to be one of our best customers for lilies of the valley. He used to buy them for his wife, who was the daughter of Lillian Archibald. They were her favorite flower too. He stopped buying them for a while after she died, then he started again.''

Charlotte jotted down the date. Liliana Doyle's skull had been found on the headstone at the Zion Hill Cemetery on April twenty-seventh, the next day.

"What about last September?'' Charlotte asked.

Tapping some more keys, Lisa called up the older records. ''This might take a minute,'' she said. ''There are a lot of weddings in September.'' Again, she scrolled through the sales records. ''Here it is,'' she said finally. ''September fourteenth, Victor Louria, M.D.''

Charlotte couldn't remember the date on which Kimberly's skull had been found, but she did remember Dr. Louria saying she had disappeared just after Labor Day. If, as in the other cases, the skull had been found about ten days after the victim disappeared, then September fourteenth would be about right.

She wondered about Dr. Louria's alibi. If he had been in Brazil at the time of Kimberly's death, as he claimed, he couldn't have put the skull in the cemetery. But maybe his alibi wouldn't hold up.

Lisa looked up again at Charlotte. "I read that he was being questioned by the police in connection with the murder case," she said. "This isn't going to look good for him, is it?"

"No, it's not," Charlotte agreed.

"Do you want me to see if he placed any other orders?" she asked.

The telephone was ringing again, but Lisa didn't answer it. "When you get a chance," Charlotte replied. "There's no need to do it right now. I'd like to know about every order he placed, starting in February 1990."

"No problem," Lisa replied, as they made their way back out to the conservatory. "The computer makes it pretty easy. I could probably get the information to you in a day or so."

"That would be great," Charlotte said. "I'd appreciate it if you'd let me know if you get any other orders too."

Lisa handed Charlotte her card. "If you don't hear from me, give me a call. I'm apt to forget," she added.

After paying for her flower baskets, Charlotte thanked Lisa and left.

So it *had* been Dr. Louria, Charlotte thought as she drove back to the police station with her hibiscus plants in the passenger seat. The iron mask had been removed, exposing this urbane Brazilian for the monster he really was. The lily of the valley bouquets were the artistic finale to a drama in which he had created the Lily look-alikes, then killed them, and dismembered them in the summer house. The choice of the summer house was hard to explain, unless he had chosen it for psychological reasons. Maybe it had been the scene of some unpleasant incident with his late wife for which he wanted to take his revenge. A bitter argument, perhaps, or plans for a romantic evening that had gone awry. She shivered at the grisliness of it all. How had he killed them? she wondered. She remembered the article she had read in his waiting room about botulinum toxin being used by plastic surgeons to paralyze facial tics. The article had talked about the dangers of using too large a dose. It had captured her interest because of the exotic nature of the botulinum toxin, but a doctor would have easy access to drugs that were more mundane, and almost as deadly. Curare, insulin, digitalis, and any number of barbiturates had all been used as murder weapons, and those were just the drugs that immediately occurred to her. "A little shot—just to help you relax," and—finis—that was it.

Her discovery that it was Dr. Louria who had ordered the lilies of the valley also solved another dilemma: what to do about her own surgery. There was no way she was going to be operated on by someone who was very possibly the murderer of three innocent young women. Coming up to a convenience store, she pulled in and parked next to a telephone booth. Then she dialed Dr. Louria's office and told the receptionist that she had decided against having the surgery. Her feeling as she hung up was one of profound relief. If she'd gone ahead with it, she would always have felt dishonest, as if she were being deliberately misleading. Other people may have been deceived, but she never would be. The lines may have been erased, but she would never be able to look at her face without remembering where they had been.

A few minutes later, she had arrived at the police station. She met Jerry as she was heading in. One of his hands held the door open for her, the other cradled a round package under his elbow. "What took you so long?" he complained. "I've been waiting for you."

She smiled mischievously. "I had lunch at Sebastian's. I wanted to make you jealous."

"You have," he said. "I had a meatball sub at my desk. I'm headed up to the Octagon House." He looked down at the package under his elbow. "I've got the skull of our third victim here. Do you want to come along? I'll only be half an hour or so."

Charlotte checked her watch; she wanted to make it back to the city by dinner, but it was only a little after three.

"Sure," she replied, and walked with him out to the police car.

Once they were under way, she said: "I've had a productive day," and then proceeded to tell him about her meeting with the pastor, and his reference to a possible motive for Dr. Louria. Then she described her follow-up discussion with Connie. "Jerry," she said, "it gives him a real motive."

Jerry wasn't overly impressed with the jealous rage theory, but his attitude changed when she told him about Dr. Louria's purchases of the lily of the valley bouquets. "They have records of this?" he asked.

"It's all on their computer," she said, amused at seeing his detective's brain kicking into gear.

"And when were the flowers purchased, exactly?" he asked.

Charlotte consulted her notes. "The second bouquet was purchased on April twenty-sixth, which I believe was the day before Liliana's skull was discovered at the Zion Hill Cemetery."

Jerry nodded. "It was found on the twenty-seventh."

"And the first bouquet was purchased on September fourteenth. I couldn't remember the exact date that Kimberly's skull was found."

"September fifteenth," he said.

"The day after," Charlotte said, "which was supposedly when Dr. Louria was still in Brazil. Have you confirmed his alibi?"

"One of the county detectives is working on it. He's confirmed the airline reservations. But they could have been falsified. I've got him calling Dr. Louria's friends and relatives now. By the way," he continued, "I talked with the lawyers for Lily Louria's estate."

"And?" Charlotte said.

"They said her estate was valued at a little over two million. They also confirmed that Sebastian was her sole beneficiary."

Charlotte whistled. "Not bad for a girl who didn't care about material things," she said, remembering what Lothian had said about Lily's habit of wearing the same pair of blue jeans all week long. "I guess that puts Sebastian on our suspect list."

"I'd say so," Jerry said. "Especially since he'll need to borrow against the inheritance to open his new restaurant."

"Getting back to Dr. Louria," she said. "He ordered two dozen flowers each time. Do you know how many were in the bouquets that were found in the cemeteries? The bouquet in the undercroft looked like about two dozen to me."

Jerry shrugged. "We can check easily enough. We still have the bouquets in the evidence locker. We also have the crime scene photographs. Did you check the sales records for this month?" he asked.

"No," she said. "I figured that the murderer would simply have picked them, since they're in bloom now. But I asked the clerk to check the records for all of Dr. Louria's purchases dating back to the date of Lily Louria's drowning."

"Good." The face that looked out over the wheel was thoughtful. "It's incriminating evidence, but I'm not sure it's incriminating enough. There are probably dozens of florists where he could have bought the flowers."

"Ah. That's where you're wrong. Winter Garden is the only supplier in the country for out-of-season lilies of the valley. They developed them as a specialty because they were Lillian Archibald's favorite flower."

"The only supplier in the country, huh?"

Charlotte nodded. "Other florists can get them, but they have to order them from Holland, and it takes a minimum of two weeks."

"Which is longer than the interval between the disappearances and presumed deaths of the girls, and the flowers' appearances with the skulls." Jerry smiled widely and looked over at Charlotte. "Good work, Graham."

No sooner had he spoken than he pulled the police car into the nearest driveway and backed it out in the opposite direction.

"Where are we going?" she asked.

"To see the good doctor," Jerry replied. "I think we've got something concrete to talk with him about, thanks to you. Maybe he'll confess; it would save us a lot of trouble."

———

Five minutes later, they pulled into the driveway of Arch-field Hall. They planned to try the residence first, and then the office. After parking next to the fountain, they ascended the stone steps and rang the bell at the magnificent front door. The door was answered by the housekeeper, Marta, who had been questioned by Jerry the day before, and who now greeted him warmly. She escorted them to an elevator at the rear of the entrance foyer. "He's in the tower," she said as she pushed the button. A moment later, they could hear the elevator be-ginning its descent from an upper story. When it came to a stop, Marta opened the door, which was of clear glass in a frame of hammered monel, for Charlotte and Jerry. Then she entered the elevator behind them and pushed the button marked "tower."

Her sweet face bore an anxious expression. "I'm so worried about the doctor," she said as the creaky elevator started to rise. "He's like he was after she die. He no go to work. He cancel all his appointments. All he do is sit in the tower and think. Think, and drink."

A moment later, the elevator had lurched to a stop, and Charlotte and Jerry got out, followed by Marta, who an-nounced: "Chief D'Angelo is here to see you." Then she got back into the elevator and launched the antique conveyance on its downward journey.

The tower room was square, with a stone floor, a low ceiling of carved teak, and floor-to-ceiling windows on four sides that looked out through the columns of the triple-arched openings. A spiral staircase in one corner appeared to lead to an outdoor observation deck on the next level.

Dr. Louria was slouched on a rattan couch in front of a television set, holding a glass of whiskey in one hand. He was unshaven, and the front of his polo shirt was spotted with stains. The morning newspapers were spread out on the coffee table in front of him, along with an array of liquor bottles.

With a start, Charlotte noticed that he wasn't wearing his artificial ear. A metal bracket was affixed to his skull at the rear of the scarred place where his ear should have been, but where there was only the opening for the ear canal. The ear lay on the table among the liquor bottles.

He glanced up at them, and then returned his attention to the television set. He was watching a golf tournament.

Walking over to one of the windows, they gazed out at the view beyond the hand-tooled metal railing. Tendrils of mist rose from the river, giving it the otherworldly air of Chinese landscape painting.

"Terrific view," Jerry said.

Without taking his eyes off the television set, Dr. Louria waved an arm, as if to say, "Be my guest."

After admiring the view, Charlotte and Jerry took seats in the rattan chairs on either side of the couch. Charlotte wondered if this was where Dr. Louria had watched the videos he had made of the Lily look-alikes.

A golfer was lining up a shot on the putting green. As they watched, he gently swung his putting iron, propelling the ball directly into the cup. As the audience clapped quietly, Jerry said: "I understand that your late wife liked lilies of the valley."

Dr. Louria nodded.

"The clerk at Winter Garden Florist reports that you ordered bouquets of lilies of the valley on September fourteenth and April twenty-sixth."

For the first time, Dr. Louria looked over at them.

Jerry continued: "Those dates immediately precede the dates on which the skulls of Kimberly Ferguson and Liliana Doyle were found in the cemeteries. On both occasions, the skulls were found with bouquets of lilies of the valley."

The audience at the golf tournament was tense as the next player lined up his shot. "If he sinks this putt, he'll have an eagle," said the golf announcer's hushed voice.

"We believe that you killed the Lily look-alikes, and dismembered their bodies at your summer house," Jerry said. "We also believe that you placed the bouquets of lilies of the valley next to their skulls."

Dr. Louria took a swig from the glass of whiskey in his hand.

"Do you have anything to say?"

The doctor didn't reply.

"In the cup!" the announcer said as the audience applauded.

They waited for Dr. Louria to respond. When it became clear that he wasn't going to say anything, they left. "So much for a confession," Jerry said as they rode back down the elevator. "It was like talking to a zombie."

Marta met them at the elevator door on the first floor.

"Marta, did Dr. Louria ever order lilies of the valley?" Jerry asked.

"What is this lilies of the valley?"

"A white flower, very small, with a beautiful fragrance." He sniffed an imaginary bouquet and then rolled his eyes in mock appreciation.

"Ah, *el muguete*," she said. "Yes. Once a week, the flowers come. Four, maybe five bouquets. I put them all around the house: the bedroom, the dining room, the Great Hall. Miss Lily, she love *el muguete*."

"And since her death?"

"At first, no. But later, when the girls start to come here"—a shadow crossed her face—"the doctor, he order the flowers again."

"What girls would these be?" Jerry asked.

"The girls who look like Miss Lily," she said.

After leaving Archfield Hall, they continued on down River Road toward the Octagon House. A few minutes later, they were standing on the porch, waiting for Lister to answer the door. Though the rain had stopped, the knoll on which the house was perched was still enshrouded by fog, through which the trunks and branches of the black locusts that studded the lawn loomed like a giant army advancing on a hilltop citadel. The door was answered by Lister, who was wearing blue jeans and a black turtleneck that emphasized the billiard ball quality of his clean-shaven head. After they had exchanged greetings, he led them through the Phrenological Cabinet to the central stairwell, and down the spiral staircase to the basement where the sculpture studio of the "recomposer of the decomposed" was located.

When they had reached the studio, Jerry set his bubble-wrapped package down on a worktable next to an unoccupied cork collar. "This time, we know who the victim is," he said.

"How?" Lister asked as Jerry proceeded to unwrap the skull.

"Lothian Archibald had seen a young woman who she thought was Lily in the drugstore and followed her home. When we figured out that the murderer was killing Lily look-alikes, we tracked her down through her landlord, thinking that she might be the next victim."

"But we were too late," Charlotte said.

Jerry handed Lister a photograph, which showed a young woman in a two-piece bathing suit sitting on a beach. "This is a 'before' photograph of the victim that was sent to us by the family." Then he placed two fingers in the eye sockets of the skull and lifted it out of its plastic nest.

"May I remind you that the superorbital ridge is not to be used as a handle for picking up a skull," Lister chided him. "You're treating a human skull as if it were a bowling ball."

"Sorry," said Jerry as he handed the skull over to Lister.

"It's just that they're fragile," Lister said, "And these skulls are especially fragile because they've been bleached so heavily." He set the skull down gently in the collar, and then leaned over to study it.

"Obviously, we don't need the reconstructions for identification purposes. But it would make an impression on a jury if we could show three 'befores' with three 'afters.' There's a chin implant here," Jerry said, pointing to the wedge that had been inserted in the chin.

"Cheek implants and posterior mandible implants too," Lister said. "The first victim was the only one who didn't need posterior mandible implants. That's what made the faces of the Archibald women so unique: that wide, square-jawed look. I always thought they would have made a good ship figurehead."

He was dancing around the skull, in order to study it from various angles.

"They had the bust lines for it too: a big, high bust," he said. "Speaking of other parts, do we have the rest of her?"

"Bits and pieces: an arm, a foot," Jerry replied. "They

washed up in Corinth Municipal Park on Friday."

"Where was the skull found this time?"

"In the undercroft at the Zion Hill Church," Jerry replied. "The sexton found it early this morning."

Lister nodded. As they looked on, he ran his fingers over the brow and then the cheekbones of the skull. Then he gently ran the knuckle of his forefinger along one side of the jaw, and paused with it on the chin to gaze into the empty eye sockets.

It was as if he were a lover, and the skull was the face of his beloved—a face that he was about to kiss. Charlotte almost felt as if she should excuse herself from the intimate scene.

At last, he stood back and stared at the skull in admiration, his wild gray eyes beaming. "What a beauty!" he exclaimed. Then he continued: "Botticelli had his Simonetta Vespucci, Whistler had his Joanna Heffernan, Rossetti had his Lizzie Siddal. And I . . ."

Jerry completed the sentence for him: "You have your Lillian Archibald."

"Or her daughter," he said. "Or her daughter's look-alikes. Not one of them, but three of them." He clenched his fists and did a little jig. "And now I get to sculpt this face again!"

Charlotte would hardly have called it a face, but she didn't think that skulls had their own personalities either.

"Do you know what Rossetti said about Lizzie Siddal?" he asked.

They shook their heads.

"He said: 'All my life, I have dreamt one dream alone.' We all have one dream: we're all destined to fall in love with a certain kind of face, and the face of Lillian Archibald is my one dream."

"You have to sign this, Jack," said Jerry, handing him the chain of evidence form used by law enforcement officials to keep track of who is in possession of the evidence in criminal cases.

"When do you need these by?" Lister asked as he signed.

"As soon as possible. I think we're about to make an arrest, and we'd like to have the reconstructions ready to present to the prosecutor."

Lister's bald head jerked up. "Really?" he said, with great interest. "And may I ask who it is that you're about to arrest?"

"Sorry, Jack. You'll find out soon enough," Jerry said. "How long will it take you to finish them?" he asked.

"Usually a week for each. But for you—and also because my other business is slow—four days for both."

They headed back out a few minutes later, leaving Lister gloating over his newest acquisition.

"He's a very strange guy," said Charlotte as they passed back out through the Phrenological Cabinet.

"You'd be strange too if your hobby was recomposing the decomposed."

The radio was crackling when they got back in the police car. It was Captain Crosby, Jerry's right-hand man. "Sorry to interrupt you, Chief," he said. "But I have some important news for you about Dr. Louria's alibi from Bill Warner over at the county."

"What is it?" Jerry asked impatiently.

"His alibi's ironclad. He couldn't possibly have done it. He was in Brazil, just like he said. Warner said he talked with a dozen people. They all backed up the doctor, and they all backed up one another."

"Were they all relatives?" Jerry asked.

"No," Crosby replied. "Warner even talked with the officials at the hospital where the doctor's mother was a patient. He performed a couple of ear reconstruction operations on their patients while he was there. For free," he added.

"Thanks," Jerry said. He replaced the microphone in its cradle. Then he pounded his fist on the dashboard. "Hell, shit, and damnation," he said.

11

CHARLOTTE DIDN'T THINK about the case on her drive back to the city, didn't think about anything, in fact. She was worn-out: all she wanted to do was sit down, put her feet up, and fix herself a Manhattan. But the case wouldn't let her alone: the newsstand on the corner of the street where her parking garage was located displayed a special edition of the *Post* with a story about Dr. Louria entitled "Murder in the Undercroft." Never mind that the murder hadn't taken place in the under-croft, it made a good headline, despite the fact that most New Yorkers probably didn't have the faintest idea of what an un-dercroft was. She bought a copy and tucked it under her arm. Back at home, she ignored the blinking light on her answering machine, fixed herself a Manhattan, and sat down with the newspaper. The story featured an artist's rendering of the skull on the altar, with its offering of the bouquet of lilies of the valley. It also included a write-up on Dr. Louria, and an ex-terior shot of Archfield Hall, with its medieval-looking tower jutting into the sky. The fact that Jerry had said that Dr. Louria wasn't a suspect didn't seem to matter. Nor did the fact that this was a rehash of the material that they had printed the day before. The press was in a feeding frenzy, and with no keeper to hand-feed them, they had set upon the most available target.

As she sipped her drink, she scanned the article on Dr. Louria, which went into great detail about his plastic surgery career. Turning the page, she came across a "before" and "after" photo layout of some of his most famous clients. So

164

much for the much-vaunted discretion of his office staff. Charlotte scanned the faces, many of which were personally familiar to her. Thank God she hadn't gone through with the surgery, she thought. Otherwise, her ''before'' and ''after'' photos would probably have been splashed all over the paper as well.

She stopped at the third photo in the second row from the bottom of the ''before'' section: it was a photo of her old friend, Kitty Saunders, whose relentless lobbying on Dr. Louria's behalf had had much to do with why Charlotte had gone to see him in the first place. She and Kitty had been friends for fifty years. They had met on Cape Cod, where they had played in summer stock together. They had both been stars in the forties. But Kitty had dropped out after the birth of her second child, and had never gone back.

No sooner had Charlotte seen the photo than the phone rang. She had a good idea of who it was.

''Where have you been!'' said the accusatory voice on the other end of the line. ''I've left four messages on your machine.'' Kitty's affectedly stagey manner of speech had only become more pronounced over the years, like that of the British expatriates whose Mayfair accents become more clipped the longer they spend on American soil.

''I just walked in the door,'' Charlotte said.

''Have you seen the story in the *Post*?''

''I was just reading it,'' Charlotte said. ''Where are you?'' she asked, thinking that Kitty couldn't possibly have already seen the article in Maine, where she spent most of the year.

''Visiting Laura,'' she said, naming a daughter who lived in Connecticut. ''Did you see the picture of me?''

''It was a good picture, Kitty,'' said Charlotte. ''You know what they say: 'Bad publicity is better than no publicity.' ''

''Oh, Charlotte,'' Kitty whined. ''How humiliating.''

Charlotte listened patiently for five minutes as Kitty went on about the sorry state of the fourth estate. Finally, Kitty asked: ''Where have you been?''

''In Zion Hill,'' she replied. ''Jerry D'Angelo is the police chief there now, and I've been helping him out on the case.''

''Are you going to have the surgery?''

"No," Charlotte replied.

"Because of this?" she said accusingly.

"Not because of this," she replied. Though it had been her suspicion of Dr. Louria that had resulted in her decision, she had realized when she made it that it was the right one. "Kitty, years ago a doctor gave me some very valuable advice about how to make a decision regarding a medical procedure."

"What?" asked Kitty.

Charlotte went on: "He said to flip a coin: heads it's yes, and tails it's no. If the coin comes up heads, and your reaction is 'Oh, shit,' then you shouldn't go ahead with the procedure."

"And what happened?" asked Kitty.

"The coin came up heads, and my reaction was 'Oh, shit.' "

"I did my best," Kitty said haughtily. "You can lead a horse, and all that." She paused. "Charlotte," she continued, "I just can't imagine that Dr. Louria would do something like this. He's such a sweet man."

"He didn't," Charlotte said.

But the damage had already been done, she thought. Even if he didn't commit the murders, the fact that he'd made the Lily clones was enough to ruin his reputation.

Charlotte knew how these things worked. She'd been a victim of false rumors enough times herself over the course of her career.

"What's going to happen to him?" Kitty asked. "Will he ever be able to practice again?"

"I don't know," Charlotte said.

It was two days before Charlotte had a chance to put her feet up and think about the case again: two days of pouring rain that she spent running around the city, tending to affairs that she had been putting off. It wasn't only that she didn't have the time: she had also felt as if she needed a break. But on the evening of the second day, after a lovely dinner spent reminiscing with an old actor friend, she found herself thinking about Dr. Louria again. If he didn't do it, that meant that somebody else did, somebody who wanted to make it *look* as if he had done it. Hence the choice of the summer house as the place to dismember the bodies, hence the bouquets of lily of the valley that were left with the skulls. Who else would have wanted to see Lily dead? she asked herself again. And for what reasons? With the memory of her asparagus lunch still fresh, the first suspect to come to mind was Sebastian. Because of the evidence implicating Dr. Louria, they hadn't taken him seriously as a suspect thus far. But he might very well have gotten wind of Dr. Louria's scheme to set up the Lily clone as his amnesiac wife. If Dr. Louria had succeeded with his plan, Sebastian would have been cut out of his inheritance from Lily, which he presumably needed to go ahead with his plan to launch his restaurant in Manhattan. Reverend Cornwall had described Sebastian as having Lily's same reckless streak, though to a lesser degree. The fact that such a young man was willing to entertain the notion of competing with the top New York restaurants was evidence enough of that. But was he reckless enough to have committed murder? Upon further consideration, she realized that there were a couple of problems with the Sebastian scenario, first among them the issue of plausibility. Wouldn't it have been simpler and easier to expose the Lily look-alikes as imposters rather than risk a life sentence for multiple murder? Instead of killing them, he could simply have hired a private investigator and tracked down their real identities, as Dr. Louria had suggested. If there were any doubts, he could have resorted to blood typing, X-ray records, dental records: there were lots of ways to prove that the clones weren't Lily. The second problem was one of what might be called delicacy. It struck her as unlikely that Sebastian would have murdered young women who looked so much like the sister to whom he had been so attached, particularly in such a brutal way.

From Sebastian, her thoughts turned to Connie, who appeared to be in love with Peter De Vries. If Peter still carried the torch for Lily, as Connie had said, then it made a kind of sense that Connie might want to see the Lily look-alikes dead. But there were numerous problems with the Connie theory, which was pathetically weak to begin with. Though she would have to check with Jerry (who had taken courses on criminal psychology), Charlotte suspected that it was highly unlikely that a woman would dismember her murder victims. At least, Charlotte had never heard of such a thing (Lizzie Borden excluded), and she'd been reading the tabloids for fifty years. The second problem with the Connie theory was that her love for Peter hadn't struck Charlotte as being passionate enough to serve as a motive for murder; it seemed to fall more into the category of a nostalgia for *les temps perdu*.

Nor did it seem likely that Peter, in his eccentric role as the one-armed Leatherman, would even be tempted to enter into a liaison with any of the Lily look-alikes. Which brought her to her third suspect: Peter himself. If it was true that Lily had jilted him because she couldn't bear being married to a man without an arm, it was very possible that Peter could have been taking his revenge against Lily out on her stand-ins. Hadn't the Leatherman murdered the woman who had jilted him? If Dr. Louria's father had considered his son's lack of an ear a reflection on his masculinity, what would be the effect of the loss of an arm on Peter, especially if he was jilted on account of it? Moreover, the Peter theory would explain the dismemberments. If Lily had jilted Peter because he had been dismembered, albeit by a bolt of lightning, wouldn't it make a kind of sense that he might try to get back at her by dismembering her look-alikes?

Her mind racing, she got up to fetch herself another drink and a bowl of potato chips. There was also the fact that Peter had been the landlord for the Lily look-alikes, she thought. Dr. Louria had said that the Lily clones had been kept under wraps—both literally and figuratively—that they had seldom gone out, except to see him. Everything they needed had been delivered. (Except hair coloring, she thought, remembering Lothian's sighting of Doreen Mileski.) But Peter, being their landlord, would have known of their existence.

Her drink mixed, she took it back to her chair. She felt like Jack Lister must have felt when he started getting a sense of what a face looked like. She was also getting the sense of a face, the face of a murderer. As the pastor's pamphlet on the Leatherman had put it: someone who has escaped from the constraints of society. She swirled the ice around in her glass, and then took another sip. Peter would also have known exactly what Dr. Louria was up to, and recognized that he would make a convenient scapegoat for the murders. Hence the orders for the lilies of the valley in his name, she thought. Reminded of her visit to the florist, she found herself transported back to the greenhouse, with its exotic smells and the sound of the raindrops thrumming on the glass roof. Suddenly, she made one of those mental connections that she probably wouldn't have made had not the rational side of her brain been dulled by the alcohol. The pieces fit together as neatly as two of the pieces from one of Lister's fractured skulls. The first was a leaky greenhouse roof made of glass and iron, and the second was a man who fixes stained-glass windows.

Getting up from her chair, she retrieved her handbag from the table in the hall, and, after a bit of rummaging around, produced Lisa Gennaro's business card. She checked her watch: it was five past nine—not too late to call. She dialed Lisa's home number, and was relieved when she picked up right away.

"I have two questions," Charlotte said, after reminding Lisa who she was. "The first is about Dr. Louria's orders for the lilies of the valley. Were they always delivered, or did he sometimes pick them up?"

"Both," Lisa replied. "Usually we delivered them to Archfield Hall, but there were a couple of instances in which he said that somebody would be stopping by to pick them up."

Yes, the skull was beginning to take shape, Charlotte thought. She continued: "Then he didn't pick them up himself?"

"No," she said. "Or rather, I don't really know. We have a kind of anteroom by the front door. Maybe you remember it."

"Yes," Charlotte said.

"He said that he or someone else—I don't really remember which—would be coming by just after we closed, so I left the flowers out there in a water bucket with his name on them. They were gone the next morning."

"Was that the case with the most recent order?"

"Yes," she said. "It was."

"Then how did he pay for them?"

"Oh," she said, as if she thought the answer to that question was clear, "he had a standing account. We billed him every month."

Aha, thought Charlotte.

"My next question is a personal one," she said. "I have a little greenhouse in my kitchen window [which was true] and I need someone to repair the glass [which was not true]. I was wondering who does your glass repairs."

"Sure," she said. "His name is Peter De Vries. He's a local person. I don't have his number handy—it would be at the office—but I'm sure you could find him in the phone book. He's actually a stained-glass artisan."

"Thanks," Charlotte said, "you've been very helpful."

Jerry was considering Charlotte's theory that Peter had murdered the Lily look-alikes because of their resemblance to the fiancée who had jilted him, just as the Leatherman had murdered the fiancée who had jilted him. She had driven up to Zion Hill early the next morning to regale him with her theory and run into him just as he was going out. He had invited her to join him, and she had presented him with her theory as they drove south on the Albany Post Road. It was a theory to which she'd devoted the best part of a sleepless night.

"The sight of a woman with long red hair and a strong jaw sends him into a murderous frenzy," he said, recapping the gist of her idea. "It's good, Graham," he said. "Very good. In fact, it's the best theory we've come up with yet." He went on: "That was exactly what happened in the Ted Bundy case," he said, naming the infamous serial killer. "He couldn't take out his rage against the fiancée who had jilted him—she had too much power over him—so he took it out against women who looked like her. All his victims had long, straight, brown hair that was parted in the middle, and all of them wore gold hoop earrings, just like his fiancée. The difference is that Ted Bundy had to go out and find victims who looked like his fiancée, while in this case, Dr. Louria was serving up victims whose faces were custom-designed to meet the demands of Peter's fantasies." He looked over at Charlotte. "By the way, Bundy decapitated his victims too. And that's not all he did to them. But out of consideration for your stomach and the earliness of the hour, I won't go into the rest. Your theory about why Peter dismembered his victims makes sense too," he added. "Though mutilation is fairly common in cases where the murder reflects a hatred of women."

For a moment, they rode in silence. It was a glorious morning, the heavy rain of the previous two days seeming to have scoured the landscape of the lingering grime of winter, and to have given the sluggish spring a much-needed nudge. The drifts of daffodils that lined the roads of Zion Hill were now in full flower, and the buds on the flowering cherry trees were about to burst. "I didn't finish telling you my theory about the flowers," Charlotte said finally. "The way I figure it is this: knowing Lily as well as he did, Peter probably knew that lily of the valley was her favorite flower, and that Dr. Louria ordered them for her through Winter Garden. He probably found out that Dr. Louria was ordering lilies of the valley for the Lily look-alikes as a result of working at the florist. Maybe he overheard someone taking an order, or saw the tag on a bouquet that was about to be delivered. Once he had decided to kill the Lily look-alikes, it was natural to try to pin the blame on Dr. Louria, and what better way to do it than through the flowers? He knew that the police would eventually figure out where the flowers had come from, and when they did, that the blame would fall squarely on Dr. Louria. It was very safe: not only was it unlikely that the florist would have questioned the order—Dr. Louria had a standing account—it was also unlikely that Dr. Louria would even have questioned the bill. If indeed he even paid the bills himself," she added, thinking of her own devoted secretary, Vivian Smith, who paid all of her bills—God bless her heart.

She went on to tell him about her skull analogy: "I feel as if I've pieced a good part of it together, but that there are still some gaps where the pieces are missing. Like where he killed the victims, how he killed the victims . . ."

Jerry interrupted her. "We've got the 'where' piece," he said. "At least, I think we might have the 'where' piece."

At Charlotte's inquiring look, he pulled into a driveway flanked by tall stone pillars on which were mounted discreet

brass plaques engraved with the words: "Zion Hill Country
Club. Founded 1909. Members Only."

"Is this the 'where' piece?" she asked.

Jerry nodded. "I got a call this morning from the grounds
supervisor, a man named Tom Sullivan. He said he found
something by the skeet-shooting range that he thought might
be of interest to us."

"But he didn't say what?" Charlotte said.

Jerry shook his head.

"I didn't realize this was the Zion Hill Country Club," she
said, as they headed up the winding drive. Though she had
driven by the course a number of times and had also looked
down on it from the church on the hill above, she had never
noticed the sign.

"It's one of the finest courses in the country," Jerry said.
"It was founded by Edward Archibald, like everything else in
Zion Hill. As you may have gathered, the Swedenborgians
don't harbor the guilt that some Christian denominations do
about the possession of wealth."

"So I've noticed," said Charlotte, remembering Peter's
joke about how the church bells ring every day at six to signal
the cocktail hour. Though taking time out for the cocktail hour
didn't necessarily imply wealth, it did imply a leisured lifestyle.

"The Swedenborgians don't believe that wealth itself is in-
herently bad," Jerry continued. "There's none of this 'eye of
the needle' stuff; it's whether or not you use your wealth for
good ends that counts."

"I can appreciate that point of view," Charlotte commented.

"They're also very liberal-minded," he added. "Not only
do you not have to be a WASP to be a member of the country
club, you don't even have to be a Swedenborgian."

The driveway led upward through the woods to the clubhouse, which was built of stone in the same English Gothic
style as the church, which seemed appropriate, at least for the
many people (Charlotte's own father having been one of them)
for whom golf was as close to a religion as they would get.

After parking under the porte cochere, they entered the clubhouse. To the left of the entrance hall, a group of gray-haired women were playing bridge at tables that had been set up in a library in front of a fireplace in which a fire burned merrily. A waiter was serving coffee from a silver pot.

Seeing them, Charlotte was struck by a "there, but for the grace of God" feeling. It was a life she had been born to and bred for, a life that in many ways would have been more comfortable than her own, but it was also a life that she would have found utterly stifling.

Continuing on to the reception desk, they were directed to an office at the back, where they met Tom Sullivan. The grounds supervisor was a tall man in his fifties, with a weather-beaten complexion, watery blue eyes, and a thick Irish brogue.

After explaining that he'd read about the case in the paper, he invited them to take a ride in his pickup truck to see what he had discovered. "I don't know if this will mean anything or not," he said, as they headed out to a parking lot in the back, "but I thought I ought to report it."

"You did the right thing," Jerry assured him.

The three of them climbed into the front seat, and Sullivan set out down a narrow road next to the driving range at the rear of the clubhouse. Drawn out by the fine weather, men in slacks of cranberry-red and lemon-yellow were already out perfecting their drives.

Past the driving range, the road climbed uphill along the side of a long fairway, where a flock of Canada geese was resting on the grass. As the pickup drew even with the geese, they suddenly rose en masse into the air and flew off to the east, as if they were leading the way.

"They're headed to the quarry pit," said Sullivan, looking up over the wheel. "They move around several times a day, always at the same time and to the same places. They'll spend a couple of hours at the quarry pit, and then they'll head over to the water hazard on the tenth hole."

"Creatures of habit," said Charlotte.

"Just like the rest of us," said Sullivan.

A few minutes later, they arrived at the skeet-shooting range, which consisted of a clearing in the woods with a log cabin clubhouse on one side of the road and the skeet range on the other. Continuing on, Sullivan pulled to a stop at a truck-width-sized gap in a stockade fence that lined one side of the road. Beyond the fence was what appeared to be a dump: a flat, cleared area where there were heaps of brush, leaves, cast-off pallets, tree stumps, broken-up asphalt, old stovepipe—even a child's tricycle.

Getting out, Sullivan entered the dump area and led them to a spot just behind the stockade fence, about fifteen feet in from the edge of the opening. "There," he said, looking down at the bare ground. At his feet were a brown extension cord with shoelaces tied to either end, and a small change purse made of bright orange fabric with a key ring attached. "I noticed this when I came out here this morning with one of my men to dump some clippings," he said, nodding at a nearby pile of evergreen branches. "I didn't touch anything."

Taking a plastic evidence bag out of his jacket pocket, Jerry picked up the change purse and opened the Velcro flap, revealing a plastic-covered pocket that held an identification card. The name printed in blue ink on the card was Doreen Mileski, and the address was 33 Liberty Street, Corinth.

"Is it the Mileski girl?" the grounds supervisor asked.

Jerry nodded and squatted down to look at the extension cord.

"She was garroted with the extension cord?" Charlotte asked.

Jerry nodded. "The shoelaces are just to make it longer, and to allow the killer to get a better grip." He looked up at Charlotte. "Now we have the 'where' and we have the 'how.' "

"Why would he have left the extension cord behind?" she asked. "As a clue to his identity, out of a subconscious wish to get caught?"

"That's a myth," Jerry said. "I've yet to meet the criminal who wanted to get caught. At least, while he was committing the act. I've known criminals who've felt remorseful afterward, but that's different. Usually, they leave stuff behind because they're so caught up in the moment."

"You mean, they're too busy concentrating on what they're

doing?'' she asked, with a shiver of horror.

"Exactly," he said as he stood back up. "You'd be amazed at the number of times we've found the perpetrator's wallet at the scene of the crime." He looked over at Sullivan. "How did you know she was Doreen Mileski?"

"Dr. Louria had made special arrangements for her to walk here. He's a member of the club. Ordinarily, we don't allow nonmembers on the premises, but we made an exception for her. He said she was a patient who needed to get her exercise in before catching the train into the city for special treatments."

Jerry nodded. "He told us about the arrangements he made with you when we questioned him." He turned to Charlotte. "He didn't want the girls going out. But the first one complained so vociferously about being cooped up that he allowed her to walk on the golf course, as long as she did so before seven."

"I remember her," Sullivan said. "She used to come here last summer. The paper gave her name as Kimberly Ferguson. She was a pretty girl, straight blond hair. Both of them used to have their faces bandaged up sometimes."

"When was the last time you saw Doreen?" Jerry asked.

Sullivan thought for a moment, and then said: "It must have been a couple of weeks ago. She came every morning at six. She always took the same route around the course. When I read in the paper that she was one of the victims, I thought about those walks . . . '' His voice trailed off. "Then I saw this."

"Why didn't Dr. Louria say anything about this when we talked with him the first time?" Charlotte asked.

"I guess he didn't want to implicate himself further, for which I can't really blame him," Jerry replied. "But when we brought him in yesterday, he speculated that Kimberly and Doreen might have been abducted on one of their early morning walks."

"Also, Doreen's neighbor said she had last seen her when she was setting out for a walk on the golf course," Charlotte said.

Jerry nodded, and then turned back to Sullivan. "I was

about to come over here to make some inquiries when you called.''

"Two girls killed on our course," Sullivan lamented in his melodious Irish brogue. "Sweet mother of Jesus."

"What about Liliana?" asked Charlotte.

"Dr. Louria said she had no interest in taking walks," Jerry replied. "She only liked to watch television. I have no idea where she might have been killed." He turned back to Sullivan again. "How did they get here?"

"They drove," he replied. "They parked out in back of the clubhouse."

"I wonder how the murderer got the cars back?" Jerry said.

"I think I know the answer to that question," Sullivan said. "I remember seeing the first girl's car being towed by a tow truck one morning. It was on Labor Day weekend, which I believe is about the time she disappeared."

It would have been simple, Charlotte thought. The murderer could have identified himself on the telephone as Dr. Louria. After describing the car, he could have asked the towing company to tow the car to Corinth, and send the bill to him.

Jerry nodded. "Do you remember the name of the towing company?"

Sullivan gave him the name of a local company, and he wrote it down.

"Did you ever see anyone following her?" Jerry asked. "Or did you ever see anyone else out walking at that hour?"

Sullivan shook his head. "Never," he said. "If we had, we would have stopped them and asked them what they were doing here. Once in a while, we get a dog walker, but that's about it."

Jerry turned to nod at the dirt track that led through the middle of the dump area and into the woods on the other side. "Where does that road lead?" he asked.

"It comes out on the old Quarry Road," Sullivan said. "That's how we truck our waste out of here. Tires, white goods, old lumber—whatever our regular garbage contractor won't take."

"Bodies too, I suspect," Jerry added.

For the next half an hour, they searched the area between the scene of the murder and the Quarry Road for footprints, tire tracks, and other clues. But the heavy rain of the past two days had obliterated any evidence that might once have existed. Their search was accompanied by the deafening roar of bird song; it was the first really warm day of spring, and the birds were exultant. Although Charlotte's good shoes were ruined as a result of traipsing through the mud, she thoroughly enjoyed being out in the woods on a fine spring morning. And if their search didn't yield any clues, it did produce a picture of the murderer's likely modus operandi. They concluded that he had probably parked his car on the Quarry Road, walked in to the dump area, and concealed himself behind the stockade fence with his extension cord. When his victim had come by, he had jumped out, garroted her from behind, and then carried her body back to his car. The Quarry Road was an ideal site for carrying out such an activity unobserved, Jerry noted. A deeply rutted dirt track, it ran from the Zion Hill Road through the woods that blanketed the hillside behind the church to the old quarry pit that had been the source of the granite that was used for the exterior of the church, and for the exteriors of many of Zion Hill's other buildings. Along this road, teams of horses had hauled the rough-hewn stone to the site of the church, where it had been cut and set into place by stonemasons such as Jerry's grandfather. The road ended at an old church retreat house, and the only regular traffic came from local people who used the old quarry pit as a swimming hole during the summer months.

After their exploration of the area, they returned to the clubhouse parking lot with Sullivan, where Jerry radioed headquarters and asked the dispatcher to send the county crime scene unit over to take photographs.

"Wait till the police beat reporters pick up that on their scanners," Jerry said, and proceeded to give Sullivan some pointers for dealing with the press, which was becoming more and more intrusive.

They were headed back to the police station when, struck by a sudden idea, Charlotte asked Jerry to turn the police car around.

Ten minutes later, they arrived at the church. Finding no one around, they tried the door to the tower and found it un-locked, as they did the door to the belfry stairs. So much for what Peter had said about keeping the tower doors locked, Charlotte thought, as they started up the stairs. Round and round they went, like a snail in its shell, the narrow spiral staircase leading them ever farther upward. Charlotte was get-ting dizzy, and her calves were beginning to ache when they finally came to the door at the top, and opened it onto the open belfry. Walking under the big iron bells with their bell ropes hanging down, they crossed over to the parapet. Below, the church lawn stretched down to the fairways of the golf course, where the eager beavers were already out in their golf carts, tiny motorized ants on a carpet of green. From this height, the course took on the appearance of a garish modern fabric design, in which the chartreuse discs of the putting greens, the beige, amoeba-like shapes of the sand traps, and the pink crowns of the flowering cherry trees that dotted the fairways were the major motifs. At the foot of the hill, the clubhouse lay nestled in its wreath of greening trees.

Charlotte had wanted to climb the tower for a reason, and she wasn't disappointed in her purpose: from here, they had a bird's-eye view of the blacktop road that encircled the golf course like a necklace of gray pearls, with the clubhouse as its clasp. There was only one place where the road was hidden from view for any distance—cut off by an encroachment of the adjoining woods—and that place was the skeet range.

"He could have watched her from here," Charlotte said. "Until he got a sense of the pattern: what time she arrived, what time she reached the skeet-shooting range." She paused, and then said: "Watched and waited."

Jerry nodded. "Sullivan said she always arrived at the same time, and followed the same route."

As he spoke, the wavy ranks of Canada geese appeared over the woods to the southeast, their long, slender, black necks extended in flight. They were returning from their morning idyll at the quarry pit.

As Sullivan had predicted, they alighted at the water hazard at what Charlotte presumed was the tenth hole, and settled down to preen their feathers. "Creatures of habit," she said.

12

IT WAS LATE morning when they arrived back at the police station. Charlotte had asked to look at the crime scene photographs, and Jerry was getting them out for her. Though Peter was now at the top of their suspects list, she still felt that the key to the murderer's identity lay with his crime scene "signature." A police detective had once given her his formula for solving a crime. It was "What happened plus why it happened equals who did it." They were making progress on both the "what" and the "why," but she felt she might learn something new about the "what" from the crime scene photographs. Jerry had described the circumstances in which the first two skulls had been found to her, but she had never actually seen the photographs.

Jerry had just placed the stack of photographs in her hand when he was interrupted by a knock at the door. "Yeah," he said. "What is it?"

The dispatcher stuck her head around the door. "Mrs. Snyder is downstairs, Chief. She's the lady who found the skull at the Zion Hill Cemetery. She says she's got something else for you to look at."

"Send her up," he said.

The red-faced, overweight woman entered Jerry's office a few minutes later. She held a leash in one hand, to which a small black and white dog was attached, and a brown paper bag in the other. She held the latter out at arm's length, as if it contained a vicious animal that was about to strike out at her through the bag. Crossing the room, she deposited the paper bag on Jerry's desk. "My name is Doris Snyder," she announced. "I'm the one who discovered the skull in the Zion Hill Cemetery." She looked down at the dog, who sat quietly, his white vest seemingly puffed out with pride. "Or rather, my dog, Homer, did," she added.

Jerry sat behind his desk, wearing an expression that fell somewhere between boredom and exasperation.

"Now Homer's found something else that you may find of interest," she said. Then she added: "I think you ought to consider deputizing my dog."

"We'll see about that, Mrs. Snyder," Jerry said as he stood up.

"I didn't touch it, and I wouldn't advise you to either," said the formidable Mrs. Snyder as Jerry moved to open the bag.

"Thank you for the advice," he replied. "But I'm well aware of police procedure." Opening the bag, he peered inside. Then he went to the door and shouted to the captain in the adjacent office. "Harry," he said. "Can you get me some newspapers, please?"

The captain appeared with the newspapers a few minutes later, and spread them out on Jerry's desk. Donning a rubber glove, Jerry reached into the bag and pulled out a bloodstained meat cleaver, which he set down on the newspapers. "Where did you find it?" he asked.

"I didn't find it," she said. "Homer found it."

"Gramps is in the well?" Jerry said.

The woman nodded.

At Charlotte's perplexed expression, Jerry explained: "Those are the terms in which Mrs. Snyder described her dog's behavior to me when he found the skull. He raced back to her and circled her several times to let her know that something was wrong. Like on the show *Lassie*."

Charlotte remembered the show from the early days of television. "Gramps fell in the well, and he's got to be saved." she said.

"You've got it," Jerry said. "Let me rephrase my question,

Mrs. Snyder,'' he said. ''Would you like to tell us where *Homer* found the meat cleaver?''

''At the foot of the railroad embankment,'' she said. ''About fifty feet south of the summer house where the bodies were chopped up.''

She'd obviously been reading the newspapers.

''We searched that area thoroughly,'' Jerry said, baffled. ''We even went over it with a metal detector. I wonder how we missed it.''

''I think I know the answer to that question,'' Mrs. Snyder said. ''Homer likes to play hide-and-seek. He'll find an object that he likes, and he'll toss it into the air, or pick it up in his mouth and drop it again. He'll play with it for a while, and then he'll hide it.''

''But he'll remember where it is,'' Jerry said. ''I used to have a dog that did that,'' he replied in answer to her inquiring look.

''A few days might elapse, a few weeks,'' Mrs. Snyder continued. ''But when he's in the area again, he'll go back to where he hid the object, and start to play with it again.''

''In other words, your dog hid the meat cleaver. I don't think we should deputize him.'' He looked down at Homer, who wagged his white-tipped tail. ''I think we should arrest him for tampering with the evidence.''

Mrs. Snyder gave her dog a look of mock sympathy.

''Would you be able to find the place again?'' Jerry asked.

She nodded. ''It was right in front of an old canoe by the side of the tracks. I think he probably hid it under the canoe.''

Jerry turned to the captain. ''I want you to go down there with Mrs. Snyder, Crosby. Search the area again, take some pictures.''

The captain nodded.

Then Jerry thanked Mrs. Snyder, and she and Homer left with the captain. Once they were gone, Jerry said: ''It's a meat cleaver from the restaurant.''

''What restaurant?'' Charlotte asked. She was looking through the crime scene photographs. Skipping the ones of the body parts, which she had no desire to see again, she studied the photo of the skull that had been placed on the headstone in the Zion Hill Cemetery.

"Sebastian's," he said. "I've used it a dozen times to chop the vegetables for stir-frying. It's a Sabatier," he added, naming the well-known brand. "It's also my favorite chopping implement. I love the heft of it." Picking it up again, he tested its weight.

Charlotte looked up. If the cleaver was from Sebastian's, that meant that the killer might have been Sebastian himself. "Do you know for sure that it's from Sebastian's? I mean, does it have some identifying feature? Or are you saying that it's similar to a cleaver that you've used at Sebastian's?"

"No," he snapped. "I don't know *for sure* that it's from Sebastian's. The name of the restaurant is not engraved on the blade. But I can check to see if their cleaver is missing. If it is, I believe it to be a reasonable conclusion that they are one and the same."

Charlotte ignored the tone of his voice. "Did you know that Peter was a frequent visitor to the restaurant?" she asked, and proceeded to tell him about seeing him there.

"I've seen him there too," he said.

"Jerry!" she said. "I've just thought of something else."

"What?" he asked.

"The key to the undercroft. Peter would have had access to the key cabinet. He also would have known where the diagram was. But why wouldn't he have used his own keys?" she asked, remembering the ring of keys that had hung from his belt loop.

Jerry shrugged. "To divert suspicion from himself." He gave her one of his disarming smiles. "We might have been led to suspect him if the door to the undercroft was unlocked and he was the only one with access to the keys. Don't you think?" he asked.

"Touché," she said, and returned her attention to the photograph. The bouquet looked to contain about two dozen lilies of the valley, which was the number that had been ordered in Dr. Louria's name. "Have the fingerprint results come back?" she asked.

He nodded. "The only fingerprints on the key cabinet were

Peter's," he said. "Which is exactly what you would expect: he was the only one with legitimate access to it. The same goes for the door to the undercroft. There were no fingerprints on the votive candles, or on the skull."

Charlotte was now looking at the photograph of the first victim's skull. Something about the gravestone on which the skull rested looked familiar, and she strained to read the inscription. Then she realized that it was the gravestone on the cover of the pastor's pamphlet.

Getting up, she passed the photograph across the desk to Jerry. "Take a look at this," she said. "Do you know whose gravestone that is?"

Jerry looked at the photograph and shook his head.

"It's the grave of Jules Bourglay, the Leatherman."

Jerry held the photograph up to the light in order to read the inscription: " 'Final Resting Place of Jules Bourglay of Lyons, France. The Leatherman.' " A big smile broke out on his face. "Well, I'll be damned," he said as he passed the photograph back to Charlotte.

"Who was it who recently said that a criminal never deliberately leaves any clues at the scene of the crime?" she asked.

As he had predicted, Jerry's summons of the county crime scene unit to the country club had alerted the press to a new development, and the dispatcher informed them that several reporters were now waiting downstairs to talk with Jerry. At Charlotte's suggestion (she was an old hand at diversionary techniques), Jerry asked one of his sergeants to turn on the siren and the lights of his police car. While the reporters were thus distracted, Charlotte and Jerry slipped out the back. After picking up some sandwiches, they headed out to the Octagon House to pick up the "before" and "after" reconstructions of Doreen Mileski's face, which Lister had finished a day sooner than he had said he would. They drove in silence, eating their sandwiches and enjoying the ride. It was a beautiful afternoon, and the sun glistened like gold dust on the river. After hovering tentatively over the Hudson River Valley for so long, spring had finally arrived in full force, and the air was warm and sweet with the smell of the damp earth. In her youth, Charlotte had preferred autumn to the other seasons, but as she had grown older, spring had replaced autumn in her affections. She supposed it was because the waning of the year had come to be linked in her mind with the waning of her life, and she always preferred to think in terms of new beginnings.

As they came to the end of River Road, Jerry finally spoke: "There's still one aspect of the Peter theory I find puzzling," he said.

"What's that?" she asked.

"The skull business. I can understand why he would kill his victims. I can understand why he would dismember them. I can even understand why he would want to keep the skulls as a kind of trophy. I mean, I don't understand, really. But if I were a murderer . . ."

"Which we understand that you're not," Charlotte said. "So what don't you understand?" she asked.

"I don't know why he would put the skulls in the cemeteries. According to what I know of criminal psychology, he would have hoarded them. A murderer likes to keep something like that around as a souvenir."

"Like the beachcomber keeps a piece of driftwood."

"More like the hunter who looks at the head of a moose hanging on the wall, and takes pleasure in reliving the memory of having killed it."

"He probably wanted to show off," she speculated. "Wasn't that the point of leaving the skull on the Leatherman's grave?"

"A point that we would have missed if it wasn't for you."

"You wouldn't have missed it," said Charlotte. "You probably would have noticed it eventually—like after the case was closed." She loved to tease Jerry. "I see it as almost a taunt."

After passing Archfield Hall with its gloomy-looking tower, they headed up the access road to the Octagon House. A few minutes later, they were comfortably settled in Lister's living room, which was high Victorian in style, with heavy, ornate furniture upholstered in tufted velvet, dark red velvet draperies dripping gold fringe, and layer upon layer of Persian rugs— everything, in fact, but the doilies and antimacassars.

Unlike the galleries below, which had been squared off by

locating closets in the angles of the octagon, this room had oddly angled walls that were pierced by tall windows. The feeling was rather like a room in a fun house: all the angles seemed a little bit off. Charlotte reflected on what Jerry had said about one virtue of an octagon house being that the space in the corners wasn't wasted. This was true, but there were no right angles either.

The feeling of the room being a little bit off was exacerbated by the paintings hanging on the walls, which were reproductions of famous paintings that featured skulls. A huge reproduction of a Rembrandt hung over the fireplace. There was also a Bellini and a Holbein—even a Dali.

Once they were seated, Lister brought out the reconstructed face of Doreen Mileski, and set it down in a cork collar on the marble-topped parlor table around which their chairs were grouped.

"I finished her just last night," he said. "I've been sitting in the library, looking at her—staring at this face being one of my favorite occupations. Which is why she's not down in my studio." He looked up at Jerry. "By the way, did you make your arrest yet?"

Jerry shook his head.

"You were going to arrest Dr. Louria?" he asked.

Jerry nodded. "His alibi checked out," he explained. "Which leaves us back at square one. This is the 'after,' I presume," Jerry said, nodding at the reconstruction, which was identical to the other two look-alikes.

Lister nodded. "As you can see, she has that same jutting chin. Lily and her mother were both women who led with their chins. Strong chins are an indicator of stubbornness."

"Were they stubborn?" Charlotte asked.

"As mules—both mother and daughter—though the mother was stubborn in a different way." He looked at Charlotte, and then said: "If I read you correctly, you're wondering at the coincidence of the fact that a facial characteristic that is linked with stubbornness—a prominent chin—turns out to belong to people who do in fact have stubborn temperaments."

"Something like that, yes," she said.

"I maintain that it's not a coincidence," Lister said. "More often than not the popular wisdom proves true: nine times out of ten, you'll find that the redhead has a temper, that the shifty-eyed person is not to be trusted, that the person with a high forehead—what the Victorians called the 'dome of thought'—is a thinker, and so on."

"So the phrenologists were more accurate than we think," Charlotte said.

Lister nodded his bald head. "The idea that physical characteristics are a sign of character is not a popular notion nowadays. There are too many ways in which such ideas can be misused—we have the Nazis to thank for that. But there's a lot of truth in the notion, nonetheless."

"And the idea that physical beauty is an expression of goodness?" asked Charlotte, thinking of the contrast between Lily's sluttish reputation and her angelic appearance.

"Such an idea is why, of course, we're drawn to beautiful people—be they in the movies"—he nodded deferentially at Charlotte—"in art, or in person. We subconsciously feel that a beautifully formed face ought to be accompanied by beautiful thoughts and feelings. That's why two generations of Listers have nourished their creative imaginations on the same remarkable face."

Their attention shifted to the face on the coffee table.

"But does a beautiful face reflect goodness?" Lister asked. "I would have to say yes, but only in middle age and beyond. The virtuous beauty can preserve her looks through her virtuous thoughts, but the base-minded beauty will find that a sulk distorts the lower lip, suspicion narrows the eyes, distrust creases the brow."

" 'The very book indeed, Where all my sins are writ,' " said Charlotte. "And that's myself."

"Aha," Lister said with a smile of recognition. "*Richard the Third*. Yes," he continued, "Lillian Archibald was a stubborn woman, but, had she lived, she would have remained beautiful because she had a beautiful soul."

"And Lily?" asked Charlotte.

Leaning over, Lister carefully picked up the "after" sculpture and held it out at arm's length. "Yes, quite a beauty you were, my dear. Or, I should say, the woman after whom you were modeled. But virtuous?'' He looked up at them and shook his head ''No. I doubt that Lily Louria would have been beautiful in old age. Too many sins to write on that beautiful face.''

''What about the 'before' reconstruction?'' Jerry asked.

''She's still downstairs,'' Lister said. ''I'll go get her.'' He excused himself and headed down the spiral staircase to his basement studio.

As they awaited his return, Charlotte became aware of a sweet fragrance in the room: it was the fragrance of lilies of the valley. Turning, she noticed a small silver vase of lilies of the valley on the table at her elbow, and then several other bouquets in vases around the room. Skulls and lilies of the valley seemed to be a popular combination in Zion Hill, she thought.

Lister was back momentarily with the ''before'' sculpture, which he set down on the table next to the ''after'' sculpture.

Charlotte marveled at the difference. It was amazing how the implants on the eyebrow ridges had set poor Doreen Mileski's protruding eyes back, and the implants on the posterior mandibles had increased the definition between her neck and her jaw, as well as widening her jaw to give her that square-jawed look of the Archibald women.

''Now this young lady wasn't stubborn,'' Lister said. ''I imagine that she was quite sweet, in fact. But wishy-washy. Look at that jaw; or rather, that lack of jaw. A young woman with no direction in life.''

''It's hard to believe this is the same young woman whom Lothian Archibald saw in the drugstore and mistook for her niece,'' Jerry commented.

''Dr. Louria did an amazing job,'' Lister said.

''As did you, once again,'' said Jerry. Their business concluded, they packed up the sculptures and headed toward the door that led to the spiral staircase. At the door, they paused to say goodbye in front of a table that held yet another bouquet of lilies of the valley.

''I see you have lilies of the valley,'' Charlotte said. She leaned over to smell the nodding, bell-shaped flowers. ''The fragrance is lovely.''

"Yes," he agreed. "They were Lillian Archibald's favorite flower," he said. "For that matter, they were Lily's favorite flower too."

"Where did you ever find so many?" she asked.

"I picked them along the railroad embankment." He nodded in the direction of the river. "There's a colony of them growing over by Archfield Hall. I imagine Lillian Archibald must have planted them. Unfortunately, this is the last of them. I went this morning for more, but they were all dried up."

He must have been referring to the same colony she had seen growing next to the path leading down to the summer house, Charlotte thought. "It's a shame that their blooming period is so short," she lamented. "Wouldn't it be wonderful if you could get them all year round?"

"You can," Lister said. "At least, you can in this area. There's a florist in Corinth that specializes in growing lilies of the valley out of season for the New York florist trade. They're used in bridal bouquets. Winter Garden Florist," he said. "I order them sometimes from there."

Charlotte took out a notebook and jotted down the name. "That will be nice to keep in mind for a dreary January day," she said.

"But they're very expensive," he added.

After thanking Lister, they descended the spiral staircase and made their way back out through the Phrenological Cabinet to the police car.

"That was interesting about the lilies of the valley," Jerry said as they headed back along River Road.

"I just wanted to find out how common the knowledge is that Winter Garden Florist supplies out-of-season lilies of the valley," she said. "If Lister knows, I guess it's pretty common knowledge."

"You did it very well," said Jerry. "Much better than I would have. See? It pays to have a woman working with you. I couldn't have feigned an interest in lilies of the valley if my life depended on it. It appears to be common knowledge that they were Lily's favorite flower too," he added.

"Which means that almost anyone—not just Peter—could

have ordered them in Dr. Louria's name,'' Charlotte said.

"Speaking of whom . . .'' said Jerry.

Finding the church locked and no one around, they proceeded on to the Manse, where they found the pastor pruning the rose bushes that climbed up the trellises mounted to the wall on either side of the front door. He was wearing a faded blue plaid flannel shirt over his black clerical garb. Seeing them, he set down his pruning shears and moved the pile of clippings to one side with his foot so that Charlotte and Jerry's ankles wouldn't be snagged by the thorns when they came up the front walk.

"I'm pruning the deadwood,'' he said when they reached him. "This past winter was very hard on roses. On everything, for that matter,'' he added, pointing to some dead azaleas by the foundation. "What can I do for you?''

"We're looking for Peter,'' Jerry said.

"Ah yes, Peter,'' he replied, brushing away the shock of dark, glossy hair that hung over his face. He stared off in the direction of the church, his profile, with its hooked nose, turned against the background of shrubbery.

"He might be in Corinth looking after his rental properties.'' He checked his watch. "But he usually takes care of that in the morning. Since it's after noon, I'd guess he's down at the glass shop.''

"Glass shop?'' Jerry asked.

"It's where the glassblowers blew the glass for the stained-glass windows. Peter uses it as a workshop.'' He turned and pointed to the Zion Hill Road. "Continue over the ridge. It's about a quarter of a mile, on the corner by the Quarry Road. You'll see a sign for 'The Retreat.' ''

At the mention of the Quarry Road, Charlotte and Jerry exchanged surreptitious glances.

"Thanks,'' Jerry said.

"Chief,'' said the pastor, as they were leaving, "I had a thought about those tall votive candles that were left with the skull in the undercroft. I think they use votive candles like that down at Immaculate Conception,'' he said. "It might be worth checking out.''

"Or any of the other nine million Catholic churches in America," Jerry muttered under his breath as they got back into the car.

"What's the matter?" Charlotte teased. "Getting tired of the interference of amateur assistants?"

He smiled. "Only some of them."

The glass shop was a long, shed-like building that was nestled in the woods in a vale behind the church. It had vertical wood siding weathered to a dark gray, and long rows of six over six windows, their woodwork painted white. The same old red pickup truck they had seen at the church when they talked with Peter before was parked outside. After parking next to it, they entered the building, and found themselves in a large room cluttered with sixty years' accumulation of junk. Peter was at the other end of the room, working on a large stained-glass window that lay on a long worktable. He held a soldering iron in his hand, which he was using to repair the lead bars in the stained glass. As before, he was wearing a leather apron.

Picking their way around the junk, they crossed the big, open room to the worktable. "Reverend Cornwall told us we might find you here," Jerry said after they had exchanged greetings.

"It's usually a good bet," Peter said.

Charlotte and Jerry took places on either side of him at the table. "What are you working on?" Jerry asked.

"This is a stained-glass window from the church," he replied. "The one I had just removed when I saw you the other day. After a while, the solder that secures the lead at the joints gets brittle and has to be replaced. I'm also cleaning the glass and oiling the leads with linseed oil."

The window showed an angel with Lily's face. She was wearing flowing robes and striding toward the viewer through a field of lilies of the valley. Her wings were outstretched, and her head was surrounded by an orange-gold nimbus. She was flanked by two angels on each side, who had Lily's face as well.

This must have been the window that Lisa Gennaro had

mentioned at the florist shop, Charlotte thought.

"This is the angel of the ascension," Peter said. "It's the central light in a triplet. The other two show the stairs to heaven. As you know, we believe in Christ, but our emphasis is on the resurrection rather than the crucifixion—on death as a new beginning. That's why you don't see any crosses."

As he spoke, Charlotte noticed the inscription at the bottom, which read: "Death like a narrow sea divides this heavenly land from ours."

"Would you like to see it against the light?" Peter asked.

Charlotte and Jerry said they would, and Peter lifted it up with Jerry's help and leaned it against an electric light panel on the wall.

"You miss the effect if you don't see it with the backlighting. But even this light doesn't do it justice. I like to look at it when the rays of the sun are falling directly on the glass. The sun turns each of these individual pieces of glass into glowing gems."

Charlotte marveled at the opalescent quality of the glass, which gave the window such an ethereal air. "It's magnificent," she said.

"Yes, it is. The Zion Hill glassblowers rediscovered techniques that had been lost for centuries. The striated ruby, for instance: you can't tell it from the striated ruby at Chartres. They also discovered some new techniques. See this shade of yellow?" he said, pointing to a ray of the angel's nimbus.

They looked at the lovely color, a rich apricot-yellow.

"The master glassblower had tried and tried to get this shade, without any success. One day, he was mixing up a batch of yellow pot metal when a piece of his hair fell into the crucible—he had just come from the barbershop. The instant the hair fell in, the batch turned exactly the right shade."

"So he used his hair from then on?" Jerry asked.

"Yes," Peter replied. "I don't know if it had to be his hair. If it did, it must have had to grow pretty quickly." He smiled. "We have a lot of this shade of yellow in our windows."

Jerry stood with his hands in his pockets, studying the stained-glass window. "All the angels look like Lily Louria," he commented.

"The model was her mother, Lillian Archibald. But yes, they do look like her. Portraits of Lillian are everywhere in Zion Hill. Would you like to give me a hand with this?" Peter asked.

"It's actually about Lily that we're here," Jerry said, as he helped Peter with the window. "We'd like to know about your relationship with her."

"What would you like to know?" Peter asked as he resumed his work. After propping a piece of soldering wire into place with a small block of wood, he proceeded to melt it with the soldering iron.

Charlotte was fascinated by the practiced skill with which he compensated for the lack of an arm, and wondered briefly if he had done the same with the bodies.

"In the kingdom of the unskilled, the one-armed man is king," Peter said with a smile, as if he had been reading her mind.

"How long you had known her," Jerry said in response to Peter's question. "How close you were. That sort of thing."

"I've known Lily since the fifth grade when my parents moved here from upstate. My father had converted to the New Church when he came across some of Swedenborg's writings in the local library. We had been on a waiting list to move here. Lily and I went through the Zion Hill School together."

"Were you very close to her?"

"Are you familiar with Swedenborg's works?" Peter asked. He looked up from his work, his long blond hair hanging over his face.

"Only very generally, I'm afraid," Jerry said.

"Swedenborg believed that everyone has a soul mate, and that everyone will eventually be united with their soul mate, if not on earth, then in heaven. When two soul mates come together in heaven, they merge into one angel, and live in conjugial bliss into eternity."

"Conjugial bliss?" asked Charlotte.

"It's a term from Swedenborg's writings. It's the expression of conjugial love, which is heavenly love, as opposed to mere conjugal love. He believed—we believe—that the true love between a man and a woman is the foundation of all other love, and that to experience this love is to experience the highest state of God's grace.''

"Are you saying that Lily was your soul mate?" Jerry asked.

"Yes," he said. "She was. To use a phrase of Swedenborg's, we were like the 'two hemispheres of the brain enclosed in one membrane.' We were engaged to be married at one time."

"What happened?" Jerry asked.

"She broke off the engagement after I lost my arm. Then she met Victor Louria and married him, as you know."

"How did you feel about that?"

Jerry was beginning to sound like a shrink.

"I was angry about it for a long time. But she and I are working it out. I've come to understand her motives for marrying Victor better, and she's making amends for how she treated me."

Something was wrong with his tenses. "*Is* making amends?" Charlotte said.

"Yes. The love between soul mates doesn't end with the death of one of them, because the spirit of the dead continually lives with the spirit of the living. I still talk to her; every day, usually."

He sounded as if he were talking about making a long-distance call. Charlotte and Jerry stared at him, nonplussed.

Peter straightened up and set aside the soldering iron. Then he took a seat on a nearby stool. "Let me explain," he said.

"Please do," said Jerry.

"Swedenborg believed that there's a veil that separates this world from the next. The veil is essential; without it, we wouldn't be able to function. But some people can see beyond the veil."

"Swedenborg was one of those people. He communicated with the spirits for twenty-nine years. He frowned on the practice of trying to initiate contact with the spirits. He considered it dangerous. But sometimes, under special circumstances, when there is a need, and 'when it is the Lord's good pleasure,' as he said, the veil is lifted."

"And that's what happened to you?" Jerry asked.

He nodded. "After I was struck by lightning. Out of the blue, literally. There wasn't a cloud in the sky. But that's more common than you'd think. It's a problem for airplanes, which are often struck. I have an article about it right here." Reaching into his back pocket, he pulled out his wallet and removed a newspaper clipping, which was dog-eared and yellow.

He passed them the article, the headline of which was: "LIGHTNING IS UNDERREPORTED." It went on to describe the phenomenon, which the pastor had already told them about, and to say how it posed a particular problem for aircraft. It concluded with a quote from a researcher: "Lightning apparently does not command the respect it deserves as a dangerous killer."

After reading the clipping, Jerry passed it back to him.

"I almost died," Peter continued, as he returned the clipping to his wallet. "In fact, my heart stopped beating. During that time, I had a near-death experience. I found myself speeding through the dark tunnel, coming out into the light, and being greeted by celestial beings on the other side." He paused for a moment, and then said: "Then I was called back."

"Against your will?" asked Charlotte, who had read in magazines about people who had undergone near-death experiences.

Peter nodded. "Being struck by lightning is a very unusual experience. They say it's as close to death as you can come and still live. People who are apparently dead for long periods of time can be brought back to life with little or no lasting damage. My doctor described it as being one of the few two-way streets to heaven." He continued: "I lost my arm, of course. I also have burn scars on my left calf: the lightning exited through my left foot. My shoe was burned right off my foot. Vaporized." He snapped his fingers. "Poof."

"Whew!" said Jerry, shaking his head.

Peter went on: "I have other residual health problems: my left eardrum was perforated, so I'm hard of hearing in that ear, and I still have seizures occasionally, though much less often than I used to. I also have some peripheral nerve damage in my left leg, which is why I walk with a staff."

"Not because you're trying to affect a resemblance to the Leatherman?" Charlotte asked.

He shook his head. "Though the nerve damage is getting better too. After the accident, it was five weeks before I could put on a pair of pants. Apart from the loss of my arm, the physical damage was minor. But being struck by lightning changed my life. I started hearing voices, seeing celestial beings. At first, I thought I was going mad. But once I established contact with Lily, I realized that I'd been blessed with the privilege of being able to see beyond the veil. Lily has been my guide to life on the other side."

Charlotte remembered what the pastor had said about damage to the cerebral cortex causing psychotic behavior.

"What's it like?" asked Jerry, playing along.

"Just as Swedenborg said," he replied. He gestured at the stained-glass window in front of them. "A paradise inhabited by 'bright, lucid stars, glittering according to the charity of their faith.' I haven't yet had the privilege of getting to heaven. Lily still lives in the world of the spirits, which is an intermediate world where I'll join her when I die. As we perfect our spirits, we'll become one angel in the first heaven. Eventually, we'll evolve into higher forms, and move up into higher heavens, which are even more beautiful. That is, if we seek to improve our spiritual natures. There are lower places where one can end up too."

"Who dwells in these lower places?" Charlotte asked.

"Demons," he replied. "Being able to communicate with demons is the down side of being able to see beyond the veil. That's why Swedenborg didn't approve of attempts to pierce the veil: it isn't all sweetness and light. You're in danger of losing your sanity. The demons are vile little creatures that will keep you awake all night with their nasty chattering. 'Globules of coal-fire,' Swedenborg called them. They know just how to punch your buttons."

Charlotte and Jerry exchanged looks.

"Did they ever encourage you to do bad things?" Charlotte asked. Now it was she who was sounding like a shrink—one who was in over her head.

"Oh, yes," he said. "They know all your weaknesses, and

they prey on them. But I never had any trouble resisting them. I know why you came here. You think I killed the Lily look-alikes. Because of the legend of the Leatherman, who killed the fiancée who jilted him.''

He may have been crazy, but he wasn't stupid, Charlotte thought.

''The whole Leatherman thing is the invention of overactive imaginations,'' he said. ''But I humor them. It doesn't do any harm, and I get some free meals out of it.''

''I've seen you eating at Sebastian's,'' Jerry said. ''At the bar.''

''Yes. Sebastian is an old friend of mine.''

''When you eat at Sebastian's, do you always eat at the bar, or do you sometimes eat in the kitchen?'' Jerry asked.

Peter seemed puzzled at the sudden change of tack. ''Actually, I usually eat in the kitchen. Sebastian doesn't like me to eat out front when the dining room is crowded. Though he's too kind to say so, he's afraid my appearance would put off the customers.''

''Do you sometimes watch the meals being prepared?'' Jerry asked. ''The cutting and the chopping and so on.''

''I not only watch, I sometimes help out when Sebastian is in a pinch. With the chopping of the vegetables.''

It looked as if Sebastian put everybody to work, Charlotte thought, reminded of how Jerry had also helped out in the kitchen.

Jerry let out an involuntary little snort, and moved on to another line of questioning: ''As near as we can tell, the first victim was murdered around Labor Day, the second at the beginning of April, and the third during the third week in April. I presume that you were here at those times.''

''Where else would I be?'' Peter asked.

''You weren't on vacation in Florida, or anything?''

''I was here,'' he said. ''I'm always here. I don't have an alibi. But you're wasting your time questioning me.''

''Why?'' Jerry asked.

''Because I didn't do it,'' he said simply.

''I think you can understand why we have to question you,'' Jerry said. ''You were one of the few people who knew that

Dr. Louria was turning these young women into Lily look-alikes.''

"One of the few, but not the only," he said. He looked up at them. "I told you, I can resist the demons. But not everyone is as strong as I am. There are some who are tormented by them."

"And who might they be?"

"I'm not at liberty to reveal what was revealed to me as a result of my contact with the spirits on the other side; it's privileged information."

"May I remind you that this is a murder investigation?" Jerry growled.

Peter looked up at him defiantly. "Then take me into custody," he said.

"I'm afraid that's what we're going to have to do."

13

PETER HAD GONE willingly with them to the police station, where he was being detained while Jerry and his men gathered the evidence that would be presented to the grand jury. The money to post his bail was being raised by the parishioners of the church under the leadership of the Reverend Cornwall. Though the evidence gathered thus far was all circumstantial, there was a lot of it. As their landlord, Peter would have been one of the few people who knew that Dr. Louria was turning the young women into Lily look-alikes. As the church sexton, he had access to the key cabinet and could have seen two of the victims taking their early morning walks on the golf course. As a result of repairing the broken glass at the florist's, he could have discovered that Dr. Louria ordered lilies of the valley for the Lily look-alikes, as he had for his wife before them. And finally he had access to the kitchen at Sebastian's, which was where the murder weapon had probably come from. Most incriminating of all, he had a strong motive, the same motive that the Leatherman had had: to take his revenge against the woman who had jilted him. He also had a motive for mutilating his victims: to do to their bodies what had been done to his by an aberrant stroke of lightning, and thereby to humiliate them the way he himself had been humiliated. Finally, he was probably a little crazy as a result of having his brains fried by a lightning bolt, as the locals put it. Though he claimed to be able to resist the demons that supposedly dwelt in the lower depths, the fact that he had admitted to communicating with them at all was enough to make Charlotte doubt his sanity.

Though it would take some legwork, Charlotte and Jerry were convinced that the hard evidence would come. To use the analogy of the pastor's braid work, they had separated the individual strands from the tangled skein. Each strand had been attached to its own bobbin on the braiding stand. Now all they had to do was plait them into a braid. The golf course personnel would have to be interviewed to see if any of them had noticed Peter on the grounds. Peter's fingerprints would have to be matched to those on the cleaver and the extension cord, if there were any. His pickup would have to be checked for bloodstains. But Charlotte was happy enough to leave the details up to Jerry and his men. She had been going nonstop for a week and a half now, and she was tired. She was ready for a nice dinner out, perhaps with her stepdaughter Marsha. Or rather, her ex-stepdaughter, since she was now divorced from Marsha's father—an event that fortunately hadn't affected their relationship. Then maybe a visit to the Metropolitan Museum of Art. It was a Friday; the museum would be open late. She hadn't been to the Douglas Dillon Galleries lately, and she always found looking at Chinese landscape paintings to be soothing for the soul. Or a show on Broadway: there was an English farce that she had wanted to see at the Broadhurst. Now *there* was a remedy for a mind saturated with death and dismemberment: an English farce.

She was about to head back to Manhattan when a call came in for Jerry from the dispatcher. "Chief," she said, her voice taut with excitement, "I think you'd better get right over to Archfield Hall. We've got another thirty-seven."

A "thirty-seven," Charlotte remembered from the call about the body parts that had been found at the Corinth Municipal Park, was a dead body. *Well*, she thought, *maybe the English farce could wait.*

Half a dozen police cars had arrived at Archfield Hall ahead of them, and a cluster of policemen was gathered in front next to the ambulance that was parked in the circular driveway by the gryphon fountain. A small crowd of curious onlookers had gathered on the road in front to watch the spectacle. A pair of ambulance attendants were crouched on the portico over the front door, lashing a sheet-covered body to a stretcher. It appeared that the victim, who had fallen or jumped from the tower, had landed on the roof of the protruding portico, instead of falling all the way to the ground. As they watched, the ambulance attendants carefully hoisted the stretcher over the ornate metal railing, and then lowered it with ropes to the policemen waiting on the driveway below. There didn't appear to be much blood; the shroud covering the body was unstained. But Charlotte knew that was often the case with falls, where the injuries were mostly internal. She remembered the case of the dead body of a beautiful young Japanese woman she had once discovered at the base of a cliff in Newport, Rhode Island. She had been as beautiful in death as she had been in life; even her makeup was still perfect.

As they approached, one of the policemen broke away and came up to Jerry. "It's the doctor," he said. "Apparently, he jumped from the tower."

They looked up at the thick, medieval-style tower, whose pointed roof, with its ceramic tiles in sixteen shades of celestial blue, jutted into the cloudless blue sky. It was sixty or more feet high.

"Anyone in the house?" Jerry asked as they watched the policemen untie the ropes from the stretcher and load it into the back of the waiting ambulance.

"Only the housekeeper," the officer said. "She's the one who called in the report. Apparently, she saw him hit. Crosby's in there with her now. He was waiting for you before he went up to the tower."

A few minutes later, they were taking the elevator up to the tower for the second time with Marta, whose grief-stricken face was streaked with mascara. This time, Captain Crosby was also along for the ride.

The tower room looked much as it had when they had seen Dr. Louria three days before, except that there were even more empty liquor bottles on the coffee table. The television set was tuned to a soap opera.

Seeing the mess, Marta shook her head. "Since Tuesday,

he no come down. Only to sleep. Ever since . . .'' Her glance fell on the newspapers on the coffee table, with their boldfaced headlines, and she started to cry.

Ignoring her, Jerry headed over to the cast-iron spiral staircase that led up to the observation deck on the next level. Charlotte was right behind him, and Captain Crosby in turn was right behind her.

They emerged a moment later on the observation deck, which had triple arched openings on four sides, divided by stone columns with Gothic-style capitals. They looked out on a magnificent panorama of the Hudson, with Hook Mountain rising on the opposite shore. Crossing to the other side, they peered over the railing.

"Jesus," said Jerry, shaking his head.

Then they wordlessly turned away and went back down the spiral staircase to the tower room to begin their search of the scene.

The suicide note was lying on top of the newspapers on the coffee table. It had been written on one of Dr. Louria's prescription pads, in the nearly unreadable scrawl of the busy physician.

Jerry picked it up and read it aloud: " 'Three young women have died because of me. And everything I valued has been taken away. Without Lily, and without my career, there's no point in going on.' "

As she looked up, Charlotte's glance caught the quote from Swedenborg that was carved on the face of the central beam of the ceiling: "The tower is a symbol for the interior life through which we communicate with heaven."

Only in Dr. Louria's case, she thought, it wasn't heaven he was communicating with in the tower, but his own private hell.

As Jerry replaced the note where he had found it, an item made of flesh-colored plastic caught Charlotte's eye. It was Dr. Louria's ear, which had been unhinged from the bracket embedded in his skull and set down next to the note.

Seeing it, Charlotte was reminded of what he had told her about the belief of the ancient Egyptians that only those with intact physical appearances would be able to enter the Kingdom of Osiris.

"It's signed 'Orejita mala,' " Jerry said. "I wonder what that means."

"He told me," Charlotte said. "It means 'bad little ear.' "

Charlotte did go to the Metropolitan Museum of Art that evening. Not with Marsha, but alone. On the way to the Douglas Dillon Galleries, she paused at the Chinese ceramics on the second floor balcony of the Great Hall, and ended up spending the whole evening there. She loved the ceramics for the same reason that she loved the landscapes, which was that they evoked lives of leisure spent in the contemplative pursuit of music, art, and poetry. The mere thought that people had once led such lives, even if they were Chinese artist/scholars who had lived ten centuries ago, was enough to reassure her that civilization could exist on earth. For this reason, it was the objects for the writing table that she loved the most: the brush washers, the seal color boxes, the inkstones, and, of course, the tea bowls and the wine cups. Gazing on them, she imagined a life spent in contemplation, drinking wine and writing poetry. On this particular evening, however, she found that she loved them for another reason: their exquisite proportions, their gleaming finishes, their elegant simplicity. Most of all, their wholeness. For a week and a half, she had been dealing with grisly images: heads without ears, heads without bodies, feet without legs, arms without hands. On this quiet balcony, high above the noisy, milling crowd on the floor of the lobby below, there were no chips or cracks—only smooth perfection, and she sucked it up as a visual antidote to the horrors she had witnessed the way sandy soil sucks up water after a rain. In fact, were she to have come across a chip or a crack, it was a good bet that the men in the white coats would have to be called in to haul her away, so fragile had her psychological sense of order become.

It was the first night in weeks that she hadn't gone to sleep thinking of body parts. Instead, she thought of Chinese glazes: the rich yellow of the chicken fat glaze, the deep red of the *sang-de-boeuf*, and the gleaming white ware, like the color of bleached bone.

———

No sooner had Charlotte resolved to give Jerry a break from her presence than she found herself about to head back to Zion Hill again. He called early on Sunday morning to invite her to an outdoor concert by a Swedenborgian boys' choir from England. The concert, which would be held that evening, would be preceded by a community picnic on the church lawn. During the event, the church would be illuminated from the inside, allowing concertgoers the opportunity of viewing the church's magnificent stained-glass windows from the outside. Along with the annual church holiday on June nineteenth, which commemorated the day that Swedenborg completed his most important work, *True Christian Religion*, the concert was one of the biggest community events of the year, Jerry said. He went on to explain that he usually attended with his wife and daughters, but his wife, who was a schoolteacher, would be out of town at an education seminar, and his daughters were now all off on their own. Jerry promised to fill her in on what he had accomplished since he saw her last, but he warned her that it wouldn't be much. Peter was still maintaining his innocence, and they hadn't been able to come up with any additional evidence against him. Unless they came up with something soon, Jerry said, they would have to release him.

The weather alone was enough to tempt Charlotte: it was one of those perfect days of late spring, with temperatures that were warm, but not yet warm enough to be uncomfortable. The idea of a picnic on a lawn overlooking the Hudson on the evening of such a glorious day was enticing enough, but given the fact that Jerry promised her a picnic supper from Sebastian's, it was irresistible.

It was Sebastian himself who delivered their picnic supper to their spot on the church lawn, which was marked by a purple balloon to match the signature purple facade of the restaurant. Sebastian had handed out purple balloons to all of the customers who had ordered picnic baskets, and a dozen purple balloons floated in the air above the blankets and lawn chairs that were spread out in a semicircle around the stage that had been erected at the foot of the church lawn, against the backdrop of the river valley. Sebastian was looking typically dashing. As on the previous occasion, he wore a purple bandanna tied pirate-style around his head, which emphasized the magnificent Archibald bone structure that had so intrigued Jack Lister and his father. He also wore an embroidered white Cossack-style shirt and tight black knee-length Spandex bicycle pants. If his aim was to look like Errol Flynn in an old-time swashbuckler, he succeeded admirably. All he lacked was a sword and an eyepatch. He even had an earring: a large gold hoop in his left ear.

The picnic supper came in an ash splint basket, from which Sebastian removed a blue-and-white-checked tablecloth and napkins, two place settings, and a bottle of California cabernet sauvignon. After laying their places, he removed the supper items one by one from the picnic basket: a crusty basil foccacia, a pasta primavera with seafood, a cold filet mignon with béarnaise sauce, and marinated broccoli rabe. For dessert there were cold poached pears with chocolate-raspberry sauce.

"You've outdone yourself again, Sebastian," said Jerry, as Sebastian finished setting out the food on the tablecloth. Each item was served in blue and white crockery; it looked like a spread from a glossy food magazine.

"The church concert comes but once a year," said Sebastian. "Besides, it's the least I can do for someone who's been chopping vegetables all year long, and who hasn't received a cent of remuneration." Reaching back into the basket, he pulled out a bottle of champagne and three champagne flutes.

"What's this?" asked Jerry as Sebastian passed out the glasses.

"We're celebrating," he said. "I got a loan against the money I'll be getting from Lily's estate, and I have a backer for an additional two million. I also have a site: on Park Avenue South in the Flatiron District. Construction starts next week on Manhattan's next four-star restaurant: Sebastian's II."

Raising their glasses, they offered him their congratulations.

"When will you open?" Jerry asked.

"We're aiming for October," Sebastian said as he took a seat with his champagne flute on a corner of the tablecloth. He went on to describe his plans for the restaurant, which wouldn't be formal and French, but rather an elegant space with a down-to-earth atmosphere.

Charlotte had a gut feeling that it would do well. Manhattan was in need of a first-class restaurant that wasn't overly formal.

"Connie's going to be in charge of the interior," he said. "She'll be working with the designers. She's also going to be my maître d'." He went on to describe his plans in further detail, and then announced that he had to leave. "Let me know how you like the food," he said as he stood back up.

"We will," Jerry replied as Sebastian headed off into the crowd. "Let me know if you need me to chop vegetables," he shouted after him.

Charlotte had been right when she had figured that it would be an exquisite evening. They dined on their delicious supper in the fading light, looking out at the panorama of the dusky Tappan Zee, with the stained-glass windows of the church blazing behind them. As the sun went down behind Hook Mountain, the colors of the landscape softened to a delicate blue-green that reminded Charlotte of the heaven that Peter had described, a heaven whose foundation was the romantic love between a man and a woman. Below, the blue-tiled roofs of the houses of Zion Hill glowed like the roofs of some celestial village. Charlotte thought of Edward Archibald, the founder of Zion Hill, who had wanted to make this little hamlet the most beautiful spot on earth. In the gloaming, on this velvet lawn high above the gleaming river, with the sun setting on the western horizon, it really did seem like a little bit of paradise. But it was a paradise that had now been sullied. For days, the case of the look-alike murders had been front-page news, and Zion Hill had been put under the microscope of public scrutiny. To a certain extent, this hadn't been bad. Some of the articles had taken pains to explain the complex beliefs of the New Church. But Charlotte suspected the primary effect of the sensational stories would be to reinforce the idea that the inhabitants of Zion Hill belonged to some strange cult. For a community that had striven so hard for acceptance—Charlotte was reminded of the efforts to plant daffodils along the roadsides and erect welcoming signs on the Albany Post Road—the look-alike murders were a disaster.

But then, seeing the tall, stick-like figure of the pastor circulating among the crowd, she was struck by another thought. Remembering that his outer robe symbolized the exterior or social man, and the inner robe symbolized the inner or spiritual man, she decided that it didn't matter. A community built on inner faith would not be shaken by the Sturm und Drang of the exterior world.

It was her theory of landscaping as a measure of spiritual faith again: Zion Hill had thrived for nearly a hundred years, and it would go on thriving, despite the weeds in the velvet lawn.

The conclusion of the dinner hour was marked by the ringing of the church bells at six o'clock, after which Reverend Cornwall took a place behind the lectern. After a joke about the ringing of the bells marking the cocktail hour, he welcomed the visiting choir to Zion Hill and offered a brief benediction. Then the members of the visiting choir filed out of the south door and took their places on the tiered seats on the stage.

Reading her program, Charlotte saw that the concert featured songs and hymns that had to do with angels or with heaven. The first hymn was by an English hymn writer named Isaac Watts, and was called "A Prospect of Heaven Makes Death Easy." She recognized the last line as being the quote on the stained-glass window that Peter had been repairing at the glass shop.

After the prayer, the boys began to sing, their radiant young faces lifted to the heavens. There was no accompaniment, only the clear, high, sweet voices—like the voices of angels—rising up into the pink- and apricot-tinged clouds of the early evening sky:

> There is a land of pure delight
> Where saints immortal reign;
> Infinite day excludes the night,
> And pleasures banish pain.
>
> There everlasting spring abides,

> And never-withering flowers;
> Death like a narrow sea divides
> This heavenly land from ours.

For the next forty-five minutes, the air over Zion Hill was filled with the boys' heavenly voices. The magic spell was finally broken by the intermission, which allowed the members of the audience a chance to attend to more worldly pursuits, such as going to the bathroom, buying souvenirs and snacks from the vendors whose stands had been set up at the edges of the lawn, and visiting with friends and neighbors.

Charlotte was putting the remains of their supper away in the picnic basket when she was interrupted by a greeting from a young woman with short, curly, black hair who was walking by with two young children in tow. It was Lisa Gennaro from the florist shop.

They exchanged introductions and chatted a bit about the concert. Then Lisa excused herself and headed off in the direction of the vendors. But in a moment, she was back. "I just thought of something," she said. "I don't know if this is important or not."

"What is it?" Charlotte asked.

"I had another order for lilies of the valley from Dr. Louria," she said. "I figured that since he was no longer a suspect, that it didn't matter. But since you asked me to let you know if he placed any more orders . . ."

"Did you know he was dead?" Charlotte asked.

Lisa looked shocked. "I had no idea. When did he die?" she asked.

"When did the order come in?" Charlotte snapped.

"It was late this afternoon." She pursed her lips in thought as her curly-headed daughter, eager for a balloon, tugged at her arm. "Around four, I think. He asked to pick it up in the anteroom after hours, as before."

Charlotte and Jerry exchanged looks. Dr. Louria had jumped to his death on Friday. But that was something that few people other than the police would have known. The obituary hadn't appeared in the paper yet.

"Thank you, Lisa," Charlotte said. In the last case, the

murderer had ordered the flowers the day before he deposited
the skull in the undercroft, which, if he held true to form,
meant that another victim had already been killed.

"You're welcome," Lisa said as her daughter led her away.
"If you want to know anything else, you can call me at
work."

"Peter De Vries!" Charlotte said after Lisa had left.
"You'd better have one of your men pick him up right away."

"He's already in custody," Jerry said.

"I thought the parishioners had raised the money for his
bail," she said, "that Reverend Cornwall was going to post it
for him."

"Peter refused to accept it," Jerry said.

Another possible victim, which meant another Lily look-
alike. But *was* there another Lily look-alike? Hadn't Doreen
Mileski been the last of Dr. Louria's Galateas? Charlotte's
heart was pounding as she quickly packed up the remains of
their supper. Maybe there wasn't another victim; maybe Marta
had ordered the flowers for some obscure reason. In the other
three cases, the body parts had turned up prior to the discov-
eries of the skulls in the cemeteries, or the undercroft. This
time, no body parts had been found. But why would the caller
have asked to have the flowers left in the anteroom to be
picked up later, as the caller had in the other cases? Why
would he have posed as Dr. Louria, who had jumped to his
death a day and a half before the call came in? No body parts
had been found—yet. But that wasn't to say they wouldn't
still turn up. The currents of the Hudson—"the river that flows
both ways"—were idiosyncratic. Presumably the dismembered bodies of Kimberly and Doreen had both been tossed
into the river at the summer house, but the parts had turned
up in different places, and some had not turned up at all. It
was a possibility that in this case the heavy current caused by
the rains of last Wednesday and Thursday had carried the body
parts farther downriver than in the other cases, and if they
turned up in New York Bay, they might not be linked to the
other look-alike cases, since body parts in New York Bay were
not uncommon.

But that didn't answer the question of who the victim was. Someone who looked like Lily Louria. The first person to pop into Charlotte's mind was Sebastian, who looked more like Lily than anyone else, but Sebastian was obviously still alive. In fact, she could see his purple bandanna among the heads in the crowd on the other side of the church lawn.

As she continued to think about the three young women who'd lost their lives in a quest to become more beautiful, it suddenly dawned on her. "Melinda!" she said, grabbing Jerry's arm as he put the empty wine bottle back in the picnic basket.

"Who's Melinda?" he said.

Charlotte went on to explain about meeting Melinda in the waiting room when she'd had her initial consultation with Dr. Louria, and to remind him of their encounter with her on Charlotte's second visit, when she and Jerry had presented him with the casts of the first two victims' skulls.

"The one with all the bruises," Jerry said.

Charlotte nodded. "It was even worse the first time I saw her. I remember wondering why such a young woman would have such extensive cosmetic surgery."

"Maybe she had a facial defect," he said.

"But why would Dr. Louria have been seeing her at his home office instead of at his office in the city?"

"He saw you at his home office."

"Yes, but I'm a celebrity. The day we saw Melinda there, the patients were a famous comedienne and Melinda. If you remember, he saw the other victims at his home office too."

"Why wouldn't he have said anything to us about her?" Jerry asked, still skeptical. "He knew the murderer was targeting his patients. Even his suicide note only mentioned three victims."

Charlotte shrugged.

"The same goes for Peter," Jerry continued. "Peter would have known of her existence. Well," he said, as he finished packing up the picnic basket, "we can't ask Dr. Louria about her, but we can ask Peter."

"And we know where we can find him," she added.

They found him fifteen minutes later in a jail cell at the Zion Hill police station. The only jail cell, in fact. The history of Zion Hill wasn't long on violent criminals. He was lying on his back on the cot, with his head cradled in his arm watching a baseball game on a television set that was mounted on a shelf on the cinder block wall. The remains of his supper lay on a plate on a table that had been pulled up beside the cot. Charlotte recognized what was left of pasta primavera with seafood, filet mignon with béarnaise sauce, and a poached pear with chocolate-raspberry sauce. It looked as if Peter too had been the beneficiary of Sebastian's culinary largesse. On the cell floor was an ash splint picnic basket identical to the one in which Sebastian had brought them their picnic supper. In fact, it was quite a comfortable little setup. Except for the missing bottle of beer (though wine would have been better with this meal), Peter could have been any one of millions of male American couch potatoes on a Sunday evening in May. The only difference was that he didn't have as far to go to the bathroom during the commercials: the toilet bowl was only about four feet from his bed, directly under the television set.

The Mets were playing the Chicago Cubs.

"What's the score?" Jerry asked.

Peter turned his head to look at them. "Hi, Chief," he said as he swung his legs around and sat up on the edge of the cot. "Two–zero," he said. "It's the top of the ninth. Needless to say, it hasn't been a riveting game. I thought you went to the concert up at the church."

"I didn't realize that my inmate was keeping such close tabs on my comings and goings," Jerry said. "It's supposed to be the other way around."

"Keeping tabs on the comings and goings of the people around here is the only thing to do," he said. "Except for watching television, that is."

"We'll take care of that," said Jerry. Taking a key out of his pocket, he unlocked the cell door and pulled it open. "Sorry for the inconvenience. I hope you realize why we had to detain you."

"That's okay," Peter said good-naturedly. "Sebastian saw to it that I ate well, and I knew you'd release me eventually.

Lily told me you'd be letting me go, but she said it would be yesterday."

Charlotte and Jerry exchanged looks.

"Does the fact that you're releasing me mean that you've caught the real murderer?" he asked.

"Pat," Jerry yelled out to the dispatcher, "Peter needs his things back." Then he turned back to Peter. "Not yet. But we're working on it. We have another possible victim. A young woman named Melinda. Did Dr. Louria rent an apartment for her from you?"

Peter shook his head. "The last girl he rented an apartment for was Doreen Mileski. Before Doreen, there was Liliana Doyle, and before Liliana, there was Kimberly Ferguson. Was Melinda one of the Lily look-alikes too?"

"We think so," said Jerry.

"Why would he have rented apartments for the others and not for her?"

"That's what we're trying to figure out."

"Maybe he didn't need to set her up in an apartment," he speculated. "Maybe she already lived somewhere in the area."

It turned out that Peter was exactly right. As Charlotte had already noted, he may have been crazy, but he wasn't stupid. Melinda had lived by herself in an apartment house in Tarrytown. Tracking her down had been a breeze. They had simply checked Dr. Louria's appointment book for the date of Charlotte's first appointment and found Melinda's last name, which Charlotte had forgotten. Then they had looked her up in the Westchester telephone book. Melinda Myer had shared her height, weight, and general age with the other victims, but that was where the resemblance ended. Unlike the others, she had been a legitimate patient of Dr. Louria's, which is why he hadn't mentioned her when he'd admitted to making the other young women over in the image of his dead wife. Her extensive cosmetic surgery was needed to correct scars from cuts sustained in an automobile accident. The fact that she was a legitimate patient also explained why her appointments had been recorded in Dr. Louria's appointment book, why he had referred to her in front of his other patients by name (which he wouldn't have done in the case of a Lily look-alike), and why she had been so willing to chat about her surgery, in contrast to the other victims, who had been under orders to keep quiet. The reason Dr. Louria had seen her in Zion Hill, rather than at his office in New York, was not that he wanted to keep her existence a secret, but because she lived in neighboring Tarrytown. But the murderer probably hadn't known any of that. To him, she had probably been another young woman who fit the profile, and therefore another one of Dr. Louria's make-overs.

At several points during the investigation, Jerry had talked about the psychological characteristics of the type of person who would commit such a heinous crime. One of them was blood lust: a drive to kill that was so intense that it propelled the killer to kill with ever greater frequency and ever greater audacity. With such a killer, the importance of reenacting the ritual of the murder according to his carefully scripted plan eventually came to supersede the importance of whatever the motive for murder had been to begin with. Therefore, it was possible that the killer had known that Melinda was a legitimate patient, but didn't care. She had fit the role that was called for in his sadistic fantasy, and that was enough for him.

It turned out that Melinda had worked for a Westchester party planner, doing theme parties for children in which she dressed up as Snow White, Princess Jasmine, Wonder Woman, or whoever was the favorite female children's character of the moment. Her employer reported that she liked the job because it allowed her to conceal her facial disfigurement behind the masks that she wore. He also reported that she had a wonderful way with children. He said she hadn't shown up for work in two weeks. He was glad that the police had called. He'd been getting worried, but hadn't known what action to take, if any. She was a reliable young woman for whom it was out of character not to show up for work without calling in.

After speaking with Melinda's employer, they then checked the bulletins on unidentified bodies that had come in on the Teletype from other police departments. They didn't have to look far: Jerry handed Charlotte the third one in his pile. It was for body parts belonging to an unidentified Caucasian woman of between twenty-five and thirty years of age and standing about five feet six inches tall. The body parts had washed ashore three days before on the west bank of the Hudson in Alpine, New Jersey.

"I guess we know what happened to Melinda," Jerry said as Charlotte read the Teletype bulletin. Then he leaned back in his chair, let out a deep sigh, and raised a hand over his lowered brow.

14

IF THE MURDERER held true to form, he would be depositing the skull within the next twenty-four hours. In every case, the skull had been found within twenty-four hours of the purchase of the flowers. This time, the police would be better prepared. In the case of Doreen Mileski, they had staked out only the cemeteries in the immediate area, and had been outwitted by a murderer who had deposited the skull in the undercroft instead. This time, they planned to stake out every cemetery and religious institution on the east bank of the Hudson from Yonkers to Peekskill, with the exception of family plots and small churchyard cemeteries. The category of religious institutions was bigger than one would have thought: many of the old mansions along the Hudson were now used for religious retreats, or as residences for the Catholic orders. Though many of these former monasteries had been turned into condos as the number of men taking the tonsure diminished, there was still an order of Benedictine monks in the area, as well as two Catholic colleges with their respective chapels. Any of these institutions might have ended up as the repository for Melinda Myer's skull.

Given the murderer's penchant for cemeteries, however, their main efforts would be concentrated on the Sleepy Hollow Cemetery and the adjoining Old Dutch Burying Ground, two miles to the south on the Albany Post Road, which was the only cemetery in the immediate area that the murderer hadn't yet hit. As the cemetery that had been immortalized in Washington Irving's famous story of the headless horseman, the Old Dutch Burying Ground also seemed a particularly apt place to deposit a skull. Nearly fifty police officers from the Zion Hill and county police departments would be posted at nineteen different sites.

Charlotte had stayed around for the initial discussions of the stakeout operation, but had finally decided to go home; she was only getting in the way. Jerry filled her in by telephone later that evening, after he had returned from a canvass of the cemeteries. He also regaled her with the names of fellow celebrities whose final resting places were in Westchester County. There was Jimmy Cagney and Babe Ruth at Gate of Heaven; Tommy Dorsey and Lou Gehrig at Kensington; and Judy Garland, Basil Rathbone, Joan Crawford, and Ed Sullivan at Ferncliff Mausoleum. There were even celebrity pets buried in the pet cemetery in Hartsdale, including John Barrymore's cat and Kate Smith's dog.

All of which made Charlotte wonder where it was that she would eventually end up, a thought that she put immediately out of her mind.

That night, she dreamed of Chinese vases. There were vases with white glazes, vases with yellow glazes, vases with burgundy glazes. There were vases with handles, and vases without handles. There were vases with round shapes and cylindrical shapes, and the double gourd shape that was the Daoist symbol of wishes that were magically fulfilled. There were simple celadon vases from the ancient Sung Dynasty and there were ornate polychrome vases from the nineteenth-century Manchu Dynasty. Except that instead of being displayed two or three at a time according to their dynastic period in the display cases on the balcony of the Great Hall at the Metropolitan Museum of Art, the vases in her dream were evenly aligned on shelves, each with an identifying marker. There were hundreds of them, displayed on long tiers of shelves. It was odd how these shelves were arranged: not in a straight line, but in angled sections. Nor were the vases large and small, but rather all about a foot high. Then, the dream took a peculiar turn: the vases started sprouting teeth, and developing eye sockets and mandibles and chins. Which was to say, the vases turned into skulls. Row upon row of eerie, grinning skulls.

Disturbed by the dream, Charlotte found herself sitting upright in bed. As she stared out at the streetlight whose yellow glow illuminated her bedroom, she realized where the dream had taken place. It wasn't at the Metropolitan Museum of Art, but at another museum altogether. Then she realized who the murderer was! She checked the clock on her bedside table. It was almost three. She picked up the phone and dialed Jerry.

The phone rang four or five times before he picked it up. "It's Charlotte," she said.

"Jesus, Graham," he said. His voice was husky, probably from all the talking he had done to his troops. "It's the middle of the night," he said. "What time is it, anyway?"

"Three o'clock," she said. "I'm sorry to wake you up. But it's important."

"I only just went to bed. What is it?"

"Describe to me again the psychological characteristics of the type of person who would commit a series of murders like this: a person who would kill and dismember his victims."

"A white male," he replied. "Of above average intelligence. Middle-class to upper middle-class background. Comes from a dysfunctional family, although it may very well be an intact family."

"That describes a lot of people," she said.

"Sexually backward," he continued. "Usually, they've never had a normal consensual relationship with a woman." He went on with his recitation: "Heavily into fantasy: they get off on fantasizing about the murder."

"They might, for instance, become obsessive about a body part?"

"More than that, but I don't want to get graphic. It's called fetishism. Often they take a body part as a souvenir, such as a skull, for instance." He went on: "They have the ability to compartmentalize."

"Compartmentalize?"

"Yeah. To keep their criminal activity separate from their

day-to-day life. What's this about?'' he asked grumpily. ''I want to go back to bed.''

''Wait,'' she said. ''You mentioned something else before. About hanging around on the fringes of the investigation.''

''That's not always true. But it often is. Like the firebug who turns up to watch the fire. We had a guy once who wanted to help pass out flyers about the missing murder victims. He turned out to be the murderer.''

''Do you realize who you could be describing?''

''What do you mean?''

''A white male with an obsession for a particular body part, namely the skull. A man who clearly derives pleasure from feeling a skull: the smoothness of the bone, the contours of the shape.'' She remembered the way his fingers had caressed the bone, almost as if it were flesh.

''Jack Lister,'' he said

Charlotte continued: ''A man who isn't just close to the investigation, but at the very heart of it. Remember how interested he was in whether or not you had made an arrest?''

Jerry picked up the ball and ran with it: ''Also, a man who lives right down the road from the summer house and immediately adjacent to the Zion Hill Cemetery. But how would he have known about the Lily look-alikes?''

''I don't know. That's one piece I'm missing. But I do have another piece: if he was working on the angel statues, he would have been a familiar figure around the church, and might even have had his own set of keys.''

''At the least, he would have known that he could find a key to the undercroft in the key cabinet,'' Jerry said.

''He wouldn't have had access to the meat cleaver, but maybe we're placing too much emphasis on that,'' she said. ''Isn't it the kind of implement that can readily be purchased anywhere?''

''Yeah, it is,'' Jerry agreed.

''I had written him off as a harmless eccentric with a skull fetish, but I should have known better,'' Charlotte said. ''The only groups I know of that share his obsession with skulls are the Hell's Angels and the Nazis.''

''And phrenologists,'' Jerry added. ''And deadheads.''

"Deadheads?" Charlotte asked.

"Followers of the Grateful Dead," he explained, naming the well-known rock group. "One of my daughters happens to be one." Then he continued: "But what would his motive have been?"

"He wasn't just obsessed with skulls, he was obsessed with a particular skull. He said it himself: two generations of Listers have been obsessed with the same face, and by extension, the skull."

" 'All my life I have dreamt one dream alone,' " Jerry said, quoting Lister, who had in turn been quoting Rossetti.

"Exactly," she said. "He's been sculpting that face his entire life. By killing the Lily look-alikes, he could add four skulls of the face he prized above all others to his collection."

"Numbers 503 through 506 in his Phrenological Cabinet," Jerry said. "And he would have had the added thrill of doing the soft tissue reconstructions. The recomposer of the decomposed."

"Decomposed by him," Charlotte said.

"But if the skulls of Lily's look-alikes were the prizes of his collection, why dispose of them in the cemeteries?"

"To show off," she said. "To taunt the police. Look what I've done. Nah nah. Besides, he didn't need to hoard the skulls. He knew you'd be bringing them back, and that he'd be making casts of them."

"I always thought he was out there."

"Out there is right. Like on Alpha Centauri. What about his fascination with the skull of the doctor who dismembered his wife? Besides, he looks the part," she said, remembering what he had said about anatomy being destiny.

"Aren't you pushing it a bit?" Jerry said. "If all murderers looked like murderers, I wouldn't be in business."

"Okay," she conceded. "But what about all the vases of lilies of the valley in his living room? Another taunt. Isn't it typical that they become emboldened the longer they go without getting caught?"

For a moment there was silence on the phone as Jerry considered what Charlotte was telling him.

"Has he ever had a normal consensual relationship with a woman?"

"I don't know. I've never seen him with a woman, or heard him speak about a woman." Then he said: "I don't think we can arrest him. We've made that mistake already. But we can keep a close eye on him."

"I think that would be a good idea," Charlotte said. Then she wished him a good night's sleep and said goodbye.

After breakfast the next morning, Charlotte got ready to head back up the Saw Mill River Parkway to Zion Hill. She was like a theatergoer at a Shakespearian tragedy who has sat patiently through the first four acts: she was damned if she was going to miss out on the climax now, even if it did mean spending a day hanging around the police station. Maybe Jerry could post her at a little graveyard somewhere to keep her busy. As she got dressed, she wondered if anything had happened since her middle-of-the-night telephone call to Jerry. She thought of giving him a call, and then decided against it. She would find out soon enough. Besides, he would have called her if they had caught the perpetrator in the act of depositing the skull.

Just then, the phone rang.

But it wasn't Jerry with news that Jack Lister was under arrest. It was her old friend Kitty Saunders, who was not to be diverted from her goal of improving upon Charlotte's appearance. She was calling from her home in Maine with yet another make-over scheme, her previous one having been defeated if not by Charlotte's own reluctance, then by Dr. Louria's suicide.

Specifically, she was calling to tell Charlotte about a Chinese acupuncturist who did face-lifts through acupuncture. "The theory is that you develop wrinkles because you habitually tense your muscles in a particular way," she chirruped. "By relaxing the muscles through acupuncture, the wrinkles relax too. It's not as good as a real face-lift, but it's the next best thing."

It was tempting. "How long does this take?" Charlotte asked.

"Typically, twenty or thirty treatments. The treatments are twice a week, so it ends up taking ten to fifteen weeks."

Charlotte considered Kitty's suggestion for a moment, and then said: "Kitty, I don't have wrinkles, I have subsidence."

"What's that?" asked Kitty.

"It's what happens in those Pennsylvania coal mining towns when the ground caves in over an old mine," she said. "In short, sagging flesh. No amount of acupuncture is going to correct that."

Kitty thought for a moment, and then said: "Maybe you're right."

"Thanks anyway," Charlotte said. "Besides, except for my neck, I look fine. I'd rather wear scarves and turtlenecks than go through all that."

"Yes," Kitty conceded. "You do look pretty good." Then she switched the subject. "How's the investigation going?" she asked. "If you're free, why don't you come up to Maine? Stan and I would love to see you."

"It's almost over," Charlotte said, more confidently than she felt. "I'd like to come up soon," she said, thinking fondly of her summer cottage. "I'll call you in a few weeks," she added as she rang off.

She didn't feel up to telling Kitty that Dr. Louria was dead.

Before she left, she glanced in the mirror to check her makeup. What she saw was the face of a seventy-two-year-old woman who looked twenty years younger. She had a bit of a jowl; she had a bit of a chicken neck. But so what. She should never have let Kitty get under her skin—so to speak. She didn't need a face-lift. Besides, she had spent a lifetime worrying about her looks: makeup, camera angle, lighting. It was time to stop worrying. She resolved that she was going to continue doing what she always had. Which was to enjoy her meals, enjoy her Manhattans, and enjoy life.

On the drive up to Zion Hill, Charlotte found herself considering the man whom she believed to be the murderer. Or rather, the monster whom she believed to be the murderer. He had probably come from a dysfunctional family, Jerry had said. To her, a dysfunctional family meant a mother who drank too much, a father with a penchant for gambling, a brother with a drug problem. In short, a family with the kinds of problems that almost every American family seemed to have to some degree nowadays. She had once seen someone wearing a T-shirt with a picture of a huge auditorium on the front, above which were written the words: "Conference of Adult Children of Normal Families." The auditorium had held only three conference-goers. If almost all seemingly normal people came from families that were dysfunctional to some degree, then what kind of dysfunction did it take to turn a child into this kind of monster? She couldn't imagine that every murderer's parents had been monsters as well. Or was it preordained, somehow? Was there a monster gene that became activated when exposed to family dysfunction the way a cancer gene becomes activated when exposed to a carcinogen? She knew the monster element manifested early in life: the children who turned into murderers as adults were also the ones who were torturing cats when they were five. Had Lister been one of those? And if he had harbored this predilection for murder since his youth, what was it that had removed his murderous inclinations from the realm of fantasy and deposited them in the realm of reality?

Or could it be, as many believed—Swedenborgians among them—that murderers of this nature were possessed by evil spirits that robbed them of their humanity? The black globules of coal-fire, Peter had called them, who get into your brain, and don't shut up, who know your weak spots, and keep at you until you break. Until you commit murder, and commit it again and again.

Ten minutes later, she was sitting in Jerry's office, waiting for him to get off the phone. The office had taken on the atmosphere of a command post for a military campaign: a map pinpointing the sites where the murderer might deposit the skull hung on the wall, and charts had been set up showing who was staking out which site at what time. Jerry himself was smoking a big cigar. He might have been Churchill in his wartime bunker.

He was talking with someone about travel schedules of

some sort. Finally, he hung the phone up with a heavy clunk.
He looked grim: his eyes were bloodshot, and his lips were
pressed together in disgust. Or maybe it was frustration. "We
were wrong," he said.

"About what?" she asked.

"Lister has alibis for the dates of the disappearances of the
first three victims. The only one he was around for was this
last one."

"Are they solid?" she asked.

"As the Rock of Gibraltar. He travels around the country
helping police departments with unidentified persons cases.
He's got police in three states saying he was with them on the
dates of the disappearances."

"Damn," she said. Just when she thought the strands were
starting to form into a braid. Now they would have to start
over with the tangled skein. "It's gallant of you not to say *I*
was wrong," she said as she sat down.

Jerry smiled. "You had me convinced."

"Did you talk with him?" she asked.

He nodded. "He took it well. I think he was a little pleased
by the attention, if the truth be known. By the way, he was
married for twenty-three years, and has three kids—all grown.
His wife died just before I came here."

"Oh," said Charlotte. "Now what?" she asked.

"We wait," he said.

Charlotte sat for a while listening to Jerry as he touched
base with the policemen at the various stakeout locations, and
then she got bored. Since she was easily bored, this took all
of ten minutes. Then she decided to take a little tour of the
crime scenes. "The crime scene is the mirror of the perpetrator," was one of Jerry's favorite sayings. He was full of stories
about how a small detail at a crime scene had resulted in the
solution of the crime. She remembered in particular a murder
case that involved the "do not remove under penalty of death"
tag on the cushion of a sofa. The tag had been left exposed
when the cushion had been put back on the sofa—an oversight
that was out of character for a victim who had been extraordinarily neat. Though Jerry had been present at the crime

scene investigation, he hadn't noticed this particular detail until he was studying the photographs later on. Somehow the
recognition that the victim wouldn't have left the cushion tag
sticking out had led directly to the solution of the crime,
though Charlotte couldn't remember exactly how. Maybe if
she went back to the scenes of the crimes, she would discover
something equivalent to the tag on the sofa cushion. Besides,
it was too nice a day to sit around inside.

She decided to visit the summer house first, and headed out
in the direction of Archfield Hall, which, she had learned from
Jerry, Dr. Louria had left to the town for a museum, just as
Lily had wanted. It would be easier to reach the summer house
from Archfield Hall than to park at the train station and walk
along the tracks. After parking in the car park where she had
parked as a patient on her first visit, she passed through the
gate in the stone wall between the house and the music studio
and crossed the lawn to the patio overlooking the river. Then
she followed the path down the embankment to the summer
house. The scene looked much different than it had only a
short while ago: the trees were now fully leafed out, and the
wisteria vines that overhung the half-open sides of the summer
house were now in bloom, festooning them with a fringe of
pale lilac. No longer did it look like the sinister Hudson River
charnel house of the tabloids.

Ducking to avoid the blossoms, she entered the structure.
The honey-like fragrance of the wisteria perfumed the interior,
and bees buzzed around the long panicles of pea-shaped flowers. It was a lovely setting. Through the vines, she could see
sailboats scudding across the wind-ruffled surface of the river.
The presence of the railroad detracted somewhat from its appeal, but the comings and goings of the trains were confined
mostly to commuter hours. She could easily imagine a servant
in an earlier era serving an elegant tea here to the mistress of
the house and her companions. But now the magic of this
lovely place was spoiled forever by the memory of the horrible
deeds that had been committed here. Though the smell was
gone, the evidence could still be seen in the bloodstains on
the worktable and on the cement floor.

She could easily see why the murderer had chosen this place

to carve up his victims. It was isolated: tucked into the embankment as it was, it was well-hidden, despite the fact that the road above was lined with houses. And it was far enough away from the tracks that the murderer wouldn't have been visible to the dog walkers, teenaged boys, or any others who might be walking along the tracks, especially with the wisteria vines covering the openings on the sides. Most appealing of all to the murderer would have been its proximity to the river. He would have had to haul the cut-up bodies only thirty yards or so in order to dump them, and the chances that he would have been seen in the act were very slim. A disadvantage was the fact that he would have had to carry the bodies from the parking lot at the railroad station, but this was mitigated by the fact that he could have left his car in the railroad station parking lot at virtually any time, and for however long he wanted, without its presence attracting notice.

Then there was the matter of the meat cleaver. Passing through the opening on the river side of the summer house, she continued on down the path leading to the tracks, and then walked along the tracks to the spot where Mrs. Snyder said her dog had discovered the meat cleaver. Or rather, rediscovered the meat cleaver. The spot was easy enough to find: she remembered Mrs. Snyder saying that it was just in front of an old canoe, which lay in the weeds about fifty feet south of the summer house. Why had the murderer thrown the meat cleaver away? Charlotte wondered as she looked down at a spot where the grass had been flattened, probably by the feet of Captain Crosby, who had come out here with Mrs. Snyder to investigate. Had he been afraid of being caught with it on him? But why would he have been worried about being caught? Unless the police had suddenly arrived, she thought. She made a mental note to ask Jerry if the police had been called to the area at any time immediately following Doreen Mileski's disappearance. And if so, if they had noticed anyone unusual. Then there was the chance that he had simply dropped it, or it had fallen out of a bag. She remembered what Jerry had said when they found the extension cord, about it not being uncommon to find articles belonging to the perpetrator at the scene of the crime. Looking at the spot, she imagined the bloodied meat cleaver lying there. Then she imagined its blade coming down on a well-worn cutting board. But it wasn't Jerry's hands that she saw on the wooden handle, or even Sebastian's, but a woman's hands: hands with knuckles enlarged by arthritis, and dark skin roughened by constant immersion in dishwater. She had seen that meat cleaver before! she realized.

Her mind leapt nimbly from point to point, like a child crossing a brook on stepping stones. From the meat cleaver to the person using it to the room in which she had seen it being used. Finally, it alighted on the face of the murderer.

She hoped she wasn't wrong, she thought as she scrambled back up the path. Jerry wasn't likely to be as forgiving a second time. But she didn't think so. This time, she had the gut feeling that she was right. All the psychological characteristics that Jerry had mentioned also described the new suspect, better than they had Jack Lister. But before she could go making accusations, she had to be sure. At the top of the embankment, she headed back across the lawn to her car. As she got in, she noticed that the clock on her dashboard said 11:15. Good! Connie would have some time before the lunchtime rush. Then she started her car and set out in the direction of Sebastian's.

Arriving ten minutes later, she found Connie setting the tables in a dining room that was empty except for a couple of businessmen sitting at the bar. As before, they went out to the patio to talk.

"When we talked before, you told me that Lily made a practice of coming on to men," Charlotte said. She was sitting with Connie at one of the umbrella-shaded patio tables.

Connie nodded. She lit a cigarette and tilted her long neck back to exhale. "I didn't put it as politely," she said.

"No, you didn't," Charlotte agreed. She continued: "I believe you also said that she took special pleasure in coming on to men who were unavailable."

"Yes," Connie said. "The more unavailable they were, the bigger the come-on. It was a game for her."

"By unavailable men, I presume you mean married men."

She nodded. "Married men, single men. You name it. The only men she didn't go after were the ones she knew for a positive fact to be gay. And I'm sure she would even have gone after them had she thought there was any chance they'd sleep with a woman as well.''

"I presume that she'd have to find the"—Charlotte paused to pick a word— "the targets of her pursuits to be physically attractive to her. In other words, that she didn't go after ugly men.''

"Not necessarily," Connie replied. "In fact, she liked to go after men whom she assumed had never been with a woman, usually because they were ugly or shy. She'd brag about their becoming her love slaves.''

"Is there anyone in particular you can think of who fits this description?" Charlotte asked. "Like a man of God, for instance?''

Connie looked at her closely. Charlotte could almost see the wheels turning. Finally, she answered: "If you're asking if the pastor was one of the men she pursued, the answer is yes. Is he a suspect?" she asked, her big blue eyes wide with astonishment.

Charlotte took a deep breath. "Maybe," she said. "At this point, we're grasping at straws. Tell me about their relationship," she said.

Connie leaned back in her chair and stretched her legs out in front of her. "Did you know her full name was Lilith?" she asked.

Charlotte shook her head.

"To distinguish her from her mother, Lillian. The Archibald sisters all had unusual 'L' names: Lillian, Lothian, Letitia. Anyway, Lilith was either a goddess or a demon, depending on the interpretation. I'm sure Lily's parents named her after the goddess, but it was the demon that she identified with.''

"What kind of demon?" Charlotte asked.

"A succubus," Connie said. "A beautiful young maiden with owl feet and wings like an angel, and hair 'long and red like the rose' and cheeks of white and red. It's a quote that Lily used to recite.''

"What's a succubus?''

"A temptress who's sexually insatiable, and so beautiful that no man can resist her. Once she's succeeded in seducing a man, she turns into a vampire, and sucks the lifeblood out of him.''

"Whew!" said Charlotte.

"Yeah," Connie said, flicking her ash. "It's pretty heavy stuff."

Charlotte remembered the pastor describing Lily as being hypnotic, bewitching, reckless. "Why would she have wanted to identify with such an unpleasant image?" she asked.

"Because of the power of it. As I understand it, Lilith was the antithesis of Eve, the woman who is obedient, submissive, chaste. According to the Hebrew scriptures, she was Adam's first wife, but he cast her out because she wouldn't submit to lying beneath him."

"The first feminist," Charlotte commented.

"Something like that," Connie agreed. "Lily used to say that Lilith was the symbol of the time when woman was not a slave."

Charlotte had taken out a notepad, and started taking notes.

"Anyway, Lilith's special targets were men of God. She would come to them in the night. Lily told me that medieval monks used to tie crucifixes to their genitals before going to sleep to keep Lilith away."

Charlotte arched an eyebrow.

"If she succeeded in copulating with them, they would lose their immortal souls." She paused for a moment, and then said: "I just remembered something else Lily told me about Lilith."

"What?" Charlotte asked.

Connie fixed Charlotte with her big blue eyes. "The monks would wear amulets for protection against Lilith," she said. "In the form of knives."

Charlotte shook her head. This was getting bizarre.

Connie continued: "If you look at Lily's life as a series of campaigns to corrupt men, Cornball—that's what we used to call him—was her Holy Grail." She smiled at the irony of the religious reference. "It began in—I don't know—seventh or eighth grade. He was our religion teacher."

"Was she already seducing men at that age?" Charlotte asked. If so, she would have been sexually precocious indeed.

"No, not physically. But she was already coming on to men. I imagine she'd been coming on to men since she was three. She would sit at the front of the class, and hike her skirt up above her knees. I remember him lecturing her at one point about not wearing such short skirts."

"Did she eventually seduce him, then?"

Connie shrugged. "I don't know. She claimed she did. As I said the other day, she claimed no man could resist her." She rolled her eyes in disbelief. "But I suspect she was telling the truth as far as he was concerned. She said it happened only once, after a youth group party at the quarry pit."

He said he had tied himself to the mast, Charlotte thought. But it appeared that he hadn't knotted the rope tightly enough. "How old would she have been then?" she asked.

"It would have been the summer after our junior year. Seventeen, I guess."

"Why only once?"

"I don't know. I don't know if he managed to resist her advances after that, or if she dropped him. Probably the latter: that would have been her style, to move on to fresh territory. Though that didn't necessarily mean that she would have stopped coming on to him."

"Did his attitude toward her change after that?"

"I don't know about his attitude. I know her attitude changed."

"In what way?"

She took a drag on her cigarette, and then spoke. "Before she seduced him, she was very adoring. She was always flattering his ego: telling him what a wonderful teacher he was, how much he had influenced her life, and so on."

"And after?"

"After, she would still flatter his ego, but the flattery was interlaced with contempt. She would make fun of him when she thought he wasn't noticing, but in fact he did notice."

Charlotte remembered him telling her the story about how Lily had climbed out of the second-story window while he was writing on the blackboard, and then reappeared at the classroom door a few minutes later.

"She was the one who started the whole Ichabod thing."

"What Ichabod thing?"

"He was always very sensitive about his appearance. Especially so back then, when he was even more gawky-looking than he is now. He took every whisper to be a derisive remark about the way he looked, every laugh a joke at his expense. Half the time he was right," she said.

"Even paranoids have enemies," Charlotte commented.

She nodded, and then said: "Because we're next to Tarrytown, we studied *The Legend of Sleepy Hollow* in English class. One day, the English teacher asked Lily to read a passage describing the schoolmaster, Ichabod Crane. The passage talked about his nose looking like the arrow of a weather vane that was perched on his neck."

"And she drew a comparison to Reverend Cornwall?" Charlotte asked. She remembered her first impression of him: that he should be wearing a tricorne hat and a frock coat. He did look like an old-fashioned schoolmaster.

Connie nodded. "The passage described him to a T: big ears, long legs, arms that hung down to his knees. 'Sounds like Cornball,' Lily said. After that, Cornball was known to one and all as Ichabod. In fact, there are *still* people in Zion Hill who refer to him as Ichabod—though not to his face."

"If he was so sensitive about his appearance, the constant reminder must have been extremely unpleasant," Charlotte said.

"Oh, yes," Connie agreed. "Excruciatingly so, I'd say. 'Cornball' had been bad enough, but it was relatively innocuous compared to 'Ichabod.' "

"What was her attitude toward him in more recent years?"

"You mean, since she married Victor Louria?"

"And before," Charlotte said.

"I don't think she saw much of him after she got married. But she used to see him a lot beforehand. She used him. If she didn't want to go somewhere by herself, there was always Icky to go along with her. If she wanted help moving furniture or hanging a picture, there was always Icky."

"Icky?" Charlotte said.

"Short for Ichabod," Connie said.

"It sounds as if her attitude toward him became less contemptuous, then,'' Charlotte said. "Except for the Icky part."

"Not really," Connie replied. "Only more subtly contemptuous. She would still taunt him, but she did it in a more sophisticated way. It was still very much a game of cat and mouse, and the mouse was still taking a beating. Except for one difference: he was a mouse who didn't want to get away."

"He was under her spell," Charlotte said. There were some people, Peter had said, who weren't strong enough to resist the nasty demons—demons who knew just how to punch their buttons.

"Very much so," Connie agreed.

15

SHE HAD LED him on, and led him on. Then, when he had finally succumbed to her advances, she had spurned him, Charlotte thought as she drove back to the police station. Not only spurned him, but treated him with contempt. Ridiculed his nose, and probably, though no one would ever know, his sexual performance. But Icky, as she had called him, had kept coming back for more, like the lab rats who keep pushing the lever for more heroin, in spite of the electric shocks. How he must have hated himself for not having the backbone to stand up to her, and how he must have hated her for manipulating him. Then one day the object of his erotic obsession was swept away, literally, by a wave in Cozumel. She was out of his life, leaving a gap that was filled one and a half years later by the appearance of a young woman who looked exactly like her. Everything that they had considered with regard to Dr. Louria's possible motives, namely the lashing out against the stand-ins for the fantasy he had lost, also applied to Cornwall.

How he had found out about Kimberly Ferguson, the first and most successful of the Lily look-alikes, Charlotte had no idea. Maybe he had seen her walking on the golf course early one morning, and then spied on her from the church tower. But found out about her, he had. And when he did, the rage against Lily that he had kept damped down all those years finally erupted. He could never find it in himself to take that rage out against Lily. Instead, he took it out on a clone who couldn't control him the way Lily had. Instead of Lily pulling

the strings, it was he who controlled her, or rather her look-
alike. In the most brutal way imaginable. He had distilled her
down to her pure essence, her skull, and then done what he
wanted with her. Charlotte didn't even want to think about
what. Then, when he was through with her, he had discarded
her, just as she had discarded him. But he was still a Christian,
wasn't he? A man of God. If only to prove it to himself, he
gave her a Christian burial, laying her skull to rest on a cemetery gravestone, along with a bouquet of her favorite flowers.
Having killed Lily once, he had then gone on to kill her again,
and again, and again.

But how to prove it? He was cunning, she thought, remembering how he had subtly directed suspicion first at Dr. Louria,
and then at Peter. Putting Kimberly's skull on the Leatherman's grave was a clever touch, as were his efforts to raise
Peter's bail money. He had even cast suspicion on the Cath-
olics, that favorite whipping boy of the Protestant denominations, with his observation that the votive candles of the type
left with the skull in the church undercroft were used at Immaculate Conception. Though he had used a meat cleaver from
the Parish Hall kitchen, had probably even used one of Tina's
stockpots, he wouldn't have been so careless as to leave evidence of his brutal obsession around his place of residence,
especially when the Manse was used for church functions. So
where was it that he had carried on the private skull worship
that had given him so much pleasure that he had been compelled to kill again and again for the sake of it? Then the
answer occurred to her. When they had found the extension
cord at the country club dump, Jerry had said that the Quarry
Road ended at an old church retreat house. Later, the pastor
had mentioned the sign for the Retreat when he was giving
them directions to the glass shop, and Charlotte had noticed
the small wooden sign in the shape of an arrow at the Quarry
Road turnoff. It sounded like a place where a member of the
clergy might go to get away from it all, an isolated place where
Cornwall (as she now thought of him—the honorific "reverend" seeming entirely inappropriate) would be free to pursue
his monstrous obsessions in secrecy.

Though Jerry had mentioned a retreat house, he hadn't said

anything about it. Was it still in use? Charlotte wondered. Or was it a derelict building? She didn't want to go all the way over there to find out that it was abandoned. Noticing a convenience store coming up on the left, she turned off into the parking lot and pulled up to the public telephone booth. She would ask Lothian Archibald. As the daughter of Zion Hill's founder and an active member of the church, Lothian should be able to tell her about it.

Lothian picked up right away.

Charlotte identified herself, and then asked: "Do you know a place called the Retreat? It's on the Quarry Road, behind the church."

"I know it very well," she replied. "It's one of my favorite places."

"What is it?" Charlotte asked.

"It's a small house, a cottage really. My father built it for himself as a place to get away from it all. With his many activities in Zion Hill, his businesses, and his eight children, he needed a place like that. We used to go there for family picnics when I was a child."

"What's it used for now?"

"I guess you'd say it's an annex to the Manse. The pastor uses it as a retreat. He goes there when he wants some peace and quiet: to write his sermons, and so on. He really has no privacy at the Manse. People are in and out of there all day long for one thing and another."

"I see," said Charlotte. "Is it very private? What I mean is, are there other houses around?"

"Oh, no!" she exclaimed. "It's all woods and fields. It's part of the eight-hundred-acre parcel my father left to the church. There's a barn nearby that's rented to the same farmer who leases the fields, but that's it. In fact, my father was so fond of the view that he insisted on being buried there."

Charlotte gasped. "There's a cemetery?" she said.

"Not a cemetery, exactly. The New Church isn't big on cemeteries. A small family plot in the woods. My mother's buried there too, and my sister Lorraine, who died of rheumatic fever when she was eight, and my sister Letitia who died two years ago. I guess I'll be buried there one day my-self.''

"Where is this family plot in relation to the cottage?''

"It's kind of hard to find,'' she replied. "There aren't any headstones. Just boulders marking the graves. They don't even have names on them. Though we know which boulder marks which grave, of course.''

"Tell me exactly how to find it,'' Charlotte ordered.

"Okay,'' Lothian said. "Do you know where the turnoff is? By the old glassblowing shop? There's a sign there.''

"Yes,'' Charlotte said.

"Just proceed on the Quarry Road for about a mile and a half; it follows the valley of Zion Hill Creek. You'll pass the old quarry pit where the stone for the church was quarried. It's filled with water now. We often have youth group parties there in the summer.''

Yes, the quarry pit parties, Charlotte thought: the scene of Cornwall's seduction by the evil red-haired temptress.

Lothian continued: "The road dead-ends in a turnaround at the Retreat. The side of the cottage will be directly in front of you, and the pond will be on your right. If you go to the left, you'll see stone steps leading to a path that heads off into the woods.''

"Follow the path?'' Charlotte asked.

"Yes. It goes around behind the house to a clearing over-looking the hillside. It's about a five-minute walk.'' She paused for a moment and then said: "I heard through the grapevine that the police think there might be a fourth victim. Do you think . . . ?'' she asked tentatively.

"I don't know yet,'' Charlotte replied.

Charlotte wasn't such a fool as to go there alone. She rode over in the police car with Jerry, whom she met in the parking lot of the church; Jerry, and Captain Crosby, who sat in the backseat. They were reasonably sure this time—unlike with Dr. Louria and with Peter—and they didn't want to take any chances. After checking to see if Cornwall was at home, which he wasn't, they continued on to the Retreat, stopping about a hundred yards before the end of the road. Then they walked quietly in. As they approached, they could see a blue sedan parked in the turnaround. It was the same blue sedan that Charlotte had noticed in the driveway on her earlier visits to the Manse, and that she presumed to be Cornwall's. Though they were still some distance away, Charlotte could see that the cottage was built of the same warm-colored granite as the church. Like many of the other buildings in Zion Hill, it was elegant in its simplicity: a rectangle with a front door crowned by a simple pediment, two large windows in the front, and a stone fireplace on the side facing them. It backed up to the wooded hillside, and overlooked a pasture and apple orchards. When they were about fifty feet from the house, Jerry directed them to hide in the woods at the side of the road.

They didn't have to wait long. After about five minutes, Cornwall came out the front door. He was wearing a light blue windbreaker over his clerical shirt, and he carried a plastic shopping bag in one hand and a small bouquet of flowers wrapped in paper in the other. As they watched, he came around the house, ascended the stone steps that Lothian had described, and headed off into the woods. Once he had disappeared from sight, they emerged from their hiding places and followed him.

The setting of the Retreat was just as Lothian had described it, though she had only hinted at its beauty. As they came closer, they could see that the flagstone patio at the front looked out over a perennial garden which in turn overlooked a pond in which clusters of blue flag were already in bloom. Beyond the pond lay a long sweep of pasture and apple orchard. The orchard was in full flower: a sea of pale pink cotton candy under a cloudless blue sky. The air was redolent with the fragrance of the blossoms, whose petals drifted toward them like snowflakes in the gentle breezes off the river. The roof of the barn Lothian had mentioned could just be seen off to one side of the orchard.

Following the route Cornwall had taken, Charlotte and Jerry mounted the stone steps leading to the path. Crosby was right behind them, his hand on his holster. After about five minutes, they emerged at a clearing. There, resting on top of one of the

boulders that marked the graves of the deceased members of
the Archibald family, was Melinda Myer's bleached skull.
Cornwall sat with his back to them on a semicircular stone
bench facing the boulder on which the skull rested. His dark
head was bowed, and his hands were clasped in prayer.
Though he must have heard their approach, he made no ack-
nowledgment of their presence. He was giving Lily's look-
alike a good Christian burial. The empty shopping bag and
the bouquet of flowers that he had ordered in Dr. Louria's
name lay on the bench beside him. After a moment, he picked
up the bouquet and carefully removed it from its paper wrap-
ping. Then he stood up and gently laid the bouquet on the
boulder, next to the skull. Stepping back a few feet, he stood
with his head bowed and his hands clasped in front of him.
Then he slowly turned around to face them.

At Jerry's direction, Crosby proceeded to read him his
rights. Then the captain handcuffed him and led him away.

The pastor sat quietly in the backseat of the police car next
to Crosby, his long legs pressed up against the back of the
front seat, and the wrist of his right hand handcuffed to the
door handle. With his other hand, he nervously fingered the
braided watch chain that hung across his narrow midsection.
He didn't say anything at first. Then he quietly began to speak:
"How did you figure out it was me?" he asked. They were
headed back along the Quarry Road to the church parking lot,
where Charlotte's car was parked.

"From the meat cleaver," Jerry said. "The meat cleaver
threw us. We thought it came from Sebastian's, at first. They
use that kind of meat cleaver there. But then Miss Graham
remembered seeing Tina using a meat cleaver to chop vegetables at the soup kitchen." He corrected himself: "I mean
meals program."

"Aha," Cornwall said, nodding.

"Is that where you macerated the skulls?" Jerry asked. "On
the stove in the Parish House kitchen?"

"Yes. I did it on Tuesdays, which is the only day we don't
serve meals. But don't bother to look in the kitchen for evidence. You won't find any: I cleaned up after myself. Tina

gets mad if her kitchen isn't left spick-and-span. I cut up Kimberly's body there too. But it was too much cleaning up. Which is why I switched to the summer house.''

"Where did you cut up Melinda's body?" Jerry asked.

"In the Parish House kitchen, again. I couldn't go back to the summer house. Also, I'd left the meat cleaver in the summer house, so I had to go back to the kitchen to get another meat cleaver anyway.

"She was Lilith, you see," Cornwall continued after a moment. "The succubus. The seductress who comes in the night to men who sleep alone in the form of a beautiful young maiden with hair 'long and red like the rose.' " He laughed bitterly. "With wings, like an angel. And honeyed lips.'' He laughed again. "The medieval monks knew about her. 'Out, Lilith,' they would cry. 'Blood sucker, alien woman, harlot of hell.' They wore amulets in the shape of knives to keep her away. I would have done that—done anything. But instead, I was turned into a swine. I didn't know she was a demon. Until afterward. Afterward, she revealed herself for the she-demon she was. A demon who kills her victims, and sucks their blood. Such was her power that her victims laughed with pleasure in their deaths at her hands. That's what I did as I condemned my soul to eternal damnation: I laughed with pleasure.''

For a few minutes, there was silence in the car as they bounced over the rutted dirt road through the newly green woods.

Finally, he resumed, his long, pale fingers still stroking his braided watch chain: "But if she was a succubus, I became her match. I became an incubus. She was the devil's dam, so I became the devil. The angel who falls from grace because of his carnal desires. The fallen angel who can only achieve corporeal form by preying on the flesh of women.''

They waited for him to go on—to tell them how he had stalked four innocent young women whose only crime was the desire to be more beautiful, and whose misfortune, in the case of three of them, was to be transformed by Dr. Louria into beautiful young maidens with hair "long and red like the rose." They waited for him to tell them how he had stalked them, and brutally murdered them. But he didn't.

His voice had diminished to a whisper: "Instead of two halves of the same angel, we were two halves of the same devil. We were perfectly matched, you see. We were soul mates."

The next day, Charlotte and Jerry were back at the Manse with a search warrant. Though Cornwall had confessed, they needed the kind of hard evidence that would make the district attorney's case unassailable. What they were looking for were photographs, diaries, scrapbooks, or the trophies of the kill that were typical of murderers who preyed on women: locks of hair or items of jewelry or clothing that would link him unquestionably to the victims. Their plan was to search the Manse first, and then the Retreat. Charlotte was assigned to search the closets on the ground floor. She started with the coat closet in the entrance hall where Cornwall had hung up his vestments on the day she had visited him. The vestments were still there: the outer robe, which symbolized a man's superficial nature, and the inner robe, which symbolized a man's inward nature. How ironic that symbolism seemed now, she thought. Outwardly, Cornwall was a quiet man, a man who aspired to be a man of letters, a man with a taste for antique furniture and Victorian needlework who enjoyed sipping sherry with visitors in his study; inwardly, he was a monster who had murdered and hacked up four innocent young women. Charlotte remembered what Jerry had said about murderers of his type being able to compartmentalize: to keep their criminal nature separate from their day-to-day activities. He had kept them as separate as the two vestments that hung side by side on separate hangers in the coat closet.

She found nothing in the coat closet, and was about to move on to a closet in the living room when she noticed a book resting on a nearby table; it was *My Story* by Charlotte Graham. Going over to the table, she picked it up, and tore out the title page, with her autographed inscription. She didn't want any evidence lying around of her once having offered a multiple murderer her "best wishes." She was tossing the autographed page in a wastebasket when Jerry, who had been searching the antique mahogany secretary in the study, announced that he'd struck pay dirt in the form of a diary. Charlotte joined him, and together they went through the leather-bound diary, in which the routes Kimberly and Doreen had taken on their daily walks were recorded, along with the times they had reached certain landmarks, like the twelfth hole, for instance, or the dump by the skeet-shooting range. It was clear from the diary that after a week or so during which they had familiarized themselves with the course layout, each of the victims had established a routine that had varied little from day to day. On some days they had abbreviated their walks, and on some days they had eliminated them altogether, but by and large there was remarkable consistency. Like the Canada geese, they were creatures of habit.

While Jerry continued with his search, Charlotte sat down on the pale green silk damask cushions of the sofa to study the diary. In Doreen's case, the diary showed that she had passed the dump between 6:20 and 6:30 every day for the two and a half weeks preceding her murder. Cornwall could easily have driven to the site, hidden behind the stockade fence, strangled her with the extension cord, and carried her body back to his car all within the space of less than twenty minutes. Given the regularity of his victims' schedules, the risk of being caught was minimal. Then he would simply have driven back to the Manse with the body in his trunk . . . Aha! she thought. That's how Peter had known that Cornwall was the murderer! He must have seen Cornwall traveling back and forth on the Quarry Road, and wondered what he was up to. When it came out that one of the victims had been killed on the golf course, he must have put two and two together. Her mind skipped ahead. Then again, maybe he had seen Cornwall picking up the bouquets at the florist's shop or macerating the heads in the Parish House kitchen. Or, maybe the spirits really *had* told him that Cornwall was the murderer. It didn't matter. In any case, the pastor had then driven down to the train station at his convenience, and hauled the bodies to the summer house to be dismembered, or in the case of the bodies that had been dismembered at the Parish House, to be dumped in the river.

The diary showed that the second victim, Liliana Doyle, had also been a creature of habit, though a habit of a different kind. She had driven to a local convenience store every evening between eight-thirty and nine for cigarettes. Since Dr. Louria had described her as a television addict, Charlotte presumed that the timing was linked to the program schedule: that she went to the store for the cigarettes just before a favorite show. Probably, it was also a chance to get out of the apartment. She wasn't supposed to go out, but, she would have thought, who would notice a quick trip to the convenience store under the cover of darkness? Presumably, Cornwall had nabbed her during this daily outing. The diary showed that the last victim, Melinda Myer, whose face had been disfigured as the result of an automobile accident, was fond of long, solitary walks on the hiking paths of the state park in nearby Pocantico Hills. Though Melinda hadn't followed any regular schedule, the fact that Cornwall had recorded the dates and times of these walks led Charlotte to the conclusion that the state park was where he had murdered her.

Though the rest of their search proved fruitless, the diary was sufficient to demonstrate Cornwall's intention of murdering his victims, and they decided to call it a day. Charlotte was waiting for Jerry in the hall when one of the samplers hanging on the wall caught her eye. It hung above a lovely half-moon shaped antique table that held a crystal vase with a beautiful arrangement of roses. It was good-sized for a sampler—about two feet wide by a foot high—elegantly matted, and set in a gilded frame. The last couplet of Shakespeare's Sonnet 94 (the source was given at the bottom) was embroidered above a floral motif of lilies of the valley. The words read:

> For sweetest things turn sourest by their deeds;
> Lilies that fester smell far worse than weeds.

The reference was now abundantly clear, Charlotte thought. "Lilies that fester" was a reference to Lilith, the beautiful young maiden who turns into an evil destroyer of men. But if it was the words of the sampler that caught her attention, it was the execution that she found herself scrutinizing more closely. Donning her reading glasses, she leaned forward to get a better look. Then she removed the sampler from the wall and carried it over to the window by the door, where she could look at it in the light. The inscription was delicately embroidered on a ground of ivory-colored silk with fine embroidery thread the color of burnished copper. "*Point tresse*," Cornwall had called it. The reference had gone right over her head before, but now she made the connection: the translation was "hair embroidery."

He had given up the *point tresse*, he had said, in favor of Victorian hand braiding. Charlotte looked again at the other examples of Cornwall's handiwork that lined the cheerful yellow walls. There were seven in all: another *point tresse* sampler, with a highly apropos quotation from Psalm One: "For the Lord knows the way of the righteous, but the way of the wicked is doomed," and five examples of Victorian braid work. The braids, in various patterns and widths, had been molded, twisted, and knotted into elaborate designs, mostly of flowers and wreaths, and then set in deep frames. All the threads were the same dark red in color. Charlotte now remembered the ring and the watch chain that Cornwall had showed her on her visit to the Manse. She also remembered how he had nervously stroked the watch chain in the police car. It was a rope made of three separate braids, each woven out of many of the delicate copper-colored strands. She had thought it quite quaint: a suitable accessory for a pastor with a passion for Victoriana. She also remembered him working at his braiding stand, and his reply to her question about how long he'd been working on that particular braid. He'd said two weeks, which was the length of time that had then elapsed since Doreen Mileski's disappearance.

Jerry now joined her in the hall. He was carrying the diary. "What's that?" he asked, looking at the sampler she held in her hands. He read the words aloud: " 'For sweetest things turn sourest by their deeds; Lilies that fester smell far worse than weeds.' "

"It's called *point tresse*. It's from the French. The translation is hair embroidery." She hung the sampler back on its hook above the antique table. "It was embroidered with thread made out of human hair. Kimberly Ferguson's hair," she said.

"Or maybe it was Liliana Doyle's hair."

Jerry stared at her, openmouthed. Then he looked back at the sampler.

Charlotte proceeded to tell him about Cornwall's reference to *point tresse*, which she had completely missed on her earlier visit, and about his hobby of Victorian braid work.

As she spoke, Jerry wandered down the hall, looking at the other examples of Cornwall's needlework. "These are all made out of hair?"

When she nodded, he let out a long, low whistle.

Then she led him into the study and showed him the braiding stand, with its many bobbins hanging down over the padded edge, each attached to a strand made up of dozens of human hairs.

Bending over, Jerry lifted the weighted strands up with his hand. When he let them fall, the bobbins clinked together like chimes in the wind. Then he squatted down next to a large sewing basket on the floor next to the braiding stand. Setting down the diary, he opened the lid.

After searching through the contents for a minute, he withdrew a package wrapped in tissue paper, and proceeded to carefully unwrap it. It was a long tress of human hair, light brown in color, combed straight, and neatly tied at the roots with a piece of yellow-and-white-striped grosgrain ribbon.

"The raw material for the next sampler?" Charlotte said solemnly as she looked down at the gleaming tress of brown hair.

Jerry nodded. "Courtesy of Melinda Myer."

The entire sewing basket, tress of Melinda Myer's hair included, went into a cardboard box that they found in the basement, along with Cornwall's diary, and all seven of the framed examples of hair work. They would be delivered to the district attorney, along with the braiding stand with its long strands of hair. After they had finished packing everything up, they headed out to the police car, which was parked in the driveway of the Manse. Jerry carried the cardboard box, and Charlotte carried the braiding stand. As they loaded the evidence into the trunk, they noticed Peter standing on the scaffolding that had been erected above the door to the south transept of the church. He was installing a stained-glass window. An older man was helping him lift the window into its central spot in the triplet of lights.

Seeing Peter, Jerry nodded in his direction. "I want to talk with Peter," he said. "I'll just go back and lock up first." After a moment, he rejoined Charlotte, and they headed in the direction of the cloister that linked the south transept with the Parish Hall.

"Why do you want to talk with him?" she asked, as they headed down the boxwood-lined path. The air was filled with the sharp, astringent scent of the shrub, which some people found offensive, but which Charlotte loved. "To find out how he knew?"

"Something like that," Jerry responded.

As they approached, Peter stopped and turned to face them. "You're angry with me," he said as they paused at the foot of the scaffolding. He stood with one hand gripping a bar of the scaffolding.

"If you knew, why didn't you tell us?" Jerry said.

"I knew you'd find out sooner or later. I didn't think it was my role to point the finger. Besides, it wasn't as if he wasn't already being punished. As Swedenborg says, our hells are of our own creating."

"But you might have been the one who was indicted," Jerry said.

Peter shrugged. "What's the worst that could have happened to me? That I'd be executed for murder and go on to a better life?"

"No," Jerry said. "We don't have the death penalty, yet. You'd have ended up spending your life in a jail cell." He nodded in the direction of the Ossining Correctional Facility, up the river.

"We all create our own prisons too. Maybe the one you would have put me in would have been better than the one I'm in now." With that, he turned back to his helper, and they resumed their work.

"Is this the window you were working on the other day?" Charlotte asked.

Peter nodded, and turned around to look at the sun, which had just climbed above the hills that rose behind the church. "You should go in and look at it now. Before the sun gets too high in the sky."

Taking his advice, Charlotte and Jerry entered the church through the south transept door, and headed down the aisle to the eagle-shaped lectern. Then they turned around to look back up at the window.

The sun shone directly on the window, turning each piece of glass into a glowing jewel. A radiant Lily, her head wreathed in a golden nimbus, floated up to heaven, while her angel companions danced their attendance.

The apricot-colored light that streamed in through the glass was vibrant, timeless, mysterious. Charlotte sucked in her breath at the beauty of it.

"Eerie, isn't it?" said Jerry. "Lily Louria walking through a field of lilies of the valley and four young women who look exactly like her. I wonder: was she a devil or was she an angel?"

For a moment, they looked up at the window. Then Charlotte said: "I was talking with my stepdaughter, Marsha, about the Lilith legend last night. She's a college professor," she explained. "She knows about things like that."

"What did she say?" he asked.

"She said it dates back to the rejection of the ancient goddess as a result of the ascendancy of the patriarchal gods. To discredit the goddess, you turn her into a vampire, and cast her out. But there's another interpretation."

"Which is?"

"That Lilith ascends into heaven and becomes the bride of God himself, not as his vassal, but as his equal; that she becomes the moon to his sun."

The clouds shifted, and a ray of sun pierced the glass, illuminating the nimbus of the central figure. "Soul mates," Jerry said.

16

CHARLOTTE DIDN'T SEE or hear from Jerry for two weeks. He was too busy dealing with the media. With Cornwall's arrest, the case had become a media event. A lack of understanding on the part of the press about the technique of Victorian braid work—or maybe just a fondness for alliteration—had led to Cornwall's being dubbed the "purling pastor," and there wasn't a newspaper, newsmagazine, or television news report in the country that hadn't featured the "purling pastor" case as their lead story at least once, and many went on with it for day after day. It was from the newspapers, not from Jerry, that Charlotte learned that the needlework hanging in the center hall at the Manse hadn't been Cornwall's only efforts at Victorian hair work. A further search had turned up several examples of gold-mounted jewelry, including a watchband and a bracelet with a braided design incorporating the initials L. A., for Lily Archibald. Cornwall had admitted that the hair used for these creations had been cut from the heads of his victims, an admission that was confirmed by chemical analysis. Though the laboratory tests couldn't confirm to which victim the hair had belonged without a hair sample to compare it to, they did confirm that the hair had belonged to young women, and that it had been dyed red. Laboratory tests also showed that the blood from the stains in the trunk of the pastor's car and on a blue plaid flannel shirt in his closet (the same one he had worn to prune the roses), matched the blood from the stains on the workbench and floor of the summer house.

When Charlotte read these stories, all she could think about was the families of the victims, particularly the mothers. Several of the articles had included photographs of grieving family members, or comments from them. It would be hard enough for the families to get over the fact that their loved ones had been brutally murdered. But even harder to cope with, it seemed to Charlotte, was the idea that the victims' hair—the hair that as little girls, their mothers had washed, combed, and lovingly ornamented with bows and barrettes—had been woven by this monster into grisly souvenirs, which, when he looked at them, or wore them, or stroked them, allowed him to reexperience the pleasure of his heinous acts over and over again.

It wasn't, in fact, until five months after Cornwall's arrest that Charlotte saw Jerry again. He had called to invite her out to dinner at a new restaurant called Sebastian's II that had recently opened to rave reviews. Charlotte had had no idea that Sebastian had finally fulfilled his dream of opening a first-class restaurant in Manhattan. She'd been away at her summer cottage in Maine, and had missed the press hoopla. To a city as food conscious as New York, the debut of a new restaurant that aspired to four-star status was a big event. But after Jerry's call, she had come across several reviews in the newspapers and magazines that had accumulated in her absence hailing Sebastian's as the hottest newcomer on the restaurant scene, and praising it not only for its outstanding food, but for its intimate atmosphere (for which Connie must have been partly responsible), and its sense of conviviality and ease. It was located on Park Avenue South in the Flatiron District, a neighborhood that was off the beaten track for a four-star restaurant. But it struck Charlotte as a good location: close to Gramercy Park and Greenwich Village, and not far from the lower Manhattan neighborhoods where remodeled factory lofts were now worth hundreds of thousands of dollars. There would be little competition: the area was in need of an upscale restaurant.

A cab dropped Charlotte off in front of Sebastian's II at ten of eight on the evening of a day in early fall whose unseasonably cold temperatures and blustery winds had led to dark speculation about what kind of a winter was in the offing. It was probably on account of the cold that Charlotte noticed the homeless man who had set up housekeeping in a cast-off refrigerator box that lay on its side over a steam grate less than ten feet from the elegant brass-handled door of the restaurant. Though it wasn't uncommon to find homeless people squatting even on Manhattan's priciest pieces of real estate, Charlotte was a bit surprised that a restaurant that was still trying to establish its reputation wouldn't have made arrangements with the police, or even with the homeless man himself, to have him move elsewhere. Like most New Yorkers, Charlotte was desensitized to the plight of the vagrants who made their homes on the city's sidewalks. For the most part, she barely noticed them, the exception being at this time of year. Like the clouds of starlings who could be seen heading south, the appearance of cardboard boxes and nests of newspapers on the sidewalk steam grates and in unused doorways signaled that a change of seasons was at hand. In a few months, they would be gone, like the starlings, with the exception of the few that wintered over. And, as with the starlings, it was a mystery exactly where they went. Many went to shelters, of course. But it was those who didn't that she wondered about. It used to be that they took up residence in the Port Authority Bus Terminal or in the steam tunnels under the city, but those refuges for the homeless had long since been "cleaned up." She suspected that many joined the starlings in their flight to the south.

Under ordinary circumstances, Charlotte would only have taken brief notice of the homeless man on her way into the restaurant, but on this occasion her presence in his company was prolonged by the sight of Jerry rounding the corner from East Twenty-third Street. As she waited for him to join her, she found herself giving closer scrutiny to the man who sat cross-legged under the eave of his cardboard castle, his lowered face concealed by a curtain of dark blond hair. He had only one arm; one sleeve of his dirty army-issue parka hung emptily at his side. Lost in Vietnam? she wondered. In a car crash? A coffee can sat on the pavement in front of him, awaiting donations from conscience-stricken passersby. Like many of the city's homeless, he talked quietly to himself: a subway mutterer in his secondary habitat. Suddenly, a gust of wind swooped down from the ominous-looking clouds that scudded across the sky, levitating the trash in the gutters, and sending garbage cans spiraling down the sidewalk. After watching Jerry deftly dodge one of these fugitive garbage cans, Charlotte returned her attention to the homeless man, who had risen to his knees to hold the flap of his cardboard house down with his only hand. It was then that she saw his face.

It was a long, pale face with deep-set dark blue eyes, a young face that was still handsome, but was beginning to show the signs of age. Though it was now concealed by a reddish-blond beard, it was nevertheless a face that she knew well: it belonged to Peter De Vries. Noticing the flap of brown that stuck out from under the front of his parka, she realized that he was still wearing the leather apron that had prompted the sobriquet of the Leatherman. The staff that he carried to help him maintain his balance lay at one side of the old sleeping bag that was spread out on the floor of the cardboard box. Seeing him, she remembered what the pamphlet about the Leatherman, *The Road Between Heaven and Hell*, that she had read at the Manse had said about the Leatherman representing the little bit in all of us that would like to escape the constraints of society. Peter's ties to society had been weak to begin with, but it now looked as if they had been severed altogether.

Now she knew why Sebastian hadn't asked him to move elsewhere, she thought. He probably ate his meals in the restaurant's kitchen, as he had at the other Sebastian's. Maybe Sebastian even let him sleep there. She hoped he had somewhere to sleep other than this steam grate.

Stepping forward, she looked directly at him and said: "Hello, Peter." She spoke loudly, remembering that his accident had left him hard of hearing in one ear. But although it was clear from the way he tilted his head that he had heard her, he didn't reply.

After the gust of wind had died away, he resumed his cross-legged position on the sleeping bag, under the shelter of the box flap. As she stood there, Charlotte considered what to do about him. She would have to consult with Sebastian and Connie, who were presumably looking after him. She wondered if they had tried to find a more comfortable place for him. Perhaps Peter preferred his cardboard cave to a warm bed, she thought, remembering what he had said about "creating our own prisons." But certainly he could use a donation. She was considering how much to give him, and whether to give it directly to him or to Sebastian, when she was joined by Jerry, who greeted her with a hug and a kiss.

As Charlotte drew away, she gently squeezed Jerry's shoulder to gain his attention, and then nodded at the man in the cardboard box, who stared up at the sky, a slight smile playing around his lips.

Jerry looked at her quizzically, and then turned to look at Peter.

"It's Peter," she whispered.

As they looked on, Peter raised his dark blue eyes to the angry clouds, and continued with his muttering. With his pale skin, reddish beard, and beatific expression, he looked like one of the mass-marketed portraits of Jesus that adorn the walls in the homes of the pious.

Charlotte could make out only one word from his torrent of gibberish. It was repeated over and over again: Lily, Lily, Lily.

"Jesus," said Jerry. "How did he end up here?"

"He must have followed Sebastian," she said.

"That's not what I meant."

"I know," she replied. She had no idea what it was that had sent him over the edge, but she guessed that he had been hovering on the brink for some time. It might have been the stress of the accident, the death of Lily, the murders of the Lily look-alikes, or a combination of all three. It might have been cerebral cortex damage that had finally caught up with him.

Or it might have been demons.

For some reason, the sight of Peter reminded her of that family cemetery in the clearing in the woods behind the Retreat, with its graves of dead Archibalds marked only by boulders.

Then the answer came to her to the question that had been haunting her for months, the question of how the tortured families of the dead young women could ever expect to find peace of mind. They could find it in the same way that Peter had: through the belief that the flesh, be it swept away by a riptide, brutalized by a madman, or ravaged by the passing of the years, didn't matter. That it was, so to speak, immaterial.

As they watched, a ray of sunshine broke through the roiling mass of dark clouds over Madison Square Park and illuminated Peter's pale face, like the morning sun piercing a stained-glass window in a darkened transept.

"Is he praying?" Jerry asked.

"No," Charlotte said. "He's communing with the angels."